Honor ON THE CAPE

USA TODAY BESTSELLING AUTHOR
MK MEREDITH

This book is a work of fiction. Names, characters, places, and incidents are the product of the author's imagination or are used fictitiously. Any resemblance to actual events, locales, or persons, living or dead, is coincidental.

MK Meredith
P.O. Box 1724
Ashburn, VA 20146
Visit my website at www.mkmeredith.com.

Edited by KR Nadelson and Jessica Snyder
Cover design by Kari March Designs

ISBN: 978-1-7328980-2-8
Manufactured in the United States of America
First Edition March 2018

PRAISE FOR HONOR ON THE CAPE

"MK Meredith penned a fun, flirty, second chance at love novel that strikes a beautiful chord! This companion novel to *Love on the Cape* hooked me from page one, and her innate ability to fuse wit, angst, sizzling passion, and small town charm in one addictive page-turner is simply remarkable!"
~ Epic Romance Reviews

"Ms. Meredith is a true Master of Description. She writes with such vivid colors and pays attention to the smallest detail with such precision, I feel I could walk into the town of Cape Van Buren and actually find the Flat Iron Coffeehouse, Blayne's shop, and even the North and South Coves."
~ Amazon Customer

"MK Meredith has topped herself."
~Amazon Customer, 5 stars.

INTRODUCTION

Hello!

I am so thrilled to share my happy ever afters with you, and I hope you love this book! If you haven't yet, enjoy your introduction to the wonderful town of Cape Van Buren with *One Jingle or Two* **FREE** on all e-retailers. Once you fall in love with Alora and Nate (they're irresistible, LOL!), you won't want to leave.

Which makes me so excited to offer you the opportunity to meet Blayne and Jamie! Just sign up to my mailing list, and I'll send *Honor on the Cape* to your email for download to your favorite reading device!

BTW . . . all of my series are inter-connected.

Hugs, loves, & peanut butter!
MK

To RAH, Romance Authors of the Heartland.
You ladies were my first home, my first realization of a dream come true, my
first forever friends in the writing industry, and I will carry you and the
support and love you've shown me in my heart with every word I write.
Please know how much I love you.

PROLOGUE

"There's no honor in it, Blayney. Leavin' the way ya are."

The anguish in her da's gaze tore at Blayne MacCaffrey's heart, but she loved Jamie. Truly, deeply, head over heels, life-changing, forever kind of love. Desperate, cross an ocean and live in another country kind of love.

She was a woman, a grown adult. Eighteen years of experience and knowledge, and she was more than ready for this next adventure.

Jamie said they'd be together forever.

Deep in her soul, she knew they'd last even longer than that.

But it killed her to see her da hurting. She'd been his shadow her whole life, and he her hero.

Especially after Ma's death.

She tried to breathe through the pain in her chest, but it was as if all the air in Ireland had been sucked away, along with her da's love. Digging her nails into her palms, she tried to make him understand. "Yer wrong, Da. I love him."

"Love 'im?" His bellow carried a tremble with it that belied his anger. "Ya don't know 'im."

"Mr. MacCaffrey, I know it might seem sudden, but we've thought long and hard about this, and we have a plan."

Noah MacCaffrey turned his deep blue eyes on Jamie as if in slow motion, and for a moment, Blayne considered throwing herself in front of the man she loved to shield him from her da's wrath if need be.

Her da narrowed his gaze under thick brows and his cabbie. "Ya think takin' my daughter across the ocean is a good plan? Droppin' outta university, leavin' her family, her home?"

Grabbing her da's hands, she tried to make him understand. "Ya always told me to shine, to be myself. Ya always loved my independent streak, my spunk and spirit. Ya always said." She swiped at the tear that escaped with a shrug. "This is it, Da."

She wanted—no—needed him to understand, to be happy for her. "This is me."

He shook her off, and it was as if he'd stuck a knife in her heart instead. Crossing his arms over his large chest, he turned his face away, leaving only the profile of his straight nose framed by his shaggy salt and pepper hair and striped beard in view. His lips were set in a hard, thin line, but he couldn't hide the small tremble in his chin. Even through his whiskers.

It was hard to talk with her throat closing and tears stinging behind her lids. "Da. I'll call you every day. I'll get enrolled in university right away. You'll see. Dreams come true in America."

Jamie's warm hand closed around hers, giving her strength. She looked into his steadfast eyes, and a calm settled the earnest desperation in her heart.

Pulling her shoulders back, she stepped in front of the one man she'd always trusted, the one who'd bandaged her knees when she thought she could climb the ivy that ran up the side of the house, and the one who'd rubbed aloe on her fair-skinned arms and nose every time she spent too many hours in the sun.

And she broke his heart.

"I'm going, Da."

"If ya walk out that door, Blayney, dontcha be thinkin' to walk back through."

The thing he didn't understand was she felt as if he'd just shattered hers. With the pain of loss fueling her words, she shouted, "If ya really feel that way, Da, then an ocean won't be wide enough. I won't want to come back!"

CHAPTER 1

"*P*lease don't leave."

Blayne MacCaffrey sighed at her best friend's softly spoken plea, the pain in her chest a tangible reminder of how very much she loved Larkin Van Buren. But it was time to go home. To find her way back to Ireland and her family.

Her da.

Ten years past time to be exact.

She forced out a light chuckle. "In a month, you'll be so busy with your new baby and the conservation center, you won't even notice I'm gone."

Larkin yanked her close, surprisingly strong for someone so willowy, and held tight. "You're going to miss meeting the baby. I'll notice every second of every day. You're my best friend."

The thickened tone of Larkin's voice threatened Blayne's tenuous hold on her own tears. Missing the baby would be hard, but she was afraid if she waited, she'd never go. It was past time she moved home and found a way to reunite with her family.

She squeezed her hard. "I'm not bleedin' leaving yet, not until we make this center a success. So, stop it. You and I'll always be close. An ocean can't change that. You know I'll visit."

"What about Eclectic Finds?"

"What about it? I'm training my new manager. Evette Kingsley's niece. She's stepping in and running things while I work the launch. I don't have to live here to keep it going."

She hid her face to blink back tears, needing to think of *anything* else, as she tightened the laces of her scuffed, banana-yellow derby skates. In any other business meeting, she'd have worn her vintage, sky-high Mary Janes and red Wiggle dress. A throwback to a power combination that guaranteed success.

However, this deal was already in the bag, *and* she loved nothing more than annoying Larkin's husband, Ryker.

And nothing annoyed Ryker Van Buren more than when she skated in the community center of Cape Van Buren—aka his old house and her ticket home.

She stood, gliding her feet back and forth to get the blood moving in her legs again, careful to make room for Puzzle as the cat weaved between her skates.

Larkin shook her head. "Ryker's going to kill you."

Nodding with juvenile enthusiasm, she agreed. "I can't help it. The bloke's fun to annoy."

"Ha, that's only because you don't live with him."

Blayne waved at Larkin's growing belly. "Yes, it seems to be such a hardship."

A blush scalded her friend's chest red and raced its way to her hairline.

Blayne took in the lighthouse at the end of the cape. "I really love this place." The beautiful building, which stood high on the rocky bluffs, overlooking the majestic Atlantic Ocean, provided a strong foundation, a solid core, and a bright, shining light to help guide those in need. She wanted to do the same.

The Archer Conservation Park of Cape Van Buren and the plans dreamed up by Larkin were much bigger than anything she had ever worked on before.

Bigger than herself.

Maybe even bigger than the ocean separating her from her family.

Literally and figuratively.

The park was more than the preservation of the richly wooded peninsula, it was an everlasting symbol of happiness, family, and community. It would enhance the quality of every life in Cape Van Buren—including her own. And once she made the launch successful, her most fervent hope was that she'd finally be able to show her face in Ireland and see pride instead of heartbreak in her da's eyes.

"Okay. It's now or never."

A pang of loneliness squeezed her as she pushed open the door and rolled through ahead of Larkin. The familiar *tsk tsk tsk* of each hardwood seam under her skates eased the ache. She missed her da most of all. His full white beard, his deep blue eyes slightly faded but clear as ever. At least that's how they looked in the pictures her little sister sent. If not for Emma, she'd never have known his beard went all white and lost the stripes of black he'd had when she was a teen.

When she'd been ten, her ma had died of complications from her brother Dylan's birth. She'd always been da's little girl, but after the loss, she and her da had grown a bond so strong she never thought it could be broken.

Back before she'd devastated her family by following a boy to America.

"Sorry we've kept you waiting." Larkin approached Ryker with her hand on her perfectly round tummy and the look of a well-loved woman on her face.

"Kiss-up," Blayne teased. "We're right on time." She glided into the kitchen and spun one full circle in front of Ryker. "I left the rink early just for you." She tapped him on the chest.

He glared through a dark, furrowed brow. "How many times have I told you—"

"Not to skate in the house?" She smirked and gently patted his cheek. "But you're so bleedin' handsome when you're growly." She jabbed her thumb over her shoulder at Larkin. "This one's been keeping you so happy lately I missed the old grumpy Ryker we used to know and love."

He shook his head with a grimace and slid his arm around Larkin's thickening waist, drawing her in close. "You're such a pain in the ass."

Blayne curtsied with her arms spread wide. "Thank you, sir. But don't you lie, I know you're mad for me."

She glided toward the sliding doors then pivoted to return. "I'm excited to jump in on this launch. I've a lot of ideas and promise not to let you two down."

"Blayne." Larkin stepped from Ryker's side with concern shining from her eyes and reached out to her. "There's something we need to tell you."

Blayne shrugged, the rush of a challenge fueling her more than the organic energy drink she'd consumed that morning. "I'm all ears. You can relax and focus on the baby. I may be a one-woman show, but I'm all Team Van Buren. It helps that I work best alone."

"About that..." Her friend's chest flushed red again.

Something was up. Larkin only blushed when she was nervous, embarrassed, or...guilty. This sounded a heck of a lot like guilt.

Her stomach twisted, but she wasn't sure if it was from determination or irritation. She would manage the opening of this enterprise better than any shiny-shoed number-pusher any day of the week. They knew it, and she knew it.

So, what the hell was going on?

She stared from husband to wife and crossed her arms over her chest. "You know I'm the best fit for this job." She shoved off a foot and skated toward them.

The front door slammed, making her flinch. She threw her arms out to catch her balance, teetered, then over-corrected just as a someone walked through the kitchen door.

"Sorry I'm late." The deep, husky voice sliced through her, hurtling her back a decade to a time when she'd believed in true love and happy-ever-afters, right before she slammed into a rock-hard chest.

"Umph." She grunted on impact, and the two fought to stay on their feet, but her skates had a mind of their own and raced out from under her as if running for their lives. "Bloody hell!"

"Shit." The word vibrated against her cheek and skittered along her spine as they crashed to the kitchen floor in a tangle of limbs.

For a moment, no sound was heard except the whir of spinning wheels.

"Oh my God." Larkin rushed toward them.

Disbelief lodged in Blayne's throat with all the words she'd never been able to say.

It couldn't be him.

Not now.

She shoved back, fighting to gain solid ground and cursing her fucking skates. Why of all days had she chosen today to tease Ryker? Karma was meaner than Ryker's grandmother Maxine Van Buren when someone threatened her moonshine.

She shoved the dark hair that had escaped its pins from her face and sucked in a breath.

"Are you alright?" Larkin grabbed her arm, trying to help her up.

But she could barely hear over the roaring in her ears.

As the bloke straightened, she took in the thick head of sun-kissed brown hair that reminded her of digging her toes into the sand off the north side of the cape, and light gray eyes that had always seen too much and said too little, and her heart stopped. For the second time in her life.

"Jamie."

One thousand one, one thousand two...*lub dub, lub dub*. Okay, she was still alive.

"Blayne. Blayne!" *Snap, snap*. Larkin's fingers made the jarring gesture in her face until she finally blinked.

The bloke lost all his golden boy color as his eyes took her in from head to toe like a starving man would a table of food. He reached for her. "Blayne, I had no—"

She jerked back, the motion almost landing her on her ass for the second time that afternoon. "Don't." Her voice was stern but soft. She thanked the universe for hiding the tremble surfing the edge of her words.

Ryker joined Larkin and laid a hand on Blayne's arm. "Are you okay? I told you wearing those damn things on this floor wasn't a good idea."

Looking from Blayne to the new arrival, Larkin gently led her husband away. "Ryker. Now's not the time."

"Not the time for what, Cupcake? Wearing the damn skates?" he grumbled, shaking his head in irritation.

The deep clearing of a throat caught Ryker's attention, and he glanced at his friend. "Jay, you alright, man?"

Blayne could only stare as Jamie brushed off the front of his tailored shirt, giving a hint of how hard his abs remained and dousing her head with a waterfall of memories.

The gentle glide of his thick fingers through her hair, the hard pressure of his chest against hers. The way he'd promised to get her back to Ireland someday.

Her heart ached at the sight of him. Why was he here, now, after all this time?

Anger and devastation and an annoying layer of awareness wrapped around her in a binding sheath of emotions, making it difficult to breathe.

Jamie ignored Ryker's question and approached her, keeping his hands to himself this time.

He'd always been a quick learner. Back in Ireland, he'd had her big sister, Ruby, wrapped around his finger, always getting the first bite of her bread

7

pudding when their little brother, Dylan, never even stood a chance. And it was well known in Glengarriff that the miracle baby of the MacCaffrey family always got what he wanted when it came to Ruby.

The memory tugged at her heart, making the poor organ feel as though it were engaged in a game of tug o' war.

"How are you?" His voice poured over her like warmed caramel, but there was more to it than the silky timbre she'd dreamed of for years. There was something deeper with age and raspier with his own emotions.

If he still had any.

She frowned. That was unfair. His openness with his feelings had always been one of her favorite things about him. That and the way his full lips felt as they slid across her collarbone.

But that was once upon a time.

And she'd learned the stone-cold truth about fairy tales.

Pulling from her strong Irish reserves, she squared her shoulders, locked her eyes with his, and stood as confidently as she could in her barely-there practice skirt and derby skates. She'd have killed for her Wiggle dress in that moment.

"I've never been better."

Liar, liar, pants on fire.

~

*J*f James Alexander Wilmington Astor III had woken up in the emergency room and been told he'd taken a sledgehammer to the head, he wouldn't have been surprised.

And it would have hurt a helluva lot less.

He rubbed the ache in his chest as he took in the sight of the only woman he'd ever loved.

To say the years had been kind to her was an understatement. Blayne looked more gorgeous than ever. Even with the pain in her expression that she so desperately tried to hide every time she glanced in his direction.

He cleared his throat. "I can see that." His voice still came out in a husky declaration.

She stared at him as if contemplating how to kill him, then turned away.

He didn't take his eyes off her, drinking in every inch of flesh he'd missed over the years.

He'd always been a selfish bastard, and regarding this woman, worse than most.

And here he was again.

Returning to Cape Van Buren to fulfill and reclaim the love of his life was loaded with risk. Especially since it had been that sense of duty and his selfish tunnel-focus on success that had cost him her love in the first place. But he hadn't counted on crashing headfirst into her on the very day he moved home.

Holding the woman who'd haunted his dreams for over a decade in his arms once again had been worth the pain of their earlier mishap.

"You've been busy."

She spared him a fraction of a glance over her shoulder, then turned to face him head-on. "That's what people do."

His low chuckle had her tensing so tight that anyone else would have snapped, but not his Blayne.

Ryker had reached out to him about teaming up with a local businesswoman to ensure a successful launch of the Archer Conservation Park of Cape Van Buren, and when he found out it was her, he couldn't refuse.

Now here she was, even more stunning than the night he'd witnessed her washing a beer down with a shot of whiskey at the Blue Loo Pub during his graduation trip to Ireland. That night, life as he knew it had changed forever.

He swallowed hard, ignoring the unbearable feeling of his heart crumbling under the weight of accusation in her stare. The precision in her arched brows and the crystal-clear seafoam green of her eyes had always ignited a fire in him like nothing else.

At the same time his heart was dying, his damn dick was rising to an occasion that had no chance of happening.

He put a real effort in keeping his gaze latched on hers, but the temptation was too great, and he took in the miles of toned thighs that popped out from a derby skirt that had the letters XXX on the front and back.

She had a tattoo on the outside of her left thigh of a Celtic knot weaved with yellow roses—her late mother's favorite flower—and dripping with ivy. He'd spent many nights tracing the design with his tongue. Nothing had ever tasted so good.

Fucking-A.

Ryker yanked open the refrigerator door and peered inside. "What can I get you, Jay? Want a beer?"

He slid onto a stool at the large island with the white granite top. He forced himself to act like nothing was wrong when it was about as wrong as it could get. Guilt slithered its way up his spine to sit like a lead brick on his shoulders, making the considerable weight of regret grow even heavier. It was going to be a long time before he'd be able to walk free of it. If ever.

Popping the top off two beers, Ryker took in the group with an uncharacteristic grin. Married life must have given the man permanent beer goggles because he was oblivious to what was going on here.

"This partnership will be easier than we thought with the two of you already knowing each other." He nudged Larkin. "And you were worried."

His wife visibly blanched, watching Blayne with worried eyes. She knew every incriminating detail of the day Jay left—and then some.

"*Partnership?*" Blayne ground out while she bent at the waist to unlace her skates. The round profile of her fishnet covered ass peeked out from her skirt with her efforts, leaving him to shift in his seat once again. If she kept it up, he'd be permanently chafed.

Jay exhaled roughly. Man, this was going to be a long couple of months. He owed Ryker, he owed the Astor family name, and most of all, he owed Blayne.

It was time to pay up his debts.

But more than any of it, he was determined to win her back no matter how hard it was to face the woman he'd exchanged for a taste of success.

He'd jumped at the opportunity to attend university abroad while helping expand the family investment business into Europe, setting a precedent as the youngest on the team, and showing he was more than just an heir. He was a leader like his father.

The moment he'd been tempted, he knew she'd deserved better than an ass like him. And the morning he'd woken up back in Europe, he'd realized leaving her in the states was a grave mistake.

But after what he'd done, it had been too late to ask her to take him back. Not until he could stand on his own two feet and prove that leaving had been worth something, be a success in his own right instead of simply because he held the Astor name.

"You always did like to do things on your own. It's good to see that hasn't changed," he said.

She stilled for a moment, then unlaced the second skate. She slid them both off, stepping down to the floor and a height that would have been less intimidating in any other female. But not her. She was fierce.

Now to remind his brain of that fact because the sight of her in bare feet ignited every protective instinct deep inside, catching him off guard. Especially since she'd only ever needed protecting from the likes of him.

With a lift to her pert little chin, she slid onto a stool, so close he felt the heat of irritation radiating from her skin. No doubt, it was the last place she wanted to be. Tough and stubborn. That was his Irish warrior, his *Bean laoch*. He'd called her *Bean* ever since learning *Bean laoch* meant "woman warrior" in Gaelic.

She'd kick him for that thought, too.

"Enough of the small talk. What's going on, Ryker? The last time we spoke, I was launching the center. I've the skill and the experience. And you know it." She glared through impossibly long lashes.

Jay dipped his chin. "And I have the financial knowledge to ensure the sustainability of your plan."

She scoffed. "Knowledge I can attain. I'm not without connections."

"Neither am I," Ryker pointed out, nodding toward Jay. "What's the problem?"

Jay and Blayne ignored him.

"You always were so headstrong," Jay said, watching her eyes flash with a memory. Her stubbornness had turned him on, and he used to push her on purpose just to get a reaction out of her way back when. A reaction he'd then had the immense *pleasure* of helping her burn off.

She turned her head slowly and pinned him with a look. An explosion was coming, and he was primed and ready for it. In fact, he welcomed it, anything to relieve the guilt, the wanting, to distract him from the need to yank her into his arms and beg for forgiveness.

Looking from Larkin to Ryker then to him, she jerked in a breath. "Fine."

"What?!" Jay and Larkin said together.

Apparently, he wasn't the only one expecting a fight.

She spread her hands wide on the pristine white granite. "It's the last Friday of April, the launch is in four weeks. I can handle anything for that long. What's important is this center, Archer's memory, and what this will do for Cape Van Buren. Not my feelings."

She turned toward him and held his gaze until something shifted in hers. A cold, empty void. "And certainly not yours."

Her berry red lips formed each word, but he couldn't believe his ears. Blayne MacCaffrey *never* gave in.

And then the truth of it all slammed him upside the head once again.

The woman he was determined to win back wasn't giving in, she was declaring war.

CHAPTER 2

*A*fter a night of tossing and turning, Blayne yawned and dragged the white primer-dipped paintbrush over the dark stripes of the Van Buren front parlor like an eraser. If only there was a primer she could use on the decisions of her eighteen-year-old self who'd been blinded by love and deafened by youth.

Youth should be added to the DSM for psychological disorders. Delusional didn't even begin to describe the ego-fueled declarations of certainty she'd shouted at her da back then. He'd warned her that there was no honor in her and Jamie's actions, but she hadn't listened.

She hadn't cared.

She'd loved Jamie. And it was a feeling unlike anything she'd ever experienced in her life. All-encompassing, all-knowing, with a happy ever after that would last an eternity.

She dragged the brush in the opposite direction, forever blotting out another section of the navy-and-eggplant stripe.

He'd loved her, too. She never doubted it.

But not enough. Not like she'd loved him. And even if he had, it didn't make it any easier to remember the pain of watching him walk out the door of their tiny little apartment. She'd begged him to stay, resulting in a humiliation so great she'd promised herself never again. Then she'd screamed at him, even giving him an ultimatum that if he left to never come back.

Just as her da had given her.

She closed her eyes against the pain of it all.

Her anger toward Jamie had been fueled by despair, fear, and heartbreak. Another awful combination for decision-making.

Neither of them had shown honor that day either. It had been a bad pattern from the start.

And now her first love, her only love, was back in town.

The painful irony was that it was moments like this that she needed her Da. How many times had he held her close after some bloke had broken her tender heart as a teen? Too many times to count.

He'd rub his big hand over her hair, his deep voice a rumbling whisper. "Ya know, Blayney, yer very special. It's hard for a young lad to know how ta handle a lass like you. I think ya scare 'em, I do. Ya need a strong lad, an exceptional one that sees how brilliant a feisty spirit like ya have is. So be patient. He'll come."

He'd always seemed to be so sure that her naïve little heart believed every word. And just like that, she'd hop back on her feet.

He'd been right. The right boy had come and then left.

Now she had to work with him.

Unless she could change Larkin's mind.

"When did Claire say she'd be by?" Larkin asked as she poured primer into her plastic paint pan.

Claire Adams completed their little trio. Having been targeted by Larkin's need to heal after losing her son, Archer, the woman had never stood a chance against being brought into their fold. It had been Clair's fiancé and Larkin's husband in the accident that made them both lose too much. And Larkin had been determined to make sure something good came out of such loss.

Blayne stepped away from the wall and her musings and set her brush down. Tightening the yellow bandana to keep her hair out of her face, she glanced at the grandfather clock in the foyer. "After lunch. That's last I heard anyway. By the way, we need to put tarps or sheets or something on these floors to protect against paint spills." She buried her hands in the front pockets of her overalls and strategized on how to best broach the subject. "Listen..."

Larkin dropped her brush into her bucket then, abandoning her painting post, turned to face her. "Oh my God. I'm so sorry. I was afraid if I told you Ryker's idea of a partner, you'd back out completely. But I swear I had no clue Jay was *your* Jamie!"

Blayne pressed her lips together in an effort to smile. "I know. No one called him Jamie but me. I never imagined he still had ties here. I mean, his family has a home on the edge of town, but they rarely used it even back then. They spent most of their time abroad and at their home in New York City."

Larkin released a nervous breath and gave her an imploring look. "I know it's selfish of me, but I need you on this project. *Archer* needs you on this project."

She stilled. "That was a low blow."

"Desperate times call for desperate measures and all that?" Larkin wrung her hands together, then stepped close. "Besides, I think this is a good thing."

"A *good* thing?" She could barely get her words out; her jaw was clamped so tight.

"You need to work through this so you can finally move on. It's been ten years."

"I moved on a long time ago," she huffed.

"The hell you have. Tell me one guy you've dated more than a week? You make a one-night stand look like a commitment."

The judgment burned in her chest. "Wow. Are you bleedin' mad? Since when do you care who I sleep with?"

Larkin grabbed her arm with a shake. "That is not what I meant, and you know it. I don't care how many people you sleep with, or who. I'm talking about a connection deeper than the length of a man's dick."

Blayne blinked. Did Larkin really just say that?

Her friend crossed her arms over her chest as a blush raced to her hairline. "Yeah, I said it, and I'll say more. You told me once that you worried I'd stopped living. Well, I worry about you, too. You have a wicked huge, fierce, and loving heart, but you won't let anyone in."

"I haven't met anyone worth letting in. Besides, what's the point when I need to go home?"

Larkin's sigh was heavy.

Blayne would miss her, too. But she'd been away from her family for far too long. And with the conservation project, she'd finally feel worthy of going home.

"I'm sorry. I didn't want you to change your mind, and history has taught me that if I push too hard, it only makes you push back harder."

Blayne smirked. "Takes one to know one."

Larkin stuck her tongue out. "I was grieving."

An image of Archer with his blond hair and dimpled grin immediately filled Blayne with a heavy ache. She didn't know how her friend had found the strength to move ahead after he'd died, but with a lot of love and cherished memories, Larkin was turning the death of her five-year-old little boy into a bright light for their community.

She was in awe of her.

"Besides, I didn't stand a chance with you and Maxine at me all the time." Larkin laughed, but gratitude glowed from the depths of her green eyes. "And now I have Ryker and this little bundle." She slowly rubbed the round expanse of her growing belly.

"At first, I was grieving, too. In a different way of course. One based in rejection and strengthened by broken dreams and loneliness."

Larkin shook her head. "It makes me so angry to think of what he did to you. Bringing you here and then leaving you all alone was cruel."

With a nod, Blayne walked to her paint and brush. "I was devastated. Which is why I don't want to work with him. You have to change Ryker's mind."

"I explained everything to him, but this launch is too important, and the donor program is what will keep it running."

Blayne's heart squeezed painfully. "Larkin, you have to." She stepped toward her. "I can't do this. I—"

"But you just said you weren't willing to lose this opportunity."

"It was just something to say!" Panic raised her voice. She grabbed her brush, then spun back to her friend. "I will make this launch a success. I have as much riding on this as you, maybe more."

"I know, but the donor—"

"Guarantees the center's future. I got it." She shook the brush in the air as emphasis. "And when I say I got it, I do. I can handle the donor program and the launch."

Larkin waved at her. "Be careful."

"I'm always careful. I'd never put the center in jeopardy."

"Not the launch, the floor!" Larkin lunged. "You're dripping all over the place."

Slow to catch on, Blayne stared at her friend. What the hell? The paint drips slowly came into focus. "Shit." She stepped away, bumping the small ladder that held her paint pan.

"No!" Larkin's eyes shot wide as she grabbed the brush.

The pan teetered, and Blayne twisted to get a hold of the plastic tray.

"Catch it!"

The pan slid. Blayne grabbed the edge, but paint sloshed forward, and she jerked the pan up to stop the flow. The opposite edge dropped from the ladder top. Shoving her other hand under the falling side, she slowed its descent but lost her balance, taking the paint tray with her.

Landing hard on her butt, she steadied the pan, victorious with only a small dollop of white primer next to her on the floor. "Phew!"

Larkin grinned. "That was close."

"You've got that right!"

Just then, the front door slammed. "What the hell happened in here?"

The familiar voice was still jarring to her nerves. With her emotions high, she flinched, losing her grip on the pan.

"Shit!" She swore as the primer poured all over her abdomen and onto the floor.

Jamie stood over her, his broad shoulders covered by a gray Henley and an annoying as fuck grin on his face. "Is this going to be a habit with you?" He squatted next to her.

The heat of him immediately enveloped her in a warm, familiar haze that was both heaven and hell. And despite everything, her chest constricted as the object of her frustration stared down at her, crowding her space.

The image of him leaving her all alone filled her vision, and her paint covered fingers twitched against the pain of betrayal that flooded her heart. In a reflex of self-preservation, she pressed her hands to his face and dragged the paint from his thick hair to his chiseled chin.

*J*ay sputtered through the shock and awe of Blayne's paint assault and reared back. Losing his balance, he landed on his ass—hard— his body splayed out like a fool with two women laughing louder than his frat brothers did the night of the full moon streak when they'd locked him out of the house.

Shoving up from the floor, he grabbed a towel from their work table. "You two are hilarious." He swiped at the paint, failing to keep from staring at Blayne as she bent to clean up the mess from the tiled floor. He remembered those overalls, or at least ones she used to have just like them. She'd tease him by wearing them around the apartment with nothing underneath.

There was something damn sexy about the swell of her naked breasts peeking out from the sides of the front chest pocket, the expanse of smooth skin where he could just see the shadows of her ribs, and—

"Jay, are you listening?"

He took a second to take another swipe at his face, wishing his dick didn't twitch with every damn memory, then blinked and found Larkin handing him a wet cloth.

"You can use the washroom by the back door. A little soap and water should get that right off." She giggled behind her fingers.

He grabbed the towels and shot a glare at Blayne, but she'd returned to work with an innocent expression on her face, painting the wall as if he wasn't standing there covered in primer.

But he knew better.

He had the strongest urge to spin her around and press her up against the damn wall.

And what?

He gritted his teeth.

Every idea that followed tightened his body in a wild knot of need, but he didn't have the right to help her up from the floor much less kiss the look of sweet triumph off her face. Not when he'd abandoned her at the first opportunity to move up in his family's company. He'd been a selfish bastard and had chased ambition with singular focus at the expense of anyone around him. It's when he'd also realized that she'd be a helluva lot better off without him.

"I'll be right back."

"Don't feel like you have to stay." Blayne's husky voice with the slightest hint of an Irish brogue followed him down the hall. Yeah, he imagined she wanted him to leave, alright.

Sorry to disappoint you, sweetheart, but that's not happening again.

Not in this lifetime anyway.

He made quick work of his face then, glancing down at his chest, he sighed. There wasn't much to be done about his favorite shirt. Maybe Maxine could work a bit of her magic on it; that moonshine of hers could get the purple out of a Malbec grape.

He turned the vintage, black crow-wing faucets to their off position then stepped into the hallway. He couldn't resist a quick detour into the Van Buren honey room, and a whole different kind of guilt settled in.

Back in the day, he and Ryker had been goofing around and found a stash of his dad's whiskey in a cupboard under the sink. Ryker had kept telling him to put it back, but being an arrogant teen who knew more than anyone else, Jay hadn't listened and accidentally dropped it.

He'd never forget the look of fear on Ryker's face followed by a look of resolve.

The next day at school Ryker had shown up with a black eye and a split lip. Jay later found out his buddy had taken the blame in an attempt to protect him.

With a deep indrawn breath, he lingered in the sweet scent of honey and let it ease the difficult memory.

There was something amazing about seeing the room up and running with cleaned frames in a stand on the counter and the spotless sterling pot of the honey extractor.

Jay couldn't count the broken hearts littering his footprints. It never mattered that he was clear from the beginning he wanted nothing beyond a casual fling. Every woman had thought she was the one to change him. But his attention had always been on the next win. In business and relationships.

However, if Ryker had been able to face his demons and right the wrongs of his past, even those he wasn't responsible for, well then, so could Jay.

As he made his way to the ladies, the front door slammed closed. He found Blayne all alone, having finished one full wall and well on her way with another. Grabbing a brush, he said, "Larkin left?"

"Claire came to help, but they ran out to grab another gallon of paint so we could start early tomorrow." She paused, not bothering to hide the smirk on her perfectly painted lips. "You don't need to stick around either. We both know that's not your strong point."

The needle burned, but he let it slide on through. "I deserve that."

"Yes, you do."

He dipped his chin and his paintbrush, then turned to the wall.

"I don't remember you being so..."

She turned, her brush held in front of her like a weapon. "So...what?" With slow steps, she rounded the ladder. "Determined? Strong? That's what happens when you're an eighteen-year-old woman in a foreign country with few friends and no family."

His gut turned at the thought. What the fuck had he been thinking to leave her? He'd needed to be richer? More successful? More of an Astor?

He'd struggled with the need to prove he deserved the name since he could remember. So much so, he'd turned into a selfish prick to make it true. Every decision he'd made had been so thoroughly justified, not even his mother had been able to get through to him.

He certainly had been successful at the ass part of Astor.

"At least you were already a citizen," he offered, though the sight of her sharp brows drawing together gave him fair warning it was the wrong thing to say. He immediately threw his hands out. "I'm sorry."

Fire sparked in her eyes. "Yeah, my dual citizenship was a warm blanket in our big bed when I was left all alone."

The muscles between his shoulder blades pinched tight. "I thought you would have gone home. I'll be honest, the idea killed me, but I expected it."

She shook her head, a few black tendrils fluttering about behind her yellow bandana. "There are so many things wrong with what you just said." Dropping her brush in the paint can, she turned to him, brushing off her hands. "Go home? After the stunt I pulled? I dropped out of university and left the country with a boy I'd known for a half a second." Her eyes wavered, the pain there a knife to his gut.

"I would have been no more welcomed home than I was to go with you." Even if it had been only half the truth.

"Blayne," he said softly. "I told you why you couldn't go."

"You..." she began. Then suddenly she straightened. The pain in her eyes hardened into something else as her spine stiffened and her lips drew tight.

He wanted to hold her, to beg her forgiveness, to make her laugh. Anything to get the flat, cold look out of eyes that used to sparkle like gems anytime he made a joke. But the feeling of a door closing on him sparked his adrenaline, and all he could do was push.

"I what? Came back uninvited? Fuck yeah, I did." He advanced on her. "I made the biggest mistake of my life leaving you, and I'm not going anywhere until you see how sorry I am. I'm here to stay."

Her eyes flared, and she stepped away. "It doesn't matter. You left and should have stayed gone."

He tried to control the rising tide of panic clawing up his back at the finality of her tone. "The hell it doesn't. It's the only thing that matters."

"Too bad Ryker and Larkin couldn't hear you say that. Then they'd know I should be working this project alone. And if not, maybe I need to reconsider my part in all this." She sighed in an overly drawn out, dramatic show of boredom. "Listen, I need to finish up here, then get some work in. I have a proposal for Ryker."

He recognized that tone and the threat it posed, but he couldn't let her leave the project. The best way to make her stay was to tell her to leave. Their dance was one he knew only too well.

"He's not going to change his mind. I'm here. But you know, with my background, I can easily take on your side of this project." As the words left his lips, he questioned his sanity. His drive to win would ruin any chance he had with her —even if it was a chance in hell.

He couldn't handle the barrage of emotions bombarding him in her presence. Hell, if this kept up, he'd be joining his dad under the cardiologist's knife.

"Easily?"

He'd hit a nerve, just as he'd hoped. "Look, I have the education and the experience necessary for a deal like this and—"

"And what? You don't think I'm qualified? Who the hell do you think you are?"

"I'm just saying—" He stepped toward her, faking a casual dismissal when what he really wanted to do was pump his fist in victory.

She stomped toward the front door, and just before it closed, added. "You can kiss my ass, you egotistical, uninformed, asshole. I'm not going anywhere."

As the door slammed in his face, he grinned.

CHAPTER 3

*T*he following afternoon, Blayne stood in the center of the front room of the Cape house watching Jamie and Ryker critique her priming job, growing more pissed than when a derby opponent tried to sabotage her on the rink.

Just looking at the way Jamie filled out his damn Armani suit made her blood boil. The arrogant, self-righteous...

How was it that men thickened in the most delicious way with age, but women had to fight the same fate like it was their full-time job?

"Quit staring." Maxine Van Buren, Ryker's grandmother, nudged her none too gently. "I know you think you're scowling, but it's more of an I'm-in-the-mood-for-meat and only-that-particular-meat-will-do kind of look." She jabbed her thumb toward Jamie.

"You're mad."

"No, you're mad, and you're also still in love with him."

Heat rushed across her skin with the ridiculous accusation. Thank God she didn't suffer the same fate as Larkin. When her best friend got embarrassed, it was like a gallon of red paint had been dumped on her head. At least Blayne's was felt and not seen beyond a thin bead of perspiration along her upper lip.

She scoffed. "No offense, but you've been drinking too much of your shine, Maxine. Either that or worse, you've turned into one of those women who wants everyone else happily wed since Judge Carter asked you to marry him."

Maxine raised a brow in warning.

"Jamie destroyed any love I once had ten years ago." A small hiccup escaped. *Son of a bitch.*

Her damn telltale sign of lies—even those she told herself—used to get her in the worst trouble with her ma and da as a little girl. Every hiccup told on her faster than her siblings ever could.

Maxine snorted. "If you say so." Giving her silver locks a quick smoothing, she looked around, effectively ending the topic. "Where's Ryker? I need to store a few things downstairs to keep Teddy's nose from getting bent all out of shape. I swear, if that man wasn't so good in bed..."

Blayne almost choked on her own breath as Ryker walked up just in time to hear his grandmother. She'd never seen such a big man turn green so quickly.

"Grandmother, come on." He pressed the space between his brows with a grimace.

Maxine gave a wave of dismissal. "Oh, please. Larkin is proof you already know what I'm talking about. Though the South Cove Madams are a cold lot, we North Cove Mavens have a reputation, you know."

The North Cove Mavens were a group of creative and feisty women who lived north of the cape and sparred good-naturedly with the logical and deliberate women of the South Cove Madams. Something about two sisters who'd lived on opposite sides of town and the one boy who'd captured both their hearts. The feud's history was as old as the town itself.

"Yeah, not the one you think, Grandma," he said.

Blayne didn't even try to hold her laughter in this time.

"By the way, I'm glad you're here. I want to use a little space in the basement." Maxine raised on her tiptoes and placed a kiss on his cheek.

"Like you'd listen if I said otherwise," he grumbled.

She smiled. "You always were a smart boy." She followed up the kiss with a soft pat.

Jay joined them with a heated look solely for Blayne. "Looks like I missed an invitation to the party."

"Nope, if there had been one, the slight would have been on purpose." She made her smile as sickly sweet as possible. It was so damn hard to keep her head straight when he was around. She constantly volleyed back and forth from wanting to throw herself into his arms and bash him over the head.

"Play nice." The look on Ryker's face was a brewing storm.

Jamie shrugged. "Have you thought about what I said?"

"Are you serious?" The man was mad—she cared fuck all about anything he had to say. "I think I made myself quite clear."

Appealing to Ryker, she said, "This launch is life-changing for the town."

Out of the corner of her eye, she caught Jamie's small nod of indulgence and it snapped something inside her. She crossed her arms over her chest. "Now more than ever we need

someone with a rational mind and common sense to lead this project."

"Like I said." Jamie added.

"And since that is clearly not you, I propose the launch remain in my capable hands, starting immediately."

Ryker lifted his head. "What's this?"

"Now wait a minute," Jamie said.

Blayne gestured to Ryker. "Your friend here told me he could easily do my job, and why didn't I take my pretty little face home."

Ryker shot Jamie a look that questioned whether or not he'd gone insane.

"That is not what I said." Jamie ground out, glaring at her.

"Close enough."

Larkin joined Ryker. "What's going on?"

Blayne appealed to her sister-in-arms. "Ryker's friend here said I'm not capable of doing the work."

Larkin's lips thinned, and she slowly turned her head toward Jamie. "I'll have you know..."

Jamie jerked is head up. "That's not what I said. I—"

Blayne's chest tightened to a burn. "That's exactly what you said. Are you really going to stand there and lie to my face?"

"Enough!" Ryker shouted. "You two are worse than Teddy and Maxine when he catches her selling her moonshine." He swung his hand in a wide arc. "This is not a joke! It's simple. Blayne, Jay will make you better."

Her stomach turned in betrayal. The hell he would. He did *not* make her anything. Of all the things Ryker could have said, that was by far the most ridiculous.

"And Jay wipe that damn smirk off your face because Blayne will make you better. We only want the best, and for the needs of this specific project, it isn't either of you on your own. Pull your shit together or get out of my goddamn house." The level of his voice increased with each word until she swore her spine vibrated.

Larkin slid her hand into Ryker's, and he looked down at her almost in surprise. Drawing her into his side, he gestured toward Maxine and Claire who'd just slipped in through the front door. "Everybody out."

Claire blinked in surprise, hiding behind Maxine. "But what about the room? We're supposed to be painting."

"Don't hide behind me." Maxine tried to move away, but Claire grabbed her like a shield.

"The hell I won't. He'd never hurt his own grandmother."

"Shows what you know, he'd hurt me first."

Ryker ignored their banter and walked toward the foyer with Larkin by his side. "Our two idiot friends can do it. And if they don't do it without incident, I'll find someone who can."

The threat was crystal clear.

Blayne waited until the room emptied, then glared at Jamie, pressure building in her chest. Getting home to Ireland with her head held high, being there for Larkin, doing good for the community, were all dependent on the successful launch of this project. And Jamie was tossing it about like confetti. "Nice going, asshole."

A you-can-kiss-my-ass chuckle rumbled from his chest, and the sound of it rolled along her nerves in a wake-up call. "There's the girl I know and love."

She stared at him a moment, suddenly feeling as though she were the butt of an unknown joke, then turned away. Hearing the word love from his mouth hurt more than she wanted to admit. She'd always imagined how classy and reserved she'd act if she ever saw him again.

Clearly, she was failing at that daydream.

Grabbing gallons of paint from the wall, she hauled them to the work table. The quicker they finished, the better. Since Ryker had made it clear they were working together, or not at all, it was time to swallow her pride and do her job.

At least that was something she excelled at.

She tossed Jamie a brush. "Here. Make yourself useful."

He caught the brush, squeezing the handle so tight the whites of his knuckles glowed in contrast to his tanned skin.

Aww, was she annoying him? Well, too damn bad.

Ignoring any urge to poke the sexy bear further, she opened her radio app on her phone and found Metallica. Since it had been their favorite rock band, he'd get the message. "War" would be an appropriate song.

She handed Jamie a gallon of paint then grabbed one for herself.

"You edge, I'll fill in the wall?" he suggested. And there was no way to confuse the heated look in his eyes.

She forced herself to keep her movements casual as an image of the two of them in their apartment took her back. She'd been younger and much more naive, but she'd also been so happy. Her lungs seemed to forget how to function, making her next breath an effort. She nodded, walking to the far corner of the room.

"Do you remember that night?" he asked softly.

She'd never forget it. They'd painted well past midnight and finished with the hottest sex she'd ever had, rolling around on the tarp used to protect the floor. They'd made their own art—and had a hell of a time getting all the paint out of her hair the next morning. But it had been worth it.

Inhaling deeply, she dipped her edging brush into the light gray paint then dragged it along the top edge of the old six-inch baseboards. "You don't get to do that, Jamie."

"Do what? Remember?" Using large strokes, he made a 'W' on the wall with the paint roller.

"Talk to me like we're friends. Make me remember things that made a mockery of what I thought we had between us." She continued down the wall.

"I'm not mocking anything. What we had was different. Special."

Finishing the baseboard edge along the length of the wall, she worked up the corner to the ceiling. She moved the ladder over and climbed until she could reach the top.

"*Different*. Yeah, that's one way to describe it. There was fuck all about our relationship that was like anything I usually see, that's for sure."

His lips quirked, and she wished she could drag her brush over his face, but Ryker's threat kept her in her spot. Jamie always found her Irish sayings amusing. Well, fuck all, fuck all, fuck all. Glad the demise of their relationship could make him laugh.

"Different is what made it special. Don't act like it wasn't." His tone was hard, his amusement gone, and she glanced at him from the corners of her eyes. He was barely an arm's length away, working the paint roller over the wall in time with the clenching of his jaw.

Her shoulders blades pulled tight as her skate laces. "Are you mad? You don't get to be angry." Her voice thickened with emotion, and she swallowed hard past the lump in her throat. "You ran off after your family and your career and didn't give me another thought. I was the one who was left all alone."

He dropped the roller in the pan and swung back nose-to-nose. "You don't think I know that? It killed me to leave, but it was an opportunity I couldn't pass up. We were too young. I realized it was better that way. I was selfish, and you deserved..."

His crisp, masculine scent wrapped around her, inflaming her senses, and as she breathed him in, liquid heat pooled in her core.

"Better? Better for who?" Her voice trembled. "I left my family, I left..." The memories of her ma, the safety of her da. Her brother and sisters. Shame made it hard to breathe.

The whole town of Glengarriff had been family, and she'd left. Just like that.

Just as Jamie had done to her once they got to the States.

"I'm sorry." His words were a whisper with the force of a hurricane.

Anguish shone in his intense gaze, and his full lips, framed by a day's scruff, were pressed into a thin line. It was sincere, but it didn't change anything.

Once upon a time, she would have kissed his worries away, caressed his brow.

Without warning, he grabbed her hips with thick hands and dropped his head to her chest. "I'm sorry," he repeated. His large frame filled her vision.

The old pain sliced her open from the inside out this time. She held her hands out at her sides, not sure what to do. Touching him was not an option. Giving in to his guilt was not the answer. She could never go back. There was nothing left in her for love. Even if every part of her not based in logic cried out for him.

"It's fine." She tried to swallow down her hiccup. The lie burned her tongue, but she needed him to step away before she tugged him in tighter.

Slowly, he lifted his head. "It's fine?"

No. But if he didn't give her space, if she didn't change the subject, she'd break. And since he'd returned, it was all she could do to stay in one piece.

It wasn't fine, but what the hell else could she do? It was time for her to go home, and she couldn't do that until she accomplished something truly of value to make her family proud. "Look," she said, and gestured to the wall behind him.

The wall was fresh and clean with crisp edges and a smooth surface. She forced a lightness in her voice. "If nothing else, we work well together. I wouldn't say you make me better. Ryker's a crazy bloke, but you and I are clearly in sync when it comes to getting things done. We always have been."

His eyes shuttered. "We'll launch the center. Then you can get back to your life, and I can get back to mine, is that it?" There was an edge to his tone, but she couldn't tell if he was dejected or determined.

She stepped down the ladder, needing to put some distance between them. Needing some air. Having him that close after so much time apart was torture when every bit of her yearned to give in and fall into his arms.

"But no more shared memories, no inside jokes. Don't finish my sentences or act like we go way back. We have a job to do. So, let's do it."

Jamie jerked away with a small shake of his head. "I can't do that."

"Then walk away. Those are your choices. We already know which one you're good at."

~

*J*ay kicked his feet up on the railing that ran the perimeter of Ryker's back deck, staring at the Cape Van Buren house across the North Cove and slowly swirling the Scotch in his glass.

His plan had worked—Blayne was staying. The victory of his win wasn't fulfilling him in its usual manner, overshadowed by how much pain he'd caused her. It tore him up to see her work so hard to be strong in front of him just as it deepened his admiration.

"Are you going to show me the initial outline of the donor program or sit there scowling at my home all goddamn day?" Ryker shoved Jay's legs off the railing as he walked past to get to another chair.

"Women are the most confusing creatures on the planet."

Larkin placed a platter overflowing with meats and cheeses and bruschetta on the table between them. "Oh, really? And here I thought it was the lot of you."

He had the grace to shrink a bit in his chair as he took the offered pour of another drink. "I wasn't talking about you, Larkin."

"No?" She raised a brow. "Just my best friend, then? Oh yeah, the one you insulted at the Van Buren house? Or perhaps the one you abandoned? Oh, wait…same woman. You're two for two."

He sighed. "I was making sure she'd keep working with me. You know Blayne, the surest way to get her to do something is by telling her she can't. Regardless, what I said was true. I have the corporate experience."

"Yeah…you didn't keep up with her once you left, did you?"

It was more of a statement than a question. One that gave him the feeling he'd made a grave error in judgment.

Again.

Fuck.

Carefully, he set his drink down and chose his next words. "It would have been too hard. I thought about her every day as it was."

"Well, poor you." She popped a piece of cheese in her mouth.

"Larkin," Ryker said her name softly.

"No, he doesn't get to judge. I was the one who was here to witness the destruction he left in his wake. She'd been lost. Devastated. And I had no idea how to help. She couldn't go home. She had no degree."

Jay shoved his fingers through his hair. The Scotch soured in his gut, leaving him unable to take another sip. "But she went to school."

Larkin nodded. "She did. On her blood, sweat, and tears. Thank God she'd been born here before her family moved back to Ireland. Her dual citizenship saved her. Two jobs, financial aid, an internship at Deloitte, which turned into her first job… She was—is a powerhouse. Which is why I want her running this launch."

Jay had no idea.

He was no stranger to hard work, but he'd had his parents to fall back on anytime he needed them. He couldn't imagine doing it all by himself, let alone in a country he hadn't grown up in.

His need to prove himself had turned out to be one of his greatest weaknesses. He'd always worried about people thinking he'd been handed everything because he was an Astor. Which was why he'd left her for Europe.

It had been sickeningly ironic.

The guilt of leaving had eaten at him with such intensity he'd dived into every new opportunity determined to win and prove his decision had been worth it, to prove he was worthy so he could return to her with his head held high.

Afraid to ask, but too intrigued not to, he leaned toward Larkin. "And Eclectic Finds?"

"As Blayne is wont to do, she got bored once her job became too familiar. She took her savings and her unique view of the world and opened her store. It's been a success ever since."

Jay blew out a breath on a wave of regret. "Hot damn."

"Exactly." Larkin pushed his drink into his hand. "So, you can see why she'd been a little more than pissed when you implied she had no relevant business experience."

"Fuck me."

Ryker clinked his tumbler to Jay's "Here's to the launch. Like I said, the two of you'll make each other better."

Jay grimaced. "The only thing I seem to do is piss her off."

"Well, you've always been an overachiever," Larkin suggested with a wink.

At least she didn't seem quite so pissed. It wouldn't be good to be on Larkin's bad side, not where Ryker was concerned.

"You know I'm here to get her back, right?"

She studied him. "Until your next big opportunity?"

"She is my *only* big opportunity."

"Well, then don't screw it up."

With a nod, Jay withdrew a sheaf of papers from his bag. "Here's my proposal for the donor program. It's solid and will set the center up to sustain every year we go forward."

Larkin scooted closer. "I can't believe this is really happening." Her voice swelled with emotion. "Archer loved this place so much. We want to share it with the children of Cape Van Buren."

Ryker placed a hand on her leg.

"I really want the children to have a voice." She rubbed her belly.

"A voice?" Jay questioned.

She nodded. "They're so easily dismissed by adults. You know what I mean. I want to make sure that while we make the center a success at enriching the lives of the town and making enough money to stay in operation that we don't forget to listen to what the children need and want."

Jay dipped his chin. He glanced from Ryker to Larkin, his gut twisting with a bit of jealousy. His buddy had found the one for him. There was something very special about Larkin Van Buren. "I love it. We'll be sure to keep the kids in mind."

Larkin smiled. "Thank you." She rubbed his arm. "You're not so bad, Jay Astor."

His laugh echoed off the trees and joined in the melody of the chimes placed around the deck.

"Does that mean you guys'll help me win her back?" His voice carried a note of hope.

Ryker grabbed Larkin's hand with a grin. "Not on your life. We won't do anything to hurt your chances, but that's all on you, my friend."

CHAPTER 4

*G*od damn doctor's son.

His gut rebelled at the thought. How the fuck was he going to win her back if she was distracting herself with someone else?

Jay stoked the fire a little harder than he should have and watched the floating embers glow brightly then disappear as they rose toward the flue. On a sigh, he rocked onto his heels. It was an apropos depiction of his relationship with Blayne.

And he had no one to blame but himself.

Fucking asshole, that's what he was.

No woman in her right mind would go back to a man who abandoned her. But was it wrong of him to hope she was a little warped when it came to him? At least as warped as he was when it came to her?

No such luck. She was as sharp as ever.

And as of last night, apparently, dating the doctor's son. Screwing him anyway.

He'd break his jaw if he gritted his teeth any harder.

He pushed up from his squatted position, moving from window to window around the living space to let in the ocean breeze. It was the first of May. The spray off the ocean was fresh but the air cool, so the fire was perfect.

"Jamie?" Blayne's voice carried up the stairs from the front door, taking him back to all the times he'd heard the very same when they'd lived together. He'd get them there again. He'd never lost a deal and he wasn't about to now.

"Up here." He grabbed two glasses from the cupboard then carried them over to the coffee table by the fire. He was determined to play the good host and keep his rage to himself.

The woman of his dreams appeared at the top step and breezed into the cozy, round living room of the lighthouse.

"Wow, it looks great in here." She moved along the perimeter, trailing her fingers along the back of the curved, gray sectional couch, and his neck washed with goosebumps as if she'd caressed him instead. "Larkin and Maxine did great work on the reno."

He nodded. The lighthouse was built with a large support beam that ran through the center, and the stairs spiraled up along the outer wall. Each level was round and incrementally smaller up to the lamp. "Ryker's idea to rent the place out was a brilliant one. Thanks to a cancellation, it was free. This place has been completely booked since they opened it."

She let her bag slide to the floor by the coffee table. "Whitewashing the brick was a great idea. It really opens the space up, and the grays and caramels are so soothing."

Jay studied her as she glanced from the large-leafed, green plants flanking the fireplace to the sofa and floor pillows. She wasn't wrong, the room was comfortable and inviting, but she'd never been one for small talk. Blayne MacCaffrey was in avoidance mode.

The muscles in his neck tightened as an image of her and Max Stanton popped unwelcomed into his head. Sonofabitch. He slammed the bottle of wine harder than he'd intended on the counter, and she jumped.

"Want a glass of wine? We can get started. I'd hate to keep you if you have another date on the books." He'd told himself repeatedly not to bring it up, but the thought of her with someone else pushed the words from his mouth.

Slipping her feet from her sandals she lowered onto a floor pillow by the coffee table, stretching her arms over her head with a yawn. "I'm so tired, I couldn't handle another late night, so no worries."

His jaw muscles worked through her words while he pretended to be distracted by the antipasti plate he'd brought home from Dine on the Vine. Her red-painted toes peeped out from the edge of her navy skinny pants. Her top was a checkered navy and white and tied at her waist with a sliver of silky smooth skin teasing him every time she retrieved papers from her bag and placed them on the table. The whole look was set off by her black hair smoothed back in a slick, high ponytail that she knew damn well drove him crazy.

She did it on purpose.

He tossed an almond into his mouth, crunching down with much more effort than was necessary. Carrying the plate into the living room, he set it between them as he lowered to the floor pillow across from her. "Glad to know you'll be able to focus so we can actually get some work done."

"Because you're the master at getting things done, is that it?" She popped an olive between her pouty red lips, staring at him in question.

"As a matter of fact, I am." Why did it feel like she was constantly challenging him?

She shoved a stack of papers across the table. "Well, I already have the bylaws ready to go. You'll find the document in the center's cloud share as well. How's that for getting things done?"

He eyed the stack of papers with growing frustration. "We are supposed to work on this together. If Ryker wanted you to do this alone, I wouldn't be here."

"Well, that would be preferable." She used a toothpick to stab a chunk of mozzarella drizzled with balsamic vinegar as if she wished it were him. "Besides, this isn't just about Ryker. The center is Larkin's dream."

"Yeah, a dream she built on another man's land if I understand it correctly."

Her arched brows snapped together. "Don't you fucking dare."

"Knock it off. You don't get to come up here and throw your bylaws around, rub your date in my face, and then act like I'm committing a crime by stating the truth about the conservation center."

"Larkin wants to do great things for this community."

The edge in her voice served as a warning, but he was having a hard time giving a fuck.

Pull yourself together, man.

If there was any hope of finding a way to work together, he had to move them past this bickering shit they always seemed to fall into and show her that what still lay between them was everything...

Leaving her defense of Larkin alone, he scanned the documents. They were thorough, well-crafted, and clean, but they lacked the donor program component, which would be the sustaining force behind keeping the center in business.

"They look good."

"They're perfect," she snapped.

He slapped them on the table. "*Stop*. They're good. They aren't perfect. Which is why we're being tasked to work together. Clearly, you've done your homework, but these papers still lack the appropriate information about the donor program, and there are a few things we should discuss to ensure Larkin's initial vision remains intact. Especially who we place in the final decision-making positions."

She held his gaze in some sort of silent struggle that he could admit he was glad to be left out of. The woman could exhaust a marathon runner with that mouth of hers. "Fine. But I get the final say."

Waves crashed against the rocks below, filling the silence with the rhythm of the ocean. A small breeze carried her scent along with it, permeating his senses and clearly confusing the shit out of *his* decision-making, because the next words out of his mouth seemed riskier than a hike in January.

"Fine. Beat me at poker, and once we work through each section, you get the final say. But if I win, the final say is mine."

"Poker?" She raised a brow.

They used to play poker all the time. But not just any kind of poker, the best kind of poker where his opponent was a sexy-as-sin woman with a smart mouth, sharp wit, and very few clothes. They'd rarely made it through a whole game.

Suddenly, the room seemed much hotter. Either May had arrived warmer than usual or he'd just entered his own private kind of hell.

A suspiciously arrogant curve lifted the corners of her lips. "Fine."

He opened his laptop and the document file she'd shared. "You'll find cards in the drawer in the end table behind you. You deal, and I'll open the first section. We'll work through each while we play."

"And the stakes are the final say?" she asked.

"Yep."

"You're on. But we're playing strip."

Jay's heart slammed in his chest as he considered her demand. What was her end game? It didn't make sense for her to throw strip poker on the table, but the woman never did anything without purpose. All the warning bells in the world went off at once in his head. But the chance to get a glimpse of her skin after all this time proved to be his downfall.

The whole point of the night was for them to find a way to move beyond their past and work together. Seeing her half-naked while they did it seemed more of a gift than the challenge she made it appear to be.

His body tightened in anticipation.

He'd always loved a good challenge.

"Deal."

*B*layne held her breath waiting for Jamie to agree to her terms. Every second with him made her heart ache and her body burn. Good thing she was able to separate the two because she wouldn't trust him with her love again for lifetime airfare back and forth to Ireland.

Some might say she was playing with fire, but really, she was playing to win and protect her heart. Distracting him was her foolproof plan to make sure the bylaws ended up the way they needed to be and not just the way he wanted. She hoped keeping him on the defensive might keep him too busy to pursue her... them. She wasn't sure she was strong enough to resist.

"But if I win, you have to admit you feel what's still between us."

"I don't." Her return was swift and followed by a hiccup.

The memory of how it felt to watch him walk away, powerless to stop him, terrified her.

She resented his presence in the first place. After all this time, he returned declaring he wanted them to be together? She had waited for months, hoping he'd miss her as much as she missed him, hoping he'd realize he'd made a mistake and come home.

She would have welcomed him home with open arms.

But he never did. His family name and his career had been more important.

She'd been a fool for loving him, and worse still, a deserter for leaving Ireland. With her heart open and earnest, she'd given him everything and had been left with nothing.

It was time to take back some power and move forward with this project the way she'd envisioned from the beginning.

"I'll get the cards." She held his gaze, refusing to look away first.

Larkin trusted her to make sure the conservation community center would carry out its mission and run as smoothly as possible, and she was not about to let her down.

She dealt the hand while he read through the first section that stated the company name, purpose, and location. She'd always loved his voice. It slid along her skin like soft velvet and continued to linger long after he stopped talking, leaving a wash of goosebumps behind.

This game might be a bit more dangerous than she'd imagined.

Thinking through her ideas had never been her strong point. Something she and Maxine had in common. How many times had she and Larkin talked the woman out of some crazy scheme or another? Maxine resisted society's proper plan for ladies of a certain age. She had her own plan. And that was to do whatever the hell she liked.

Blayne loved her for it and hoped to follow in her well-formed footsteps.

Starting with strip poker with a super sexy man she'd never been able to get out of her head and still dreamed of having in her bed. She wanted him ten years on, there was no denying it, but she couldn't subject herself to that kind of pain again.

Jamie finished with the description and paused. "This is going to be pretty great for the town." His voice was soft and full of appreciation as he studied the document.

Damn it. Sincerity was a damn sexy accessory. Heat spread across her chest. She hadn't counted on how his appreciation for the project would affect her resolve to resist him. Shifting on her pillow, she arranged her cards to get a better look at them and strategize.

She was already ahead, letting Jamie think she'd been out late with Max. Though it was petty, it was quite fun to see her ex struggle with what he wanted to say and what he *let* himself say as far as how she'd spent her evening. Holding back had never been his strong point. In bed that characteristic was a hard-placed plus, but in arguments it was annoying and always pissed her off.

Her whole ice sculpture festival-Max Stanton plan had been a failure from the start. They'd chatted nicely enough, and she'd caught up with Dr. Stanton, but it was evident that if she wanted to maintain positive community relations, she had to back away. The Dawson triplets made it abundantly clear that Max was spoken for. The question was, by which sister?

That was going to be a whole different kind of problem.

"Alright, woman. Put your money where your mouth is," Jamie taunted as he laid out a full house.

She stuck out her lower lip in a pout for a second, then grinned as she slapped a four of a kind down on the table. "Sucker."

She leaned against a chair. "What's it going to be, sweet cheeks?"

The look on his gorgeous face was worth every bump and bruise she'd received since he'd walked back into town.

Winning sure did feel good.

Jamie nodded in good humor. "Alright. I see how this is going to go." But instead of removing a sock as she expected, he pulled his long-sleeved t-shirt over his head.

Oh shit.

His muscles flexed.

Her heart stopped.

And her body hummed with every inch of delicious, golden skin exposed. He'd always been a fine specimen, but over the years, he'd grown absolutely succulent. Thick and wide with more muscle than she would know what to do with. They flexed in response.

She swallowed hard and forced her voice to resist the tremble that tickled her vocal cords. "Your deal."

Jamie shuffled the cards. "You okay?"

"Of course." *Hiccup.*

"What was that?" He asked with an innocent look that was anything but. That was the problem dealing with an ex. There was a good chance he already knew every secret.

She waved at him. "Let's go, Ass-tor." Swallowing down the giggle that bubbled up, she turned his laptop and read through the members section of the bylaws.

"These are good, but we have to include the director of the donor program as well as a corporate relations manager." He rummaged through his leather portfolio until he produced a few sheets. "Here are job descriptions to help give you an idea of what their responsibilities will look like. I've made notes in the margins customized for the center."

She maintained eye contact, but her periphery was busy taking in his broad, muscular chest, the dark stamps of his perfectly-shaped man nipples, and the mounds of his shoulders rising like Mount Katahdin.

"Fine. I'll look at it." She grabbed her cards, keeping her fingers crossed for a royal flush. If she could keep her damn eyes from straying to his bare torso every five seconds she'd be more than thankful. At this rate, she was worse than a starry-eyed schoolgirl ogling her first crush.

"What'll it be, MacCaffrey?" The arrogant tilt to his lips did not bode well for her modesty.

He slapped his cards down. Straight flush.

Shit.

He rose one brow...slowly, and her stomach quivered with the suggestive gesture.

With a sigh of resignation, she considered her options. Too bad she already slipped off her shoes. That would have covered two losses.

She braced herself. Hell no. No more losses.

Pushing to her feet, she unzipped her skinny pants, shooting Jamie a warning look. "Don't get too comfortable."

He pressed his lips together as she pushed the fabric down her thighs.

"Comfortable is not the word I'd use." Clearing his throat, he shoved the cards across the table. "You're up."

Seeing him squirm was incredibly satisfying. And wasn't that the point?

They went over the board of directors and committees, and she threw her hand on purpose. She'd get him completely distracted then take the game right out from under that sweet, hard ass of his.

Next to go was her checkered top. His eyes landed hungrily on her chest as she exposed her pink bra one button slide at a time. She let her shirt fall to the floor and hesitated, giving him a good view of what he'd walked away from ten years ago. Her pink bra topped a pair of hip hugger panties. Years of skating gave her a core to die for, and she was never more thankful than this very moment.

"Are you going to deal or what?" she quipped. Forcing her tone to remain neutral, every second reminded her of all the things she'd missed about him. How safe she'd felt; how easy it had been to follow him across an ocean. How much she'd loved him. Truly loved him.

His eyes were taking in every square inch of her with such intensity that she had to look down to make sure she wasn't naked. Taking advantage of his preoccupation, she grabbed a card and slid it into the band of her undies at her low back.

Cheating may not be respectable, but all was fair in bylaw war.

She held back a grin and snapped her fingers. "Jamie."

With a jerk, he swallowed hard. "Yeah?" He coughed. "Oh, yeah."

He appeared confused and, for a brief moment, the innocent look on his face reminded her of the deep, burning love she'd never really gotten over. With a vicious surge of self-control, she strengthened her resolve against her one weakness.

James Alexander Wilmington Astor III.

Now was the time to slam down the hammer.

Arranging her cards, she prepared for her big win. The bylaws were hers. The control was hers. It was time to put Mr. Astor in his place.

She lengthened one long, toned leg, turning it to put her tattoo in clear view, and flexed her foot. Jamie followed the intended target, tracing her ink with his eyes, as predicted, and she slowly slid her hand behind her back to retrieve her card.

His attention snapped away from her long-limbed temptation and landed on her with suspicion. "What're you doing?"

She froze. "What? Nothing. I had an itch."

Gray eyes narrowed, and he tilted his head, trying to see behind her.

"Seriously, Jamie. Knock it off." Her pulse raced as he raised to his jean-clad knees, his abs rippling with the movement.

"What're you hiding behind your back?"

"Nothing."

"Blayne." He crawled slowly around the table, his muscles bulging with each advance.

She swallowed hard, the crackling fireplace and crashing waves a backdrop warning her of the dangerous position she was in.

Desperate to keep him at a distance, she threw her hands up. "Stop." She really couldn't trust herself if he got to close.

His biceps flexed with each move toward her, and her mouth went dry.

Crossing her arms, she tried to distract him by pushing her cleavage together. He didn't bite.

Shit. The card began to stick to the skin of her lower back as she broke into a cold sweat. Jamie couldn't find out she'd been cheating; he'd never let her live it down. Trying her best to keep her cool, she straightened her leg until the ball of her foot met the firm and warm skin of his naked chest.

"Show me what you're hiding, woman." His low growl sent a shiver of need through her body.

Panic raised the pitch in her voice to a squeak. "There's nothing to show!"

In one fluid movement, he pushed her leg to the side and lunged. Hot, heavy man-body along with ten years of repressed orgasmic memories pressed her into the floor, and a swirling starburst of sensations shot out from her center.

"Let me see," Jamie demanded with the rumble of a chuckle.

"No!" She shoved the card farther down her underwear, hoping he wouldn't go foraging for it, then wrestled to get him off her. Not because she wanted him to move away but because she wanted him to stay.

God help her crazy-ass heart.

They struggled for control. He tried to roll her over, but she held him in a vice-like grip with her legs.

"Good God, Bean, you're strong." He gasped with effort.

"Damn straight." She applied pressure in just a way that had him rolling with her on top until, finally, she straddled his waist in victory. She almost shot her fist up to celebrate her win.

But the undeniable evidence of his own arousal pressed hard against her.

She froze.

Then dropped her forehead to his. It would be so easy to give in, to get him out of her system once and for all.

His breathing was heavy and mixed with hers in a torrent of lush red wine and heady lust. His lips parted. Hers inched closer, hovering, promising…

"Ahh ha!" Warm fingers slid the card from the beneath the edge of her panties, then held it high in the air above their heads. "You cheated!" His look of shock would have been hilarious if it didn't mean she just lost by default.

Her control, her plans were slipping away like the tides of the Atlantic. And she almost just kissed the one man with the power to break her. Again.

CHAPTER 5

*M*onday morning came with the feeling of a new beginning and a surge of purpose. Kind of like the Cape lighthouse. It went from a money pit to a lucrative investment. The month had opened up, allowing Jay to rent it until he figured out what part of town he wanted to call home.

He shoved his wallet into the pocket of his jeans, rehearsing the points about the donor program he'd prepared for Mayor Sebastian Marth. He needed to confirm a few city requirements before he finalized his plan.

Marth was the youngest mayor the town had seen, and in Jay's favor, one of his buddies from school. That was the nice thing about growing up in a small town. Chances held that you were friends with the mayor.

He navigated down the old steps of the lighthouse one by one, just as he did the unfortunate events of the day before at the Cape house with Blayne. And on top of it all, his dad decided he wanted to expedite Jay's takeover of the company —something about the second honeymoon his parents had been meaning to have. Jay shuddered. He wanted no part of that conversation. He was glad his folks were happily married, but he didn't need to know anything about how they achieved that level of happy.

Only that reaching a level of success that enabled him to take over the family business finally allowed him to consider that he was finally worthy of fighting for Blayne.

Pushing through the side door to the cape grounds, he sucked in a deep breath of the crisp, salty air blowing in off the choppy waves. He loved the rhythmic crashing against the rocks and the scent of sea spray. He'd missed a lot being away. There was nothing quite so spectacular as the coast of Maine in spring.

He looked about with a satisfied nod.

It was time to step into his father's position in the Astor company and let the man retire so his parents could go on as many honeymoons as they wanted. And it was about time his mom didn't have to live so much of her life alone. There was no telling how many anniversaries and birthdays were missed due to business. Duty was the root word of every Astor name.

But more than anything, it was time for Blayne. He had to man up and fix the shit of a mess he'd made years ago. He didn't deserve her, he knew it then and he knew it now, but she did deserve to be happy. If she ever gave him the chance, he'd work every day for the rest of his life to make sure it happened.

For a woman who at one point jumped blindly into love, he'd been shocked and relieved to find out she was still single and doing nothing to change that fact —especially when they used to dream of a house full of kids together.

He wasn't quite as surprised to find out she'd managed her career with the kind of badass success he'd come to know and love from that woman.

He rubbed his chest. She was an enigma.

Seeing the memories reflected as heartache on her face filled him with a need to protect her, to fix his wrongs, and make her see what a future together could look like.

However, she'd made it all too clear what his chances were.

Fuck. He'd just have to show her.

As he stepped through the gate toward town, he glanced down the length of the cape. The lighthouse was off, but later in the evening, the lamp would boldly cast a glow as far as the eye could see.

Ryker had brought it back to life when he and Larkin had met. Pretty telling for a guy bent on selling the place.

Jay laughed out loud, watching his cold breath float away from his face in a puff as he walked toward town. Apparently, he'd missed quite the show when Ryker and Larkin had met. From the tell of it, Larkin seemed quiet and unassuming until someone got in her way. Then nothing would stop her.

Blayne was like that.

He didn't try to resist her image floating along the perimeters of his brain. It was always more than simply memories. He could hear her voice and lose himself in her intoxicating scent as if she stood in front of him, and his body immediately tightened with awareness. It had been a constant phenomenon since he'd caught a glimpse of her at the pub the night they'd met.

Having her close now was like shoving a man out of a sensory deprivation tank right into the middle of a Metallica concert.

Jay stopped at the thought and let his head fall back. The Celtic inspired iron sign of Eclectic Finds mirrored her tattoo and swayed gently on its hinge with a gust of wind. The sign croaked as it moved back and forth, and he couldn't tell if it was a warning to run or challenging him to go inside.

He'd heard about her store, but he hadn't seen it yet. Possibly because he'd been busy but mostly because he wanted to keep his nuts. Lately, she seemed bent on destroying them—literally and by wearing her damn cheek-framing derby skirt, teasing him with glimpses of the tattoo she knew drove him wild.

His hands itched to slide underneath, stripping her panties off and tormenting her as she'd been tormenting him. Her sharp tongue was as much an aphrodisiac to him as the cape's bee balm plants were to honeybees.

How the hell was he going to be able to win her back if every time they were together he couldn't stop wanting to either rip her clothes off or shake her senseless?

He had to find a way for them to work together. Step one might need to be keeping his hands to himself. Once she remembered how well they worked as a team, maybe she'd be open to at least talking about them as a couple.

With a death wish, he pushed through the door. The first thing that hit him was her scent. It was light and fresh and reminded him of the ocean. He breathed in deeply once more, letting memories of her wash over him.

Everything from housewares to culinary specialties lined the shelves with the promise of one of a kind and never boring behind every item. As he walked along, one particular set of salt and pepper shakers caught his attention, and he laughed, loving her spunk. Only Blayne would promise that table accessories wouldn't be boring. He turned a generous pair of breasts over in his hand, then set them carefully on the shelf.

He rounded the end of the aisle just as the woman in question stepped through a door labeled Eclectic Staff Only. Her head was down, and she worried her berry-colored lower lip with her teeth. He'd never get used to it—the sight of her was a swift punch to the gut. He remembered how those lips felt, how they tasted...

"I'm sorry, we're closed." She stopped dead in her tracks, her crystal green eyes going wide. "Jamie." Her tone was breathless with surprise.

He'd never tire of hearing the Irish lilt in her voice when she called him by the nickname. He looked around with a nod. "I found myself outside and had to come take a look. You have something special here."

"Yeah, I do." She hesitated, studying him closely. "I worked hard for it, too."

"Larkin told me you put yourself through school. That couldn't have been easy."

Pressing her lips together, she pulled in a breath, her nose flaring in that adorable way he'd always loved. She jabbed her thumb over her shoulder and said, "Look, I have to get back to work. My stock doesn't unload itself." She nodded toward the front of the store. "You can let yourself out."

He had two choices. The smart choice would be to do as she said and leave, but when it came to Blayne, his intelligence was in serious question and usually found just above his balls. Following her through the small hallway flanked by a small office on one side and a break room on the other, he couldn't keep his eyes off the way her ass swayed beneath her fitted skirt.

Her style drove him wild, and her current attire was no exception. He perused the line of her long, shapely legs down to her impossibly sexy high heels. "How the hell are you unloading boxes with six-inch heels holding you up?"

She spun around with a startled look on her face. "I said let yourself out, not in. What are you doing?"

"I'm helping." He looked around at the stacked boxes and table full of merchandise. "I'll unload and unpack, you inventory."

"I don't need your help, Jamie."

"No, you don't. But you're going to get it." He stepped beside her, noting how she stiffened with his nearness.

He stiffened too, but in a completely different way. And to the point that he shifted from one foot to the other, hoping his unwieldy erection would settle in a more comfortable position.

He hauled a box off a stack then carried it to the table. Grabbing a box cutter, he flicked up the blade with a swipe of his thumb against the small, textured lever. "Look, Blayne. I'm here. You might as well make use of me." He heard it as soon as he said it.

And realized he meant it.

She ran her eyes from the tips of his shoes to his crotch—*please, God*, he cleared his throat—then on up to his chest, and finally his face.

"What's the American saying? Been there, done that?"

His bark of laughter echoed off the walls, and her painted lips quirked up at the corners.

With a sigh, she rolled her eyes. "Fine. Unpack each box, carefully handing me one item at a time. This job is about accuracy and care, not speed. Got it?" One perfectly arched dark brow raised with her question.

Something settled in his chest. It meant something for her to give in, to let him stay. "Got it, boss."

She scoffed. "Take that to the center, and I'll let you help me here any day."

He sliced through the tape of one box. "In your dreams. We're partners at the center, but I will give in to your demands here."

"Give in to my demands?" Her question sounded anything but innocent. "All of them?"

"Yes."

"Anything?" Her eyes dilated.

Fuck. Me.

"Completely." Adrenalin rushed through his body. The heat of her made him want to reach out and yank her in until her breasts flattened against him. It was as though his breathing stopped with his heart as she leaned toward him.

So close, her silky hair, her porcelain skin. Those damn lips that left his dick begging to feel her warm, wet heat wrapped tightly around him.

Then just as quickly, she stepped away, her fingers gripping a silver paperweight in the shape of an inchworm. She slapped it into the palm of her other hand, and he winced. "Perfect."

He narrowed his eyes at the victorious gleam in her own.

Two could play at that game.

With a clap of his hands, he scanned the stacked boxes, taking a small measure of satisfaction when she jumped at the noise. "Well, Blayne MacCaffrey, let's get to work."

Shrugging off his jacket, he kept his gaze on the table, purposefully avoiding her eyes. He grabbed the back of his black, sweater and pulled it over his head.

"What are you doing?" A hint of panic raised the pitch of her voice.

With the self-control of a monk, he resisted the smile that tugged at the corners of his mouth and grabbed the first box. "Getting to work. I imagine you don't want to be here all day, Bean."

Bean.

One syllable and the world reversed to a time the future held promises that were kept and declarations of love that were believed.

Blayne turned her thigh from side to side, showing off her newly acquired tattoo, the yellow petals of the two roses were bright against the black shaded Celtic knot. "What do you think? The Celtic knot means we're all connected. No matter where we are. In life and in death. The roses were my ma's favorite. One for her and one for my da." She peeked at him from beneath her lashes. "Or one for you and one for me."

He pulled her into his arms, his scent wrapping her in a haze of lust and undying love. "Bean loach."

She shook her head, bewildered by the random words.

"You. You're my bean loach, my warrior woman. My bean."

Blayne busted out laughing at the absurdity of the nickname. "I'm not a vegetable or anything that should even remotely remind you of a disgusting insect. And there is nothing warrior-like about the nickname bean. It's pronounced more like ban leekh...bean laoch."

Running his finger gently along the side of the Celtic design on her thigh, he grinned. A decidedly delicious, wicked, and lustful grin. "That's fine, but I'm sticking with bean."

With that look in his eye, she didn't care if he called her lint. She'd answer to it.

She blinked away the memory. "Don't call me that." Her voice was clear and her words succinct.

The emotion in her voice emboldened him. She hadn't forgotten. Acting as if he hadn't heard her, he continued. "I don't want to get my shirt sweaty before having a chance to meet with Mayor Marth." He shook his head. "It's so weird to think of quiet, timid Sebastian as the Mayor."

She waved with a dismissive flick of her wrist. "First, get your shirt on. Second, call me Bean again, and I'll cut you."

Ouch.

"Third, I've seen Sebastian Marth...there is nothing timid about that man."

Her light green eyes stared off into space for a brief second, causing a swift, unreasonable knot of jealousy to twist in his gut.

"The last time I saw him, he had a fifty-pound salt bag hoisted on each shoulder." She followed up with a low whistle.

And the knot twisted tighter. It shouldn't. He didn't have the right to feel one way or another. He'd lost any claim to her the night he walked away. His head knew it, but damned if his heart did.

He gritted his teeth and grabbed another box, moving it over to the table, followed by two more.

She picked up a large serving bowl made of glass and silver, studying it from every angle, seemingly unaware of the change in atmosphere. "Yep...not timid at all." Placing the bowl to the side, she reached up on tiptoe to rearrange items on the top shelf labeled serving ware. "Like...at all."

That was it.

If anyone asked, he'd say the devil made him do it. And he'd do it again, too.

Without a sound, he stepped behind her, so close his chest brushed her back.

She sucked in a breath but couldn't move because she had two porcelain dishes perched on the edge of the shelf.

"Careful now. I'm just trying to help, Bean." His voice was even, but his blood raced through his veins at her nearness. Her scent wafted around his head, her heat warmed his skin, and the silky slide of her hair tickled his biceps as he reached around her to assist with the bowls.

"Jamie." She stiffened. And he'd have sworn on his position at the conservation center she quit breathing.

"You're about to lose two bowls that were balanced against the ones in your hands. Take it easy and let me help you."

"I don't need your help." She shoved away slightly with her ass to force him to move, but all she accomplished was pushing those luscious round globes tight against his dick. And his vision went white.

Now he was the one who couldn't breathe. God damn, she felt so good.

As quickly as she pushed back, she jerked forward.

49

He wanted to grab her hips and yank her to him, so he could grind against her softness, and his poor, pathetic heart wanted to propel her back to a time when she loved him. He blinked and swallowed hard then, adjusting the bowls, helped slide the other two on to safe ground.

As if his body hadn't been on the verge of exploding, he stepped away and returned to his table.

She didn't move from the shelf for a full minute. He counted, thankful for the time to get his raging erection in check and his mind straight. Those kinds of games were dangerous, but fuck him if it didn't feel good to play.

Finally, she quietly cleared her throat and reached for her clipboard, busying herself with her list of incoming stock.

He opened another box, slipped the box cutter blade safely beneath the protective edge, then set it on the table.

With a quick, easy grace, she grabbed the box cutter and unsheathed the blade.

"What the hell?" He looked from the blade to her eyes, which glittered ominously. He let out a soft chuckle. "Don't be ridiculous."

She raised the blade a little higher from its sheath.

"I was only trying to help."

"Bullshit. You were trying to manipulate me. You were trying to muddy my head with your rock-hard abs and your damn bulging biceps."

His dick jumped.

"Come on. I was doing nothing of the sort."

The hell he wasn't.

And she knew it.

He raised his hands in front of him. "Seriously."

"Get out."

"Blayne, come on."

She grabbed his shirt and threw it at his face. "Get. Out."

There were times to advance and there were times to retreat.

And there were times to run like hell from a mad woman with a blade.

～

"*I* need to meet someone tonight, Claire," Blayne announced as they walked past a row of brilliantly carved blocks of ice. A light breeze blew in across the South Cove waters, the light, salty air carrying the savory aroma of seafood entrees from the Lobster House. Her stomach growled.

"Meet someone?" Claire asked, distracted by a very well-built sculpture of Poseidon, King of the Sea.

Blayne put some heat behind her words. "I mean *meet* someone."

Her friend stopped abruptly, the blunt edge of her sleek new haircut swinging past her face. "At the ice festival?" Claire asked with a clear tone of *you've gone batshit crazy.* "Let me make sure I am getting this. You want to have sex with someone you meet here...at the ice festival."

"Well, I don't want to have sex at the festival, but I want to take someone home. Yes."

Hearing it out loud did make the idea sound much more preposterous than it had a few hours ago when she'd kicked Jamie out of her store, but she needed to do something to erase the memory of his skin on hers, the glide of his big, warm hand, the touch of his lips.

Shit.

"Yes." She declared with a bit more determination. There were a few things in life she didn't trust. Jamie, love, and her heart concerning Jamie and love.

Claire dragged her toward the Dine on the Vine concession stand. "Clearly, we need to drink. I'd have never thought it, but this time, I think you need to sip on a glass...a whole glass before moving forward with this asinine plan."

She scoffed. "Sounds good to me. But I'm not changing my mind."

Claire handed her a Cabernet then downed a large sip from her own glass. "Larkin is supposed to meet us at six. Maybe she can talk some sense into you."

Blayne looked over the grounds for possible prospects. A few men were sprinkled in the growing crowd. Eyeing a group heading their way, she rubbed her hands together. The first one had nice, broad shoulders, but he only came up to her nose. His buddy was tall but had a very weak chin. The third bloke was a bit more filled out than she preferred, but his jaw was strong, and he did have nice hands. Hands that coaxed a cigarette out of a pack of Marlboros.

Blech.

Taking a long, appreciative swallow, she let the heavy grape slide down her throat and soothe her from her insides out. She and Jamie had loved hanging out at the town wine tasting. They'd hop from vendor to vendor then stumble home to their apartment and make love on the ivy-edged balcony with the sounds of the bustling town as their love song and the warm sun their spotlight.

She clenched her teeth together and nudged Claire. "Help me find someone. Now."

Claire shook her head but stood on tiptoe and looked around.

"Woman, the point is to go up and down the boardwalk to see each piece." Maxine shook her head as she and her North Cove Mavens walked up. "I swear, you kids get lazier every year."

Blayne shot Claire a warning look, but her friend ignored her and then some. "Oh, I'm looking for a piece alright, but not of ice. Blayne seems to think a good tossing will cure her of wanting her ex."

She choked on her wine, spraying an ice bust of Michelle Obama with her drink. "I am not—"

"Lying isn't attractive, young lady. I expect more from your Irish blood. What the hell are you, a South Cove Madam?"

"They don't lie, Maxine."

Lifting her nose with a sniff, Maxine smoothed her silver strands with jewel-ladened fingers and cocked her head to the side.

Blayne opened her mouth to argue further but hiccupped instead. "Shit."

"What's this?" Janice Brennan, one of the North Cove Mavens and Maxine's best friend, joined them, her red curls bobbing about her face. "Those hiccups only mean one thing. Spill it."

Blayne tossed back the rest of her wine, then handed Claire the glass. "Thanks a lot." Ignoring the ladies, she stomped away, heading down the boardwalk.

But nothing short of a tsunami was getting them off her back, and they followed close behind.

"Apparently, miss thing here is looking to get laid in order to stay off young James Astor," Maxine shared.

Blayne spun around. "Are you *kidding* me?!"

The older woman raised her well-groomed, salt-and-pepper brows slowly, then pursed her red-painted lips. "What? Did I miss a detail?"

Janice looked her up and down with an approving nod. "Well, you'll find a prime specimen for sure in those heels. And I love the cape you're wearing. It's so Maleficent-esque. Perfect to hunt down your prey for the night."

She stopped in her tracks, smoothing her cobalt blue cape. She loved the look of it with her pencil skirt and heels, but now she just felt ridiculous.

Claire grabbed her arm. "What about that guy?" Four pairs of eyes followed Claire's pointing finger to a tall man with blond hair, a wide chest, and a tight ass.

Maxine whistled.

Janice clapped. "I approve, then I can start planning the wedding."

Blayne laughed. "Wedding?"

All four women watched as the young man turned and walked their way.

"Aw, hell," Claire grumbled with a light blush to her skin.

Blayne watched her, curious at the reaction. "Is there something you aren't telling me?"

"What? Oh God, no. That man drives me insane. I can't understand how anyone can take him seriously."

Janice waved her son, Mitch Brennan, toward them. "I do have to say, Claire. You have spectacular taste."

Claire rolled her eyes. "Kill me now."

Mitch kissed his mother and Maxine on the cheeks and smiled with a mischievous glint in his bright blue eyes. "Who has spectacular taste?" he asked.

Maxine shrugged. "Claire was just pointing out a sweet piece of meat for Blayne to take home."

Claire looked like she was going to be sick. "Maxine!"

"What? Between you and Blayne, I swear you two think I don't know my own name. Quit shouting it at me."

Mitch looked at the two women with a brow raised. "Who's the lucky guy?"

Just then, Jamie joined the group, and Blayne swore the universe was playing a practical joke, and she was the butt of it. The sight of his black sweater stretched across the chest she now had no need to imagine made her skirt feel too tight and her cape, suffocating.

"Someone's getting lucky?" Jay asked.

Maxine opened her mouth to speak, but Claire piped up. "Blayne's got a date."

Shoving her elbow into her friend's side, she hissed, "What the hell?"

Claire returned. "It's better than anything Maxine might have said."

The smile on Jamie's chiseled jaw fell. "A date?" His voice a low rumble.

She desperately looked around for a way out of this mess. Just the mere sight of him standing there, looking so impossibly handsome, messed with her resolve to hook up with someone to get Jamie out of her head.

Where the hell was Larkin when she needed her? Claire was not the best in the wing-woman territory. She searched the crowd. Farther down the board-walk, she spotted Dr. Stanton's son, Max. Max Stanton was a tall, dark and hand-some sculpture artist. A dreamer with amazing hands and a killer smile.

Oh yeah. Now there was a man who could potentially help her get her mind off Jamie.

She stepped away from the nosy crew with a clear mission, but before she could proceed, a familiar touch on her arm slowed her, his heat and scent clouding her head immediately.

She stopped dead in her tracks and glared up at him. "What the hell are you doing here?" She hated that her question ended higher and way more whingey than she'd intended. All she had to do was stamp her foot and she'd win the contest for being the biggest baby in Cape Van Buren.

"Do you really have a date," he demanded.

"I'm about to if you all would leave me alone." She continued down the boardwalk.

Jamie searched ahead then coughed with a slap to his chest. "The doctor's son? Really? Max was a tool in high school."

She slid him her best you're-fucking-one-to-talk look and kept on walking.

"You can't seriously be—"

She whirled to face him. "Can't *what?*" She was baiting him. Challenging him. He had no right to say a damn word about her love life. He had no right to pop back into town, on her project, in her head and her dreams, making her want and need and...

With a slow inhale, she forced herself to calm down, hoping the tension along her neck would release its death grip.

Jay glanced at his feet then back with determination in the light gray eyes she used to stare into for hours. He stepped close with his voice low for her ears only. "Deny that you feel something for me, and that's why you're running toward any asshole you find on the boardwalk."

His wide shoulders blocked everyone else from view, and the sense of him surrounding her became overpowering. She gave a gentle nudge but a firm order. "Back. Off."

For a brief moment, he looked hurt, but it must have been a trick of the light because that didn't make any sense at all. Surely, he didn't think anything would ever happen between the two of them. Only a fool would go back to a man who'd selfishly abandoned her in a foreign country.

And she had already proved herself a fool once with him.

Twice would simply make her an idiot.

"I've got to go." She took a step, but he followed.

"No, you don't, Bean."

She snapped her head up. There was a time she'd loved the nickname, she'd been his Irish warrior, his bean laoch, though he butchered the Gaelic term every time he tried to say it. When he'd shortened it to Bean it had seemed so intimate. Only they knew what it meant, what it stood for. She'd crossed an ocean for him.

But then he left.

Yet she still survived. She was a warrior. But not his.

She poked him in the chest, hiding the startling sensation that ran along her arm at the feel of him beneath her fingers. "I am not your Bean. You lost any claim to that name or me. Got that?"

He grabbed her fingers, refusing to let them go, and dropped his chin once in acknowledgment, an intense look in his eyes as he searched her face. She resisted the sigh of relief her lungs burned to give as she tried to tug her hand free. Finally, he understood.

There was a rough edge to his voice with his next words. "No matter who you run to or how many times, I'm not going anywhere. You got that?"

Mitch, Janice, Maxine, and Claire stood watching them from a few yards away, waiting to see what happened next. They should be embarrassed. She shook her head, tugging her fingers from his grip. "I've got to go."

"I'll be right here." His jaw was set in fierce determination.

Why couldn't he have made that decision ten years ago?

With a strength born of necessity, she let the desperation to both run to him and away from him fall like the leaves from cape trees in autumn.

Belying a calmness she didn't feel, she lifted the corners of her lips, and turned toward her nosy audience. She loved her little family here in Cape Van Buren, but they were crazier than a moose during mating season.

Mitch waggled his eyebrows at her—the shit. The man would do anything for anyone, but he also loved a little fun at someone else's expense. Two could play at that game.

"Hey, Maxine," she called out. "Mitch was such a good helper clearing out the attic, I bet he'd be even better organizing the basement. You need room for your —" she fake coughed into her palm, "—supplies...don't you?"

Maxine's eyes grew wide along with the grin on her face.

Mitch shot Blayne a look, promising her a slow and painful death, but for some reason, she felt lighter, happier.

"Wow. That was mean," Jay whispered.

She tilted her head. These boys were going to learn not to mess with her one way or the other. "No," she said with a smirk, then hollered once more to the group, "Maxine, Jay just said he'd love to help, too."

Maxine whistled. "Perfect! Four bulging biceps are always better than two."

Slowly turning toward Jay, it took every ounce of strength she had not to laugh. The look of betrayal on his face was priceless.

"What the hell?" His strained whisper was music to her ears. That would teach him.

"Now *that* was mean." She winked and gave a little wave as she headed down the boardwalk toward Max Stanton and his artist's hands.

Too bad he wasn't a magician.

Even after ten years and a broken heart, she needed some kind of magic trick to get the hell over Jamie.

CHAPTER 6

*A*fter a long week of overtime and overcompensating, Blayne pushed off her left skate at the whistle, propelling forward with such force her hamstring threatened to boycott. If she didn't find a way to relax and get some control back, she'd lose her focus.

And she refused to let that happen when Larkin was counting on her.

With Ireland on the horizon, she'd reached out to her older sister, Ruby, trying to get a feel for her da's reaction when she returned home, but her sister refused to talk to her. It had cut deep, but what could she expect? It hadn't just been her father she'd left. Emma had been her lifeline to all the goings-on at home. She owed her everything.

Not to mention the constant struggle with Jamie's return. She didn't know what was worse, the fact they worked damn well together, the fact that he'd caught her cheating, or the fact that when he had, she'd wanted nothing more than to kiss him senseless. Her lips still tingled with the memory of anticipation.

What a bleedin' mess.

She shoved against an opposing player sending the woman on her ass.

Senseless.

That was the key word right there.

She was goddamn, fucking senseless when it came to James Astor. The reason she'd hurt her da so badly when she'd dropped out of college and moved to the States, the reason she'd begged Jamie to stay when he'd left, and the only reason she could possibly have for wanting to kiss the bloody bloke now.

She threw her hip into another skater, clearing a hole in the pack, sliding through, then breaking free.

Her plan had been doomed to fail from the start, and when faced with his beautiful, sexy lips so close to hers...

She'd lost focus.

And lost control.

Flying past the finish line, she kept skating, pumping her arms and her legs until they burned with the strain. Lap after lap melded into a blur. Her lungs burned, her muscles screamed, but what a relief compared to the burn of wanting.

A whistle blew in quick succession, yanking her from her self-flagellation, and she screeched to a stop. Every cell in her body wanted to collapse to the floor, but she rested against her knees instead, trying to catch her breath.

One of the jammers of the Van Buren Roller Beauties, Lilly Sims, slapped Blayne on the arm. "You alright there? You're shovin' around like you're a Blocker."

She shook her head and squirted water in her mouth. "I'm fine. Just practicing."

Penelope Kent, a fellow Pivot, angrily replaced her skate. "Seems to me like someone is burning off a little steam."

"Sorry, Pen." Blayne sucked in a breath, trying to calm her lungs.

"I heard a wicked sexy ass...tor was back in town. Couldn't have anything to do with that, could it?"

All the tension that had drained with her energy returned ten-fold, clamping down on her like a lobster claw.

"You know we all have an idea of what happened even though you refuse to talk about it," Lilly said, snapping the gum that always seemed to be in her mouth.

"There's nothing to say. Besides, that was ten years ago."

"So...you're over him?" Jackie Miller, a blocker known for her hip swing and uppercut, asked. "Cause he is too fine to be spending his nights alone."

It took all her hard-won self-control to keep her hands on her knees and not wrap them around Jackie's neck. "Let's drop the subject and skate, shall we?"

The Van Buren Roller Beauties were like an extended family. Not quite as loved as her own family and not quite as close as Larkin, but close enough they stuck their noses in each other's business at every opportunity.

"I don't think so, MacCaffrey. We don't get as many sexy, rich dudes in Van Buren as we should, being a port city and all. If you're done with him, it's my turn." Jackie winked at the rest of the team.

She's teasing. Pushing buttons. Breathe in, breathe out. The whole conversation was nothing more than trying to throw her off her game for the next jam.

"Well, sloppy seconds always were your preference, huh, Jackie?" she tossed back, hoping to change the subject.

Unfortunately, Jackie didn't appreciate being reminded of her last boyfriend, Benny, or the fact he'd only come running after Jackie once he found out Blayne wasn't interested in the day after a one-night stand.

Jackie shoved off her skate and rolled up to stand nose to nose. "Are you trying to start something?"

Blayne refused to back down, though the onions her friend had eaten at lunch encouraged her to do so. "I could say the same to you." Rolling the slightest bit closer, she stiffened her spine. "If you really want to do this, Jackie, then let's go."

She was itching for a fight. Her intentions were to leave it all on the track, but if Jackie wanted to have it out now, she'd be happy to oblige. Which was ridiculous. She'd never been in a fight in her life.

Anything to get Jamie out of her head.

"Knock it off, you two. We have a jam to get to. What the hell is this? Junior high?" Penelope shoved them apart.

Blayne stiffened against the contact, and Jackie bowed up.

"Speakin' of wicked sexy..." Lilly bit her lower lip and outright leered toward the double doors as if the whole altercation never happened.

Blayne had always admired her calm. Lilly had an amazing ability to shrug off life, but Blayne wasn't sure if it was incredible coping skills or that her friend just didn't give a shit.

All the women went silent and stared at the very well-cut form silhouetted against the afternoon sun shining in from the slow closing double doors. She'd know those shoulders anywhere.

What the hell was Jamie doing here? Her pulse accelerated, leaving her breathless just as she'd finally gotten her lungs to calm down.

He gave a confident wave, but few of the ladies noticed. Thirteen pairs of hungry eyes perused the poor bloke up and down like they might the options at an open wine bar. Mouthwatering and lip-smacking good.

For Christ's sake. She rolled her eyes. Breaking away from her team, she rolled toward him. "What in the bleedin' hell are you doing here?" she grated out in a low voice.

His gaze traveled from the tip of her skates to her eyes, taking a scenic route along her legs and breasts.

If he lingered any longer she'd pass out from heat stroke.

"You haven't returned my calls, and I haven't seen you at the center. If I'd shown up at your place, you'd have called the police." He chuckled, but it was strained with an effort to pull his eyes up to hers.

"Smart man."

She glanced toward the door. "Go ahead and start the next jam. I'll be right there."

Jackie rolled forward. "And miss out on meeting our new guest? Not in this lifetime, MacCaffrey." She glided around Jamie, visually measuring him like cattle at the Somerset livestock auction. Trailing her fingers along his neck to his chest, she tapped twice, then stuck out her hand in a limp, fingers down fashion. "I'm Jackie, but you can call me…anytime."

"Ohmygod. Really?!" Blayne grabbed Jamie by a bicep that was more solid than the track she skated on and tried to push him through the door.

But he slid past with a smile to her teammates. "Any friends of Blayne are friends of mine."

The ladies threw out invitations to return whenever he wanted, all of which he answered with a generous smile.

An irrational surge of jealousy had her slapping his hand down before she could stop herself. Mortified by her reaction, she gave a fierce whisper, "Are you kidding? These are not the women you want to be encouraging. I thought you had more sense than that, at least."

"If you're not careful, I might think you're jealous."

On a huff, she retorted. "I'm not."

She totally was.

He outright laughed. "Sure you're not." With a shake of his head, he followed her outside. "Besides, you're a skater," he said, as if that statement alone contradicted her point.

She rolled down the cement sidewalk in an attempt to put some distance between him and her team of salivating sirens. For fuck's sake.

Spinning, she faced him. "Why're you here? You won." She crossed her arms over her chest. "Gloating will only piss me off."

Jamie shook his head. "Bullshit. There's no winning with you." He walked to his car then climbed halfway in, leaving his rear view high and tight.

He was doing it on purpose.

Clenching her teeth against the surge of lust wreaking havoc on her body, she cast a quick glance at her team confirming her suspicions that the Roller Beauties were taking in the scene like a goddamn drive-in. If she had popcorn, she'd throw it at them.

"Jamie, I don't have time for this. We have a tournament coming up soon."

He stood and shook the pages at her. "Here. I'll email them to you, but this way you can't ignore me."

"I wasn't—"

"Again. Bullshit."

She huffed and grabbed the papers. "What's this?"

She flipped through the pages of the bylaws, one at a time. At first scan, she couldn't quite believe what she saw, so she rolled toward his Audi and leaned against the trunk to take a closer look.

Everything was there. Her bylaw plan was unchanged save a word or two. He simply added in his sections on the donor program with one additional section that tore a hole in the walls around her heart more than anything else ever could.

"Archer's Angels..." She studied the giant of a man in front of her, startled by the uncharacteristic look of vulnerability on his face. "I'm not sure I understand."

He stepped closer, leaning his hip against the car. "Yes, you do."

"You even established a president and vice president position."

With a nod, he turned more fully toward her. "The whole idea of the center is to give the community a place to learn, to grow, to unite. And a huge part of that will be the programs for children so they can find joy on the Cape like Archer did. Right?"

Her eyes blurred with tears, but she refused to let them fall. Damn trickster was messing with her emotions.

"Well, what better way to protect Archer and Larkin's ultimate vision than to have an additional committee made up of children to help us focus on their interests and needs? We can set up some general guidelines and requirements, but ultimately this will ensure that we meet the needs of the children in Cape Van Buren. Not just what *we* think...but what *they* want."

She sniffed and blinked rapidly. Larkin was going to lose her shit over this. The loss of her little boy was felt every second of every day, but she was a strong woman and found joy in his memory. The conservation center was a huge part of her ability to move forward, and for Jamie to come up with such a beautiful way to celebrate Archer's memory was almost more than even Blayne could handle.

She remained silent. What she wanted to do was to tell him something snarky to piss him off and protect her heart, but she couldn't. Not with something so special.

"This is more than..." It was true. It was so much more. How was she supposed to process this? She was at a loss. No one in Cape Van Buren would believe it.

Nodding, she forced herself to look him in the eye. "This is perfect. I'm blown away by the idea, and Larkin will be touched beyond words.

Jamie studied her. "You're okay with the changes?"

She laughed. "You and I both know you didn't make any, you only added the donor section and now this."

He grinned. "I'm glad you like it. And for the record, I didn't change anything because it didn't need to be changed. You did really good work."

She dipped her chin. "It means a lot to me. This project."

"I can see that. Larkin's your best friend."

Pushing away from the car, she cleared her throat. "She is, but it's more than that. I believe in it. The message, the service to the town, is real."

Her fingers trailed a path along his jaw, and his eyes darkened. Surprised by her own gesture, she moved away, but he caught her, pressing a kiss to her palm.

They stared at one another, unable to look away. What was happening to her? A fluttering sensation spread through her chest.

"Blayne."

"Jamie, I'm going back to—

"MacCaffrey! Are you comin' or what?" Lilly yelled from the double doors.

Jamie winced. "Gentle bunch."

Skating backwards, she was thankful for the interruption. With a weak laugh, she said, "Roller derby is not for the faint of heart."

A fact she had to keep telling herself. There was no room for softness on the track or with Jamie Astor.

One wrong slip would result in a broken and bloody mess.

"Margaritas? Larkin can't drink, she's pregnant." Claire chastised Blayne but barely glanced Larkin's way.

Blayne took a healthy sip of her own, determined to enjoy Saturday night with her friends and put Jamie and his sexy lips and sweet gestures out of her head and heart. With one week of May firmly behind them, her time to return home was only a little over three weeks away.

Larkin's pregnancy wasn't easy for Claire, and none of them expected it to be, but the longing on her face every time she looked at their friend's growing belly made Blayne want to cry.

And she didn't cry.

At least not usually. It seemed since Jamie had returned to town, she'd already filled her tear quota for a lifetime.

"Cinco de Mayo only comes around once a year, and we're going to celebrate." She hung a few beaded necklaces over Claire's head before her friend could bat them away. "Besides, the blue pitcher is virgin...which I'd like to point out is hilarious, because Larkin has clearly had *a lot* of sex."

Larkin rolled her eyes and took a sip. "Neither of you can talk, so—"

Claire cleared her throat then downed half her glass. With a wince, she grabbed her head. "Shit! Brain freeze."

Larkin leapt up from her spot on the couch as quickly as her belly would let her, then wrapped her arms around her grimacing friend. "I'm so sorry. I wasn't thinking."

Claire nudged her away. "I'm fine."

Larkin kept patting her awkwardly on the arm. "I know, but I'm usually more sensitive. My brain lately."

Claire smiled. "Stop. I'm fine."

Blayne set out chips and salsa and a pink pitcher filled to the brim with full-octane margaritas. "What am I missing?"

"Nothing." Claire sunk to the midcentury, cobalt sofa.

"Since when are we lying to each other?" Blayne cocked her head in an I'm-not-playing angle and waited.

Claire threw daggers at Larkin. "Thanks a lot."

"I'm sorry." With a sigh, Larkin continued. "John was the only man Claire had ever been with."

Blayne shot a look of surprise at her friend. She was considered part of the North Cove Mavens when based on geography she should be a South Cove Madam. Claire's fiancé had been the man driving the other car in the horrific accident that claimed the lives of Larkin's husband and son. Claire had miscarried soon after the accident, and it took a while before she could handle seeing Larkin.

But Larkin had a way about her, and Blayne had refused to put up with any meanness—a combination Claire couldn't resist in the end.

Now Claire had been smacked back into mourning with Larkin's pregnancy —though she tried to hide it behind a too-bright smile.

Blayne sighed. "What the hell am I going to do with the two of you?"

She grabbed the chips and salsa and carried them over to the vintage round coffee table. The black table was a striking companion to the blue couch and white flooring and window treatments. She loved how it felt to be in her home. Almost as good as it would feel once she stepped on Irish soil once again. "So, how long has it been?"

Claire took a healthy sip of her drink.

Larkin settled into one of the matching velvet chairs flanking the sofa and tucked her feet under her. "Has it really been that long?"

"You hadn't had sex until Ryker," Claire tossed out in an accusatory tone.

"She's got a point," Blayne quipped.

Larkin's chest blushed bright red. "But, whoa, was he worth the wait."

Blayne pretended to gag on her finger. "Spare us your syrupy happily married crap." She teased her friend, but they all were so thrilled for her. Larkin and Ryker were made for each other. They healed past hurts in a way no one else would have been able to do. She may not think she'd ever be as lucky, but she certainly wanted all the happy ever afters for her girlfriends.

Besides, if Larkin was going to take the plunge again, Ryker was a delicious man to do it with. The whole tall, dark, and grumpy thing worked for the guy in a way that left women salivating.

"Claire, it's time to get you back on the horse, so to speak, and snog a bloke... or five."

Tucking her blond strands behind her ears, Claire spoke through a mouth full of chips. "Because your hunt at the South Cove Ice Festival was so successful?"

"I still can't believe you were going to randomly pick someone to take home." Larkin carried a chip loaded with a healthy chunk of salsa to her lips.

"Not randomly, I was making a choice. Taking action." She defended. "Unfortunately, three blondes stood between me and the doctor's son, and I wasn't about to damage Eclectic Find's reputation for any man. Jade Dawson is rising fast in her design business, and I plan on keeping her and her sisters as customers."

"Speaking of action..." Larkin let her words sink in. "I heard through Maxine, who heard through Janice, who heard from Lilly's mother, Rose, that a sexy and let me reiterate—*sexy*—man stopped by to see you at the track yesterday."

Blayne emptied her glass then poured another. "Stupid man, you mean. Who in their right mind shows up at a roller derby track? A man like him strutting around the Roller Beauties is like a rabbit in a fox den."

"So, you're still attracted," Claire said.

It was a statement, not a question, and panic and denial raced up Blayne's throat. "What? No." She waved in front of a hiccup. "I mean...of course, he's good-looking. No one is going to argue that, but I am not going there. Ever. No matter how sweet his actions might be sometimes."

She hadn't told Larkin about his Archer's Angels plan. It was his brainchild, so it was important that he be able to share it himself.

Larkin offered. "He's grown up. Maybe on the inside and out."

Blayne jerked her chin to the side, her heart arguing with her head at every turn. "It doesn't matter. My da warned me there was no honor in my actions or Jamie's when we left Ireland. Jamie only proved that to be even more true when he chose his career and family business over me. That isn't a mistake I'll make again."

"What mistake did you make exactly? Loving an eighteen-year-old? I hope you don't make that mistake again," Claire scoffed.

"Gross!" Blayne threw a pillow at her.

"So, what? You'll just stay single forever?" Larkin popped another chip in her mouth.

Blayne raised her glass in a toast to her best friends. "It's working for Claire and me. Maybe it's not in the cards for us like it was for you."

Claire raised a glass. "Hear, hear."

"You two are dumb." Larkin sighed. "This conversation is proof that celibacy isn't working for either of you."

Claire smirked with a raised brow at Blayne. "I can take care of myself for the time being."

Blayne raised her glass in a toast. "That's our girl!"

"But you don't have to. Since a relationship with Jamie is off the table, I think sex with him should be on one. A big one. A big table for big sex. I'm talking an all-nighter, better yet, a 24-hour free-for-all."

Heat rushed through Blayne's chest with the thought as she laughed. She snatched Claire's drink from her. "That's it, you're officially cut off."

She saluted. "I don't care as long as you go find Jamie and *get off!*"

The vision of Jamie's naked torso clouded her vision as she tried to process Claire's words amidst the echoes of laughter. Her pulse sped, her lungs constricted, and her fingers flexed under the onslaught of sexy horizontal memories. She'd have to be drunk or crazy to consider it.

So she tossed back the rest of her drink.

CHAPTER 7

*a*t the insistent chiming of the lighthouse bell a few days later, Jay opened the door to find berry-colored lips pressed into a resigned thin line.

"This is a surprise."

So surprising, adrenalin still pumped through him. The sight of her was both a salve to his soul and punch to the gut. She had her hair piled on top of her head, and his fingers itched to remove the pins, to see those thick, shiny locks fall to her shoulders.

She'd slap him, no doubt about it.

But ever since feeling her weight against him in nothing but her skimpy underwear—the look in her eyes, the hitch in her breath—he hadn't been able to think of anything else. There was something about her that made him feel like he was unraveling, but she was the only thing that could keep him together at the same time.

Made no God damn sense.

"I'm not here for you." She cut right to the point.

He dipped his chin. For every moment she softened toward him, another only showed that her resolve to keep her distance had strengthened. He didn't blame her, but he wanted to.

He'd just have to work harder.

Opening door farther, he stepped away. "Come on in."

"Nope."

He hesitated, drinking in the sight of her.

She had on her overalls again, which only filled his head with ideas that would get him killed. Instead of her signature wedges or heels, her feet were covered in a pair of bright yellow Converse sneakers.

"No?" He rubbed his chest in confusion, delighted when her eyes followed the action and went dark with her dilating pupils.

She shook her head. "I made that mistake already. We don't seem to do well in confined places together."

The memory of her straddling his body jerked his dick to attention. "Actually, Bean, I'd say we do very well in confined places." His voice dropped an octave with the memory.

"Too well." She lifted one side of her lip in an Elvis scowl and dismissed the direction he'd hoped to take the conversation.

But he had to try. Anything to see that heat in her eyes or the unconscious way she darted out the pink tip of her tongue and licked her lips.

Fuck.

"We need to go over our options for directors, so we can vet out those we want on the board," she said.

"But we can't do this inside?"

"Nope."

It made sense, and nothing made him happier than the fact she didn't trust herself with him. His dick agreed.

If she worried, then she still cared.

And if she cared…then maybe there was still a chance for them.

"Fine. Let me grab my sneakers."

He felt her eyes on him as he shoved his feet into his Nikes, wishing he knew what was going on in that head of hers. It would take time, but he'd find out. Maybe he'd even break some ground today. They needed to develop a friendship once again if he had any hope of something more. And God damn, he wanted more.

It had always boggled his mother's mind that he insisted on taking on the hardest challenges, but he'd learned long ago, they paid off the greatest reward.

And nothing was greater than Blayne MacCaffrey.

He joined her and closed the door behind him. "Don't we need to take notes, make our list, and brainstorm?"

"I know this town. As soon as I get home, I'll get everything we discussed down on paper and you can approve it. We can set up a meeting next week to get a feel for who's interested."

"Did you just give me permission to approve something, and I didn't have to win a game or bet first? I'd say this is progress," he teased, grabbing her hand.

She resisted at first but soon fell into step.

"There's a tree Ryker and I loved to climb when we were kids. Come on, I'll show you."

They made their way past the fountain in the circle drive and the memorial going up next to the newly built well where Archer's old well used to be. Her gaze lingered. Her frown made him want to wrap her in his arms and promise that bad things wouldn't happen.

"We're climbing trees now, are we?" She tugged her hand away.

He released it, not wanting to push her limits, but the loss was immediate, and he flexed his fingers against empty air.

Leading her down the path toward the woods, he laughed. "Please, I can't think of anything you wouldn't climb. From what I hear, that includes the corporate ladder."

"For a bit. But it didn't suit."

They broke into the ethereal world of the cape woods, all the noise of reality muffled into a soft hum of life and potential. "I've always loved it here. There's something so special about this property. It's like we've stepped into another world. Reminds me of home."

The mention of Ireland was like tightening a noose around his neck. "When was the last time you were home?"

He slowed. "Please tell me you've gone home."

She ignored him as they passed a small bench and hummingbird feeders near an active apiary. A little grin spread her red lips wide. He could stare at that smile for the rest of his life and never get bored.

"What?" he asked.

"Larkin. She's afraid of bees."

"But Ryker's a beekeeper." He watched the hum and activity of the box. Ryker's grandfather used to take Ryker with him as a boy. Jay was glad to see his friend reconnecting with his good memories from the Cape. Lord knows the bad ones were too awful to think about. "Has he convinced her to give it a try yet?"

She rose a brow. "Larkin? No way. In fact, she almost killed them both running from a few irritated bees up in the lighthouse lamp room when they'd first met."

He shook his head. "Those stairs are no joke." They came upon a big oak that was wider than it was tall.

Walking to the base, he patted the trunk then tilted his head to stare up the length toward the top. "Here she is. I've missed you, Daisy."

"You named a tree Daisy?"

He shrugged. "Ryker and I always thought she looked like a flower because she seemed to bloom so wide instead of being tall. You haven't answered my question."

The limbs of the tree started at about chest height. Jay grabbed on to one, then swung his legs up to another and leveraged to a sitting position. As expected, she followed suit on a thick branch next to him. Seeing her straddle the thing made him jealous as hell.

"I couldn't."

"But I never dreamed you'd stay here all by yourself," he said.

"I never dreamed you'd leave." She returned, using the branches above her to stand, then climbing two limbs above him.

He followed, hoping the weight of his guilt wouldn't yank him to the ground.

With his arm looped around a branch, he held her gaze. "Blayne, I was a selfish, eighteen-year-old bastard."

"Why did you ask me to come with you?" Her softly spoken question shredded his soul.

It was time to splay it wide open. "I fell head over heels in love with a Bean Laoch, my warrior."

She rolled her eyes. "If you're not going to give me an answer—"

"But I am. I loved you, never stopped."

Turning away from him, she closed her eyes.

He wanted to wrap her in his arms, to take it all back. Desperation and determination warred with how to show her he'd changed. Grown up.

"No excuse I have is going to make it okay. I was selfish, driven. Too often given everything I'd wanted but desperate to prove I'd earned every bit of it. I thought I couldn't say no."

"So, you left."

Rubbing a hand over his face, he nodded. "By the next morning, I'd figured out I'd made the biggest mistake of my life, but I knew I'd have to prove my worth to you before showing up at your door."

She snapped her head around. "What?! You were going to come home?"

"I had the return tickets bought, but I kept playing our last conversation over in my head. You said if I left to never return."

Incredulous, her mouth dropped. "So, it's my fault?!"

His error caught too late. "No. Never. None of it was you. That's not what I meant."

She moved to climb down, but he grabbed her arm. "Don't touch me." She ground out, her eyes shiny with tears.

Fuck.

"Just wait a second." He kept her by his side. "I didn't mean it like that. Fuck, Blayne. I ditched you, for Christ's sake. There was no way I could show my face to you again until I proved myself. Until—"

"Stop." She trembled. "Stop with all the proving shit, Jamie. I never asked you to prove anything to me. I loved you." The words ripped from her throat, and she stopped to swallow.

"I loved you for you. I didn't care that you were an Astor or where we lived or if you were given everything you had. I loved how hard we played, how hard we worked...how hard we loved. You broke me." Her breath caught, and he reached for her.

"No." She stiffened. "Give me some space."

The pain in his chest was suffocating, but he'd deal with it tenfold if he could take away the pain he'd caused her.

Yet there was so much more, so many reasons he'd thought staying away was the answer.

Jay had loved his childhood, the events and travel and opportunities. He loved and respected both of his parents. They were an adoring, close-knit family. Always there for each other even when they were apart. "Family first" was the motto drilled into him since he could talk.

But his mom had always been left behind while his father had pursued

71

success. When his father was home, he'd take his mother on a trip as if it were the solution to all her loneliness—a passport payoff of sorts. At least that's how it had seemed.

How could he ever get her to understand that he'd refused to make her live the solitary life hoisted onto his mother's shoulders?

Or his need to prove that he was much more than just the heir to the Astor throne?

And as James Alexander Wilmington Astor the III, it had been his duty to follow suit. More so, he'd been determined to show everyone he'd deserved to. His drive to succeed in the short term had blinded him to what he'd wanted in his future.

He hadn't expected the opportunity to come when it had, and he'd thought they'd have more time. He thought he had time to establish a relationship with her and find a different way for the next Mrs. Astor to live that would be more fulfilling. But his sense of duty, his drive to succeed hadn't been her responsibility.

He'd talked himself into believing it was kinder to encourage her to go home to Ireland and live a full life than one dictated by the ties of his family's history. Always left waiting for him to come home.

He shook his head. "Blayne."

She climbed higher. "I'm not talking about this anymore."

The tightness in her voice was more than enough warning, but he had to do the hard thing and pursue it anyway.

Joining her in the middle of the treetop, he straddled the branch she was on and faced her.

"Look." He adjusted his position. "I couldn't ask you to keep following me around because of my family business." Regret piled so high, he could barely see around it.

She stared him in the eye. "You never asked. You explained, but you refused to discuss it. You decided for me...which I hated the most. As if I didn't have an intelligent thought of my own. And then you left me, Jamie. You left and never hesitated."

"I did. I told you."

"But you didn't." She leaned against the trunk. "If you had, you'd have known

I'd stayed. If you had talked to me, you'd have known that I could not go running to my da after hurting him the way we did."

The sorrow in her eyes tore at him.

"He warned me. Did I ever tell you that?" she asked softly, her voice thick. "He told me our haste and our actions were selfish. But I ignored him because nothing was going to keep me from being with you." She closed her eyes against the sight of him. "But you didn't feel the same for me."

He shot his hand out. "No. Blayne. That's not—"

"You left," she interrupted. Two words that told a story he was ashamed to star in.

All the years flashed through his mind. Holidays, birthdays, simple weekends. She'd missed them all. Trying to protect her from himself, from his mother's lonely existence, only left her lonelier than she ever would have been as his wife.

Hell, he'd hate him, too.

"Wow. That is the truth of it, isn't it?" she whispered, her lip trembling. "All this time, I've been so mad at you, but I'm the real one to blame. I should have never left Ireland."

He shook his head. "What we had was special. If you hadn't come with me, we would have never—"

Bewilderment widened her eyes. "Never what? Broken up? Been alone? None of it mattered. I devastated my father, abandoned my siblings…and for what? A boy who didn't really love me."

She blinked and gazed past him, with a shudder. Her eyes roamed the landscape behind him for a few silent moments. "But I never would have had this. I do have you to thank for that."

He tried to swallow, but his throat closed at the finality in her tone. Glancing over his shoulder, he stared across the cape toward the lighthouse and the Atlantic beyond. It was a breathtaking view and somehow made his actions worse than he'd imagined.

"I'm sorry." He wanted to shout at her for saying he didn't love her, but the truth was, he had to take responsibility for his actions back then. "I fucked up, then convinced myself I was doing what was right. I made a huge mistake, but you can't say I didn't love you. We were best friends."

"*Friends?*" she scoffed, crossing her arms over her chest. "Friends don't abandon each other, Jamie. Larkin would never walk away from me like that."

His gut twisted as she seemed to slide further away even though he could reach out and touch her.

"We work together. We dated once upon a time." She leaned toward an adjacent branch and grabbed on, then slid her legs from the one they shared. Branch by branch, she made her way down the tree until she paused and looked back up at him through the newly budding branches.

The hollow look in her gaze dropped all his hope like a stone in his gut.

"But we are not friends."

～

*B*layne forced the words out. She had to make Jamie think there was nothing between them in order to keep herself from running to him. The sincerity in his eyes, the passion in his voice had tugged at her in such a way that she wanted to abandon all thoughts of reason and open up to him once again.

She couldn't let that happen.

It was time to get on with her life. To connect with her family. She'd learned a very hard lesson about trust, about who and what she could count on.

Love certainly wasn't it. It came with conditions and ultimatums.

Larkin loved her. But she wasn't her friend's priority and shouldn't be.

Her da told if she left to never come back. The words had torn her in two and must have been a family motto since she'd been guilty of the same with Jamie.

Karma may have been sending her a message, but so had common sense. She was not destined for a forever love. A heavy weight forced a sigh from her lips as she slipped to the earthy floor, the crunch of dried leaves and pine needles reminding her of the consequence of trusting someone—of loving someone.

So here she was, faced with all the feelings she wasn't good with, and had to find a way to stay strong. The answer was keeping the one man she'd ever loved at arm's length.

He dropped down beside her, the vibration of his landing reverberating through her body. "The hell we aren't." His voice held an edge that skittered up her spine.

The stone gray of his eyes seemed to harden with the most delicious intensity when he was upset, and she tried to ignore the hold they had on her. "Look, we need to talk about the board of directors. As much as I hate admitting that Ryker is right about anything, we do work well together. So, let's work."

She ran her fingers along the spongy moss carpeting a large boulder, braced for a fight.

"Fine."

His acquiescence startled her more than if he'd yelled. She walked ahead, afraid to make eye contact, which burned her ass even more. It was time to buck up. Take charge. There was no other way to survive him. With a surge of rebellion, she glanced at him.

He was a giant in the forest, looking like a man determined to win.

Her heart sped up in her chest. She couldn't think of a time that he'd ever lost.

"Dr. Stanton," she blurted out.

With a nod, he stepped up beside her. "Good choice. I was also thinking Clint Fenwick."

She rolled her eyes. "Really? That man patrols the good people of Cape Van Buren closer than Sheriff Davenport." She didn't even try to hide her disgust.

Jamie's laugh was hard and swift and made her belly flutter.

"You just don't like anyone telling you what to do."

"Well, that's because other people are stupid." She climbed up and over a cluster of rocks, then jumped to another clearing. "They always think they somehow have the right to tell you how to live your life and what that should look like." She shook her head, continuing forward.

The sounds of the ocean called to her. She loved the rhythm and flow of the crashing waves. The crisp spray of the sea breeze, almost like a cleansing, like starting anew. "I'll never understand—

"Stop talking. Don't move." Jamie snapped in a fierce whisper.

She spun around. "Are you kidding?" Had the bloke gone mad? She certainly didn't take orders from him.

But the look on his face had nothing to do with judgment and everything to do with concern.

A few rough *bluffs* came from up the path she was on.

Slowly, she turned her head until she was looking in the eyes of a huge moose. A cow with a small calf trailing behind it.

Adrenaline raced through her limbs, leaving her hands and feet stinging with pins and needles. "Jamie," she whispered. Her heart thumped in her chest, making it hard to breathe.

The cow was too close to run from, but if it didn't turn around, that was her only option.

She moved away, but the moose stepped toward her, and she froze.

Jamie carefully stepped down from the rock beside her. "Steady," he whispered.

"What are you doing?" Her voice was barely a desperate breeze of sound, but the moose's ears laid back, and the large animal licked her lips. A sure sign that she was not happy.

"I'm here." His voice registered as if whispered from miles away.

The moose stomped on the ground. Jamie closed the space between them, now in the sights of the moose as well. She released a few hard *bluffs*, then charged.

"Drop!" In one hard push, Jamie shoved her to the ground then covered her body with his own. The moose stomped her huge hooves next to them. She couldn't see anything with her head tucked and his body blocking out the light, but she felt the shudder and felt the spray of dirt.

The commotion continued for what felt like a lifetime.

Jamie kept cover over her body with a few grunts, swears, and a prayer, then the thundering of hooves faded off in the distance.

The two of them stayed wrapped tight in their little cocoon, heavy breaths and heartbeats all she could hear. Jamie adjusted above her, then slowly moved off her to the dirt at her side.

"Holy fuck."

She peeked down the path to find their angry friend gone, and gingerly sunk to her backside. "Ohmygod."

Jamie's jaw was set, and he was holding the side of his right thigh as he watched to make sure the moose wasn't returning for round two.

"Are you okay?" She slid closer to him, the smell of earth and sea mixing with his cologne.

With a nod, he sighed.

"What were you thinking?" she ground out.

He held her gaze with a stubborn glare of his own. "She wasn't letting you move, and I wasn't going to leave you out here alone."

Her pulse refused to slow down, and tears of relief or fear or both burned behind her eyelids. What the hell had he been thinking? He could have been hurt.

She punched him in the arm, but before he could respond, she grabbed him and yanked him to her chest.

"Blayne."

"Shut up. Just shut up." She kissed the top of his head, keeping her arms wrapped around as much of his large frame as she could. "I can't believe you did that."

She'd never been so scared in her life.

He held her gaze. "I'm okay."

"You got hurt." She glanced at the tear in his cargos and the red skin visible beneath. Her throat constricted.

"And I'll heal."

"Don't play it off. Oh my god." She tried to get a better look, but he held her to him instead. She could hear the pounding of his heart in the silence of the woods.

What made him do it? Guilt for the past, a need to make things right? Whatever it was, she felt awful. She never wanted to see him hurt, especially not over her. There was plenty of pain going on in this world. What happened between the two of them didn't need to add any more to it.

She grabbed his face and held it between her palms. "Don't ever do something so stupid again."

His eyes darkened with something that wrapped around her in a warm embrace. The corner of his mouth lifted in half-smile of understanding. "Don't worry, I'm fine."

"I'll worry if I want to."

He opened his mouth to respond, but she covered it with her own.

The feel of his lips forced a small moan from her throat, and he tightened his hold.

She slid her mouth against the tempting fullness of his, relearning a terrain she'd known only too well so many years ago. His taste slammed her into a vault of memories, but with the potency of reality, the urgency of now.

Pressing into him, she took the kiss further, needing to feel what it was like to be in his arms again. Arms that were so familiar yet so changed. There was a fullness, a thickness to his body now that delighted her senses, weakened her knees, and set off a flutter of awareness so deep, no one kiss would ever be enough.

She skimmed the hard mounds of his shoulders and deep valleys and ridges of his back, an excitement of discovery fueling her curiosity.

On a growl, he leaned back, taking her with him. She pressed her breasts against his chest, trying to ease her wanting, and dove even deeper into the ocean of the kiss.

"Fuck, woman." He grabbed her hips, holding her to him as he moved against her.

Her tongue slid along his, and he groaned low in his chest. Emboldened, she stroked her tongue against his again and again. She bit his lip with a gentle tug, then soothed the area with the caress of her mouth desperate to taste him, as if she'd never have the chance again. "Jamie," she whispered against his lips.

"I'm here." His voice rasped out as he caressed her sides until they found themselves tangled in her hair. The pins she'd used that morning to stack it high on her head fell to the dirt beside them and her hair tumbled about their faces.

The large, fingers of one hand massaged her neck, while his other slid to the exposed skin along the seams of her overalls, making her body scream to be touched.

A loud crack pierced through the sensual cloud of her brain, reminding her where they were and what they'd just encountered.

She kissed his lips, then his face, easing back just a bit.

His grip on her tightened. "Bean, wait."

She stared into his eyes, always amazed by the transparency she found there. "Thank you." She kissed him. "Thank you for protecting me."

He pushed her dark hair away from her face, tucking it behind her ear. "Take it back," he demanded, the timbre of his voice low.

She stiffened. "What?"

"Tell me we're friends." The need shining from his eyes was more than attraction, it was more than a casual encounter.

Her head demanded she deny him, to protect herself. But her heart...her heart couldn't beat so close to his and lie.

"We're friends," she whispered, but moved away, brushing the pine needles and dirt from her overalls. Once she was a safe distance from him, she added. "But only friends."

His dipped his chin, but there was a stubborn glint in his eyes, and a fissure of excitement shot straight to her core. She'd almost forgotten how intoxicating it was to be wanted by this man.

Hiccup.

CHAPTER 8

*B*layne walked with Larkin and Claire along the boardwalk in front of the Van Buren Boat Club, breathing in the cool, salty breeze and admiring all the sailboats entered in the Van Buren Wave Races. Seagulls called from the water's edge, swooping to the surface then sailing high in the sky, and she followed their route, jealous of their view. She hoped to run into Cape Van Buren's very own life coach, Clay Parrington, and nail down an interview for a board position. Then the list she and Jamie created would be complete.

"Look how vivid all the colors are." She tilted her head to take in a particularly beautiful sail.

The one-design boat race was more than how fast the boat was in the water, it was also based on the best sail artwork. The boat that won the race didn't necessarily win the competition. It made the event very unpredictable and, sometimes, quite volatile. Especially when the North Cove Mavens and South Cove Madams were involved. Art was very subjective, and the feud between north and south unfailingly stubborn.

Two years ago, a riot practically broke out between the North Cove Mavens and South Cove Madams over one particular boat. There was nothing scarier than a bunch of feisty AARP members battling it out with canes and swinging pocketbooks.

"The teal and fuchsia in this cobalt design are breathtaking." She followed the line of a peacock on one sail. When the fabric was in full bloom, the peacock's feathers spread in an amazing bouquet, and when it was folded, the peacock looked as though it peeked around the mast pole.

Noticing how quiet her opinionated friends were, she turned around.

Both Larkin and Claire stared at her with open mouths.

"What?" She glanced about, trying to figure out what in the world was going on.

Claire cocked her head. "Who the hell are you...?"

"And what have you done with Blayne?" Larkin finished.

Blayne chuckled, the feeling reverberating up her throat and across her chest. It felt good to laugh. "Are the two of you mad? I don't know what you're talking about." She stepped close to Larkin and touched her arm. "You feeling okay?"

Larkin sputtered. "Me?! You just used the words vivid and breathtaking. Blayne MacCaffrey doesn't use words like vivid and breathtaking. You're more of a 'badass' and 'that's the shit' kind of gal. The only thing I've ever heard you be even close to poetic about is one of your roller derby jams."

"Jam? Who wants jam?" Evette Kingsley walked up, flanked by Maxine and Janice. Evette looked like Popeye's wife, Olive Oyl, and grew the most amazing berries in the world. "I have a fresh batch ready to bring to your store."

"Better save me some," Maxine piped up. She'd been using Evette's berries and Janice's flowers in her moonshine for years, and there was no getting the recipe out of her. It was hard enough to get any of her brew as it was—unless there was a good amount of cash involved.

Blayne appreciated the interruption. Larkin and Claire's assessment was disturbing. Why was she acting so sappy? Maybe it was surviving a moose encounter.

Moose.

Jamie.

Oh no. The image of Jamie popped into her mind with his delicious mouth and to-die-for sexy shoulders. Her lips tingled along with the rest of her body. *Shit.* She had to rein in those betraying thoughts, and fast.

But her heart had a mind of its own. She cared, and it scared the shit out of her.

They were friends. They worked together.

81

Doesn't mean you don't want him.

Oh, shut up.

Great, now she was talking to herself.

"That's great, Evette. I know we were getting low. Your jam doesn't last long on my shelves."

The North Cove Mavens could not even get a hint of her rekindled attraction for her ex or they'd be scheduling her wedding over at The People's Church.

"That's all fine and good," Larkin butted in. "Let's get back to why our Blayne is so full of smiles and sunshine."

"Blayne?" Maxine asked, suspicious.

"Oh, please. It's a beautiful day and the designs are spectacular." She arced her arm out toward the rainbow of color floating on the North Cove waters.

Maxine played at adjusting the collection of silver bangles at her wrists. "Ah, I see what's going on here. Things going well with Jay Astor, are they?"

Every flight or fight instinct she possessed charged through her system. How the hell was she going to get out of this one? "As a matter of fact. Yes. Jamie and I settled on our list of potential board members. We start our interview process on Monday."

All three women lifted their chins and fluffed up like the peacock on the sail.

"Well, I hope I hear from the two of you," Maxine gave them a pointed stare.

Evette shook her head. "A local business owner would be the perfect addition to the community center board."

"Oh really, and does that include Shelly Anne Mills?" Maxine teased. Shelly Anne was the proud owner of the Flat Iron Coffeehouse. The best coffee along the east coast, but they never dared admit it in front of Evette. She owned The North Cove Confectionery on the north side, while Shelly Anne was a South Cove Madam, and with the feud and all...

Evette huffed. "Clearly, a North Cove Maven holds the more desirable characteristics for a responsibility such as this."

Janice shook her red curls. "Please, ladies. Why don't you be more obvious?"

The three women fell into a good-natured argument, and Larkin nudged Blayne's arm. "Tell me what happened."

Claire stepped closer, put her fingers over her mouth, and gasped as if in disbelief. "Tell me more," she said louder than necessary.

Blayne shushed her. "I can't believe you."

"Oh, believe me. I can do way worse." Claire folded her arms over her chest.

Phantom sensations of Jamie's hands and lips ignited her skin, caressing, demanding...promising. She held her breath to prevent the sigh that rolled up her throat.

"Nothing happened."

Claire opened her mouth to holler.

Blayne grabbed both ladies and tugged them farther down the pier. She tucked their arms in hers. "We met at the lighthouse to work. We climbed a tree."

"What are you, Paul Bunyan's sister?" Larkin laughed.

"I didn't want to work in the lighthouse."

"Ahhhhh..." Claire said. "Now that is an interesting fact."

Blayne yanked them along, then slowed, worried it was too fast in her friend's delicate condition. "Do you want to hear the story or not?"

"Do," they answered in unison.

She sucked in a breath. "We came across a mama moose with her calf."

"Oh, crap. Mama's be crazy," Claire teased.

"Long story short, the moose charged, Jamie knocked me down and shielded my body with his own."

Larkin's eyes lit with surprise. "Oh. Wow. That's not the story I was expecting."

Off the hook.

Blayne all but sang hallelujah that she didn't have to admit to the kiss. "It was terrifying. The cow stomped a bit, hit his leg, but then left."

"How's Jay?"

That was what she wanted to know as well. "Last I heard, he's okay. We were shaken up, his thigh had a nasty bruise on it, but otherwise okay."

Claire shook her head. "My dad used to warn my brothers and me all the time about how dangerous the moose can be. They're just so big."

"A couple years ago a bull moose took on a Jeep. The Jeep didn't make it," Larkin added. She studied Blayne for a second. "So, you're telling me that Jay saved you? How does that make you feel?"

Everything.

Confused.

Terrified.

She waved to dismiss the question and tried to redirect their attention to the sailboats. "What time is the race?"

"You didn't answer my question," Larkin challenged.

Claire piped up. "Six p.m. They're finishing all the sail art judging by four, then transitioning to the start of the race. Who do you think'll win?"

"Now that is a question I can answer." She stuck her tongue out at Larkin. She didn't want to think too much about how selfless Jamie's actions were. She had to admit they were friends against her heart's better judgment, but anything beyond that was impossible. Pondering any of it too closely would only make the next few weeks harder. So she decided to live in the moment while he was here.

There was no way she was sharing that with Larkin. At least not now.

"I think Dr. Stanton's team has the greatest chance. Max is an expert sailor."

"Are you seriously going on again about Max Stanton?" Jamie's deep voice washed over her like the bubbling waves upon the cove beach.

Blayne spun around. "Jamie."

She hadn't seen him in almost seventy-two hours, and the fact she had the time down so accurately meant she was in a heap of trouble.

$\sim$

*J*ay inhaled the sight of Blayne like he would a pizza after an involuntary fast. She must have come over to the Wave Races from work since she was sporting one of her vintage dresses and stockings with the seam up the back that drove him insane.

He wanted to dive under that skirt and follow where that seam disappeared with his eyes, his hands...then his tongue.

From the lighthouse until spotting the little crew on the boardwalk, he'd repeated over and over to keep his hands to himself. A few days apart would surely help his self-control. But they needed to get moving on their interviews if they were going to make the deadline, so it was time to get to work whether he liked it or not.

Blayne's lips worked over silent words for a second, then finally added her voice behind them. "You know damn well the man is good with his hands. Makes for an excellent sailor."

The twinkle in her eye challenged him, and he loved it now as he had so long ago. "Good with his hands, hm?"

Nodding, she pretended to study a sail's painted artwork of old-school life preservers. "Great...with his hands."

She was teasing, but damn if he didn't bristle against the idea anyway. If he ever did see Stanton's hands on her, he'd be hard-pressed not to break them, then punch the guy in his goddamn face.

Larkin laughed. "Oh, please. The triplets would have you tied to a brick and thrown you out to sea if you stepped one foot near the man. You said so yourself."

Blayne's eyes shot wide. "Larkin."

And suddenly, the sun shone brighter and the air smelled sweeter.

"Is that so?"

She nibbled her lip, looking everywhere but him.

She'd let him believe she'd gone out the other night, but apparently Coach Dawson's daughters had other plans. He'd thank them all later when he had the chance.

He'd given her space after their moose encounter Wednesday. Having her in his arms again, holding her, tasting her was exactly what he wanted, but she didn't trust what was between them, nor did she trust him for that matter. Retreat was necessary to protect his progress.

Seeing her now in the flesh almost made it impossible not to gather her up and show her just how happy he was to see her, how thrilled he was to hear she never did go out with the artist.

She wouldn't admit it yet, but she'd belonged to him since they shared pints in Ireland...and he belonged to her.

The North Cove Mavens joined the group. "Asking your mom to be on the board, James?" Maxine asked.

Jay could smell something that stank of trouble in the question. He hadn't realized how interested the townspeople would be in serving on the board, but as soon as word got out that they were putting together the committee, the lighthouse phone had been ringing off the hook.

He shook his head. "No, ma'am. She and my dad will be traveling back and forth to Europe for some business and pleasure over the next few years, so she won't have the time."

The look of relief on Maxine and Evette's faces was comical. One less in the pool of competition, he guessed.

"Oh! Well, that's good that they'll get to travel. How fortunate for her," Maxine replied.

Blayne guffawed. "And you, Maxine. Subtlety is not your strong point."

"Look who's talking about subtleties. You've been panting like a pup in heat since Jay walked up."

Her jaw dropped to her chest and she sputtered. "I have not...you don't know...I can't believe—"

"Are you actually going to finish any of those sentences, dear, or is Jay's presence a little too much for you to handle?"

Claire and Larkin were laughing so hard Jay was afraid the Van Burn baby might be born right then and there. He liked the idea of Blayne being hot and bothered by him, but teasing her about it was not the way to win her over.

"To be fair, Ms. Van Buren, a board member of the Archer Conservation Park of Cape Van Buren will need to be very poised and diplomatic. Quick barbs and ribbing really aren't what we're looking for," he said.

Maxine Van Buren's mouth melted into a thin line and her eyes narrowed into slits. "Is that so, James Astor?"

Aw, fuck, he was in for it now. Where the hell was Ryker? He could work magic when it came to smoothing things over with his grandmother.

"Well, I guess you also won't be looking for any of my moonshine, will you?"

Ouch, that hurt. The woman's moonshine was the finest kind. And that was coming from a man who'd traveled the world and back.

Larkin wrapped her arm around Maxine. "Be nice, Maxine. He's making a solid point." She then whispered something in Maxine's ear that made her mouth relax into a smile and her eyes soften to their good-natured twinkle once again as she glanced from Blayne back to him.

Apparently, Ryker had passed on some of that magic to his wife. He'd have to thank her later.

Blayne took the distraction and jumped in. "Well, I'd love to stay and chat, but I need to go find Clay Parrington. I heard he'd be down here today."

She dragged him down the pier toward Beach Booty, the North Cove's go-to shop for beachgoers, from shark tooth necklaces to bathing suits and everything in between.

"Whoa, slow down." He resisted. She walked faster in her heels than he did in sneakers.

"I was not panting."

His grin was quick, and his thoughts wicked. "You are now."

Arched brows drew together in a warning. "I wouldn't even start if I were you."

Jay loved the spark in her light eyes when she was worked up, and he couldn't help but push just a little. It was better than the loss and sorrow he witnessed in the tree.

If he could keep that look from ever crossing her face again, he'd move the heavens and empty hell.

He drew a finger down her bare arm, clavicle to wrist. Technically, he was still successful at keeping his hands to himself. A finger didn't count. "I like your dress."

A small shiver shook her frame and his grin grew broader.

He grabbed her hand. "Come on, Clay is part of the team on boat seven. Let's grab an ice cream, then we'll be able to get an appointment set up when the crews gather to prepare for the race.

She didn't hesitate, but she walked slowly. "I guess I could use a small bowl from The Ice Cream Cove."

She was thinking a lot these days. Taking her time and sometimes responding in the exact opposite way that she used to. It made sense. People grew up in ten years, but it made his ability to read her a challenge.

"Thank you, by the way. Standing up to Maxine might cost you in the moon-shine department."

"Well, I'm sure you'll share," he said with a wink.

She stopped dead. "Hell, you don't know me very well, do you? Her brew is not something you share, but something you greedily keep all to yourself."

"Blayne." He laughed. But the look on her face spoke more clearly than any words could. No moonshine for him.

She slid her hand into his. "Now, about that ice cream…"

Adrenaline surged through him with the need to jerk her close, to make her promises. Promises he'd keep this time.

But instead, he played it cool, walking the pier hand-in-hand as if they did it

87

every day. The truth was, it was painful. It gave him a taste of everything he wanted in one simple gesture of acceptance.

He'd savor every second, the feel of her palm against his, the awareness of her next to him, her scent floating on the breeze. His body responded with its familiar tightening, but it was so much more. He was solidly fucked.

They stepped up to the open window of The Ice Cream Cove, and she dropped his hand to get a better look at the flavors.

He wanted to resist every time she let go.

Her eyes were bright. "I know what I want."

"You always have." He laughed, though he felt anything but light. "Peanut Butter-Vanilla Dream?"

"Every time." She snapped a finger then spun away from the counter. "In a bowl, please."

"You heard the lady," he said to the ice cream concierge. "I'd like cookie dough in a waffle cone, please."

Grabbing the ice creams, he joined her, standing in front of an impressive boat with a sail of an incredible setting sun. "Damn, that's beautiful."

She accepted her ice cream with a nod. "The art is my favorite part of the Wave Race."

He raised a brow. "Now that does take me by surprise. I figured you would be all over the physical competition of it."

"Don't get me wrong. I love a good fight, but there is something impossible about choosing a winner from an ocean of beauty. I'd never want the job, but I'm always thrilled by the announcement."

He studied her. "You surprise me at every turn. Your competence, your work ethic, your insight."

"You have, too." A large glob of ice cream disappeared off her spoon. She worked it in her mouth with a thoughtful look on her face. "Jamie, this idea you have...Archer's Angels...it's beyond amazing." Her voice was soft and dreamy. He didn't know if it was the ice cream or his idea, but hearing his name spoken in such a way only solidified his determination.

Somehow, someway, he would change her mind about them.

About him.

"I'm excited to iron out the details and propose it to Larkin. I'll make sure you know when. I'd like you to be there."

"Thank you." Her whisper struck right in his heart.

He held her eyes, and a silence stretched between them, serenaded by the waves lapping against the boat hulls and the call of the seagulls.

He slid his fingers along her jaw and cupped her chin, his big hand a contrast to her porcelain skin and ruby lips. "Blayne…"

Her eyes wavered, then she looked past him. "Oh! There's Clay."

Jay followed her gaze until the man in question came into view. A sigh rose in his chest, but he held it in with a quick nod. "Let's go then."

It only took a few minutes for her to grab Clay's attention and detail the board member responsibilities for him. Her eyes were bright with excitement. There was no way the man could resist her enthusiasm.

"Any questions?" Jay asked.

Clay shook his head. "Not about the board position, but I do have some ideas for the center's programs. I think our town could use a few opportunities to learn coping skills, how to set life goals and make them a reality. And not just for the adults, but if we could teach children early and repeat it often, the effect on their adult life is immeasurable."

Jay loved his passion.

"This is exactly the kind of thing Larkin Sinclair, excuse me, I mean Larkin Van Buren has in mind." She rummaged through her bag, then handed him a business card. "Give me a call and we'll set up a meeting. I think she'll love every word you have to say."

"Excellent. I'm excited to be a part of this. Thanks for thinking of me." A whistle blew, and he glanced at his boat. "I better get on board. Wish us luck." He saluted.

She and Jay watched him board the boat, then they hurried alongside the ice cream shop as a crowd of people rushed the pier to see the boats off.

Laughing, she blew her bangs from her eyes and leaned against the wall of the building. "This is fantastic. He's the perfect fit. Larkin's going to die."

He nodded. "I consider that interview in the bag. One down, and we hadn't thought to start until next week."

"We really do work well together, don't we?" she admitted with a grin.

Her statement set something off inside of him. Something raw and needy and selfish.

In one fluid motion, he stepped into her, melting their bodies against the side of the building. He took her mouth with his own. Her flavor exploded on his tongue, and a low rumbling growl rolled up his chest.

Her arms wrapped around his neck, leveraging her body tighter to his. The feel of her breasts crushed against him almost knocked him on his ass. His hands itched to be filled with her warm, womanly curves, and he dragged them down her sides then around her hips to cup her ass. Yanking her closer, he ground himself against her softness, trying to ease his wanting.

The small whimper that escaped her lips registered in his brain like an aphrodisiac.

So much for keeping his hands to himself.

If he was going to fail, this was the way to go.

CHAPTER 9

"Spill it," Larkin demanded.

"But you haven't even told me about your day yet." Blayne dodged the demand by busying herself with the magazine options on the table next to her chair at the Flat Iron Coffeehouse. "As for me, I finalized the paperwork for Alora Kingsley to manage my store, she's been doing a great job."

Larkin stared at her.

"Evette's niece, if you remember. Since you asked so nicely."

Ignoring the sarcasm, her friend sank into the chair cushion. "I packed a few remaining boxes at the Cape house. Some albums that I'd had over there along with some of Maxine's." She smiled sweetly. "Now spill."

Blayne tried to shrug off the wash of goosebumps that ran along her skin as the moment she'd shared with Jamie against The Ice Cream Cove played again in her mind. His kiss had rocked her harder than any kiss he'd given her before. Why was that? Was she such a rebel, or had she simply gone mad that the forbidden made him taste so sweet?

Because what woman in her right mind would go back to a man who'd left her like he had? But with each passing day it was becoming more difficult to keep her distance.

She was failing hard. A grin tipped up her lips.

Maybe it how his shoulders had filled out, overflowing her hands, or how he towered over her more than before?

She was a strong-ass woman, damn it. A man being bigger than she shouldn't make him attractive, but damned if it didn't do just that.

Or worse.

It could be his thoughtful addition of Archer's Angels, or the care and attention he was taking on the project. That was so much worse because it was a hell of a lot harder to fight against an attraction based on respect and admiration.

If only she could get Larkin to tell her to stay away. To best-friend-threaten her into keeping her distance. Surely that would help.

"I'm sick," she exclaimed.

Claire and Larkin looked at one another then back.

"Do you have a cold?" Claire looked confused.

"No." Blayne shoved up from the velvet cushion, then sunk back down. Balling her fingers into fists, she said, "I kissed him."

"What?" her two friends blurted in unison and scooted to the edges of their seats.

Larkin studied her from the corner of her eye. "Him who?"

Pinning her with a look, Blayne had to force herself to unclench her jaw. "You know him who."

"And why are you acting like you're mad at me?" her friend questioned.

Blayne smoothed the fabric of her red cigarette pants and dropped into the chair, questioning her decision-making on every plane.

Claire asked, "Are we talking about Jamie?"

"We had a successful day yesterday and we both got caught up in it all. We really do work very well together and—"

"Ha, so Ryker was right!" Larkin grinned.

Claire waved her off. "I don't think now's the time to gloat on your husband."

"Oh, right." A sheepish shrug couldn't disguise the supreme satisfaction glowing from her eyes.

Shelly Anne walked up. "What's up, girls? You three are busier than a beehive."

Blayne threw a warning look to her friends.

"Can I get another espresso, please?" Claire asked abruptly. "I can't get enough of this stuff."

Shelly Anne beamed. "Of course, honey. Does Evette know you're here?"

The former Studio 54 dancer had her long, waist-length hair braided with a few silver ribbons to go along with her bohemian-style silver skirt. She maintained a decades-old but friendly coffee competition with Evette's North Cove Confectionery. Blayne could only imagine how fierce she'd been in her heyday, and the *competition* was a no-brainer.

Larkin laughed. "She should know better if she thinks we wouldn't come. Your coffee is the best in town."

"Got that right." She sniffed as if patting herself on the back. "Anything else, ladies?"

"No, but thank you, Shelly Anne." Looking past her, she turned to Blayne. Crap.

"As I was saying...we got caught up in our success yesterday and Jamie kissed me. Hard. And long."

Claire sighed. "Hard and long are two of your favorite things."

"Claire!" Blayne laughed.

"Just because I'm not getting any doesn't mean I don't want any," she retorted.

Blayne couldn't fault her for that logic. "It was different somehow. Just like after the moose—"

"Wait, what? *After* the moose?"

This was the drawback of having good friends. They never missed a damned thing. She sighed. "Yes. After the moose took off, we kissed for the first time."

"I knew something else was going on. Did it *feel* like the first time?" Larkin teased.

Shelly Anne returned with Claire's espresso. "Be careful, honey. This is some high-octane stuff."

"I'm a pro." Claire laughed. "Don't worry."

"Well?" Larkin pushed.

"As a matter of fact, yes. It's Jamie and all the same things I was attracted to before but more. I don't know. He's filled out. A man now. We were so young. But it's more than just how drop-dead sexy he is. I wish it wasn't." Days gone by of laughing and dreaming flashed before her. "It scares me."

"Why?" Claire asked.

Because losing him had been excruciating and scary in a foreign country all by herself. Thank God she'd already met Larkin by then.

She shook her head at the impossibility of it all. "I'm going home to Ireland."

"I really wish you'd quit reminding me." Larkin frowned.

"I know, but I am. I miss my family. I need to apologize to my da." She swallowed past the pain. "Emma keeps me up to date with everything going on. Dylan's a real heartbreaker these days, and Ruby's in charge like always—but she shouldn't have to be. I hate that I've missed so much, but I can still hear my da say not to come home."

"Oh, Blayne. He didn't mean it."

"You don't know Noah MacCaffrey. He says what he means and means what he says." She tried to organize her thoughts through the web of pain and guilt that had been spun over the years. "I hurt the family. My da and I'd always been close, and I was so mad when he didn't immediately understand my need to be with Jamie back then that I lashed out. Said hurtful things."

"But by now..." Claire offered.

Blayne nodded. "By now he knows he was right. It's time for me to face the music, but I couldn't do that until I was worthy to do so. And thanks to you," she gestured toward Larkin, "I'll finally be able to face them."

"You are more than worthy. And that didn't just happen now."

She blinked a few times. "This project will do so much for this community. It is so much bigger than myself or a firm or any business I can build. It changes lives and futures."

With a nod, she strengthened her resolve. "Now, I can go home. Ruby needs a break from having to take care of everything all the time, though I think she loves it. She was always the leader of Dylan and Emma and me." She looked around the coffeehouse at the couples and families. "And I'm lonely. I don't have anybody here. There's no reason to stay."

"But that's not true. *We* are family." Larkin's voice trembled.

Blayne rushed to reassure her. "Of course. But you have Ryker and the baby on the way. Your mom and dad are here. Maxine."

"And my sister." Larkin pinned her with a pointed look.

"I'll always be your sister."

"Yeah, yeah. You two love each other. Let's get back to the kissin'." Claire drank another sip from her cup.

Larkin and Blayne glanced at one another then shot a look at their friend. Her cheeks were pink, and a thin bead of perspiration was glistening from her upper lip. She'd scooted to the edge of her chair as if afraid it would give under her any moment.

"We love you, too, Claire. You know that." Larkin rubbed her arm.

Claire looked at them like they were mad. "I don't care. I want details."

Blayne raised an eyebrow at the demand.

"Oh, count me in. I'm a sucker for details." Mitch's deep voice startled the three women as he sunk to the couch next to Claire. Larkin and Blayne quickly straightened in their seats.

Claire stiffened. Clearing her throat, she said, "You wouldn't be interested in these kinds of details, Mitch. They have to do with full lips and big muscles..." As the words raced from her mouth, she snapped her hand that was trailing down his arm back to her side.

As if her words had slowly dawned on her, she continued. "Not your full lips, I mean, not that your lips are full or that your muscles are large. I mean. Shit."

She looked at Larkin and Blayne for help.

Larkin stood, her belly making the action slow, then settled her arm around Claire. "Our friend here just had one of Shelly Anne's high-octane espressos and is apparently hornier than a bull moose during mating season."

That snapped Claire out of it. She shoved Larkin's arm away. "I am not!" she shot back with a snarl. Jabbing her thumb at Mitch, she added. "And certainly not for this guy. He's about as good a choice as Jaimie is."

"What the hell?" Mitch said. "Look who's talking. You're wound tighter than Clint Fenwick during a PG-13 movie at the park."

Blayne laughed. Mr. Fenwick watched over Cape Van Buren's morals like Janice did her plants, with a sharp eye and persistent care. Though sometimes his care seemed somewhat stifling and judgy. The poor guy needed a little lovin' to calm him down. Then maybe he wouldn't be so afraid of it.

And then there was Mitch. One of the Cape's most eligible bachelors who'd do just about anything for anyone. Except commit. He'd always hold a special place in her heart for all the free legal help he'd provided the center. Giving him a hard time had become one of her favorite pastimes, next to teasing Ryker. But this boy gave it as good as he got it. "Relax, Mitch. Claire's got a point. Your reputation doesn't just precede you, it parades ahead of you like a high school marching band."

"You're one to talk, Blayne MacCaffrey. I have buddies who'll walk a mile out of the way to avoid passing your store after they'd dated you."

Her grin was quick and sharp. "Good. I can't abide idiots."

Mitch slowly backed away. "I am regretting this whole exchange."

"Be nice or I'll tell your mom," Larkin teased.

Mitch turned on his heel and disappeared into the crowds at the front of the coffeehouse. Smart man.

Blayne and Larkin slowly turned curious eyes on Claire.

"What the hell are you two looking at?"

"Do you like him?" Larkin asked.

"Not even a little. He's irritating and cocky...and irritating."

"You already said that," Blayne teased.

"He's an ass, and so are the two of you." Claire grabbed her cup and threw it in the trash. "Stupid coffee high."

Larkin laughed. "Uh huh...sure."

"Weren't we telling Blayne how she's an idiot if she doesn't jump Jamie?" Claire said.

Panic washed through Blayne's chest. "Hell no. You were telling me how only a masochist would put herself into such a position after everything the man did to me."

"No, you're right." Larkin sunk into the velvet cushions of her chair. "But what if he's really changed? Then that means he's all the things you loved but better."

Blayne couldn't believe what she was hearing. Who the hell were these people and where did her friends go? "Are you kidding? Since when do we push each other to run into broken relationships?"

"But it doesn't sound like it was broken. Just badly timed." Claire offered.

"Look, I'm not telling you to go down that same road again. But I worry about you not thinking this through and giving yourself a chance to figure out what you really want."

"I know what I want," Blayne ground out. "And it doesn't include watching the love of my life walk away...for a second time."

Two sets of eyes stared at her as if she had the answer. Her words echoed around her head, increasing her dread.

"I'm just saying, quit fighting everything between you and Jamie. He's changed. Grown up. And I'd hate for you to lose out on this second chance because you were afraid. It's time for you to live a little too."

"I live plenty." She snorted. Gathering her things, she stood.

"I'm suggesting hold off on the fast food for a while and try something a bit more savory, probably more satisfying, and definitely tastier." Larkin winked. "Nothing is set in stone. Even if you allow yourself to really spend some time with Jamie, it doesn't mean you still can't go home to Ireland. But at least this way, you'll go home knowing for sure."

Blayne didn't know if she should laugh or swear or cry. Larkin was supposed to keep her from the love of her life, not push her toward him. The problem was, she had a bad feeling that the more time she did spend with Jamie, the more time she'd want to. It was a terrible and incredible situation to be in.

But no matter what happened, she had to go home. This time it was more than just what she wanted. She owed it to her family. Jamie didn't even know it, but he'd taught her a very important lesson when he'd left so long ago. The importance of family. He'd put his first as she should have done with hers.

Well, now was the time.

She'd get this launch off the ground with his help, and she might even let herself enjoy the time she did have with him.

But then it was off to Ireland.

~

*J*ay sat in the kitchen of the Cape Van Buren house—AKA new community center—and ran through the numbers one more time before saving the document. If his plan was executed the right way, the donor program would keep The Archer Conservation Park of Cape Van Buren running in a way that was sustainable and encouraged growth. Satisfaction settled in his chest. Now to make his plan to win back Blayne work just as successfully.

He had to find a way to remind her of how great they really were together

97

before he'd fucked it all up. Their work on the launch was a great start, but he needed something more.

Something intimate.

A loud bang sounded from the basement, followed by a louder curse.

Pushing away from the large island, he walked to the top of the stairs. "Need a hand?"

"Nope," Maxine yelled from below. "I know what I'm doing, young man."

"Never doubted it for a second." With a grin, he snatched the open, cobalt blue canning jar of moonshine from the counter and poured it into a small tumbler. He had one job. Don't let anyone disturb Maxine while she was working with her harvest. He'd stand guard all day, every day, if it promised him some of her brew.

Taking a sip, he let out a sigh as he walked through the rooms. The painting was finished, the floors restained, and Cape Van Buren-inspired artwork now hung from the walls. The navy and eggplant color scheme, though striking, had been swapped out for a softer gray and neutral palette with a lot of wood and rope reminiscent of the coastal life they lived. Beautiful in its own way, and in line with the motif set in the lighthouse.

Later in the week, the new furniture and supplies would be delivered. Then they could set up the offices, classrooms, meeting room, and the new community space.

A grin stretched his lips.

Being part of something so significant to a whole town was a different sensation than anything he'd ever experienced before. He'd closed huge deals, helped companies turn never-imagined profits, and set his own investments up to serve him a lifetime.

Yet everything still felt hollow.

Alone.

No matter what he'd accomplished, it had never left him settled or with a feeling of purpose.

But this was different.

The fulfillment, the wash of contentment, of pride, was so much more than anything else. If he wasn't careful, he could get high off something like this.

Or maybe it was simply the fact that he was a part of it with Blayne.

He'd lost count of the empty one-night stands he'd had over the years. How numb he felt, as if just going through the motions. No matter how sweet, or smart, or sexy the women he'd met had been, his dreams remained crowded with crystal green eyes and berry red lips.

But he'd persisted, searching for someone to fill the ever-present hollowness in his chest. How many hearts had he broken? And what kind of selfish bastard kept looking to fill a hole, knowing from the beginning that there was only one answer...one person who could?

Scrubbing his fingers through his scruff, he moved through the back hallway, past the honey room—that wasn't going anywhere—and into the front receiving room. An opened box along the front wall caught his attention.

With another sip of the shine, which he secretly wished had the power to wash away his regret, he lowered to the floor, leaning against the wall. He set his tumbler next to him, then pushed the cardboard flaps open. The box was filled with albums, and he took them out one by one.

The first album had pictures of Larkin and Archer visiting the Cape. He flipped through the pages. This would be great to have in the library for visitors to look through. Kind of the beginning, the "once upon a time" of the new center.

The next one hit him in the gut.

Blayne's glowing green eyes stared at him with a grin so big he'd call it cheeky—and she'd hate it. At least, she'd pretend to. She was way more sentimental than she wanted people to know. He'd always guessed it was part of her self-preservation mechanism.

He turned the page to find her and Larkin at the Cape Van Buren Independence Day Festival with fireworks bursting in the night sky behind their heads. He remembered that day clearly. In fact, he was the one who'd taken the photo.

The next picture made him pause. His chest squeezed with desire. Blayne sat on his lap with her arms around his neck. Her black beret had tilted in that sassy way of hers that left him wanting to cover her body with his, to stake his claim every time he saw it.

Selfish bastard was right.

They'd just finished a huge fund-raiser in the town square at The Fountain of Youth to provide financial assistance to families who required extensive pediatric care in town. The two of them had set it up, run it together, and ended with more funds than any other event that year. Maybe ever.

The front door opened, and Judge Carter strolled in with a look on his face that reminded Jay of a kid looking for candy.

"Hey, Judge, Mrs. Van Buren's in the cellar." He turned to the photo, loving the smile on Blayne's face as his words finally registered. Shit!

He jumped up, jogging over to intercept the man before he reached the top of the stairs. "I mean she was in the cellar...dropping off..."

He racked his brain for anything the woman could have dropped off.

"Albums. That's it." He grabbed the older man's arm and dragged him toward the boxes he'd discovered. "Remember this?" He showed the judge the photo of him and Blayne.

Judge Carter craned his head to look toward the cellar door. "Was?"

He waved dismissively. "Oh yeah. She left about an hour ago." If the judge went near those steps, Jay was a dead man.

He swore he could feel the perspiration beading at his hairline. Never partaking in any of Maxine's moonshine again would be the worst punishment ever.

He shoved the picture in front of the judge again. "Remember how much money we brought in that year?"

Judge Carter was hesitant to relinquish his search for Maxine, but he focused on the picture. "I do. I do. I don't think we've had an event quite as successful since." He scratched the whiskers at his chin. "Why would Maxine drop the albums in the cellar? I don't think they'd keep very well down there with the dampness and all."

Clearly, the judge hadn't set foot in the basement of the Cape house since Ryker taken over. Maxine had talked her grandson into letting her use the space and had the whole thing finished out with climate control and good lighting. What better way to make her brew?

Hell, they could convert it into a comfortable apartment if they wanted to someday. But he secretly hoped they didn't. It would be a huge loss if Maxine quit making his favorite drink.

Directing the man through the front door a little firmer than he was comfortable with, Jay snorted. "Sounds just like her, doesn't it? I had to go down and haul them upstairs. You know Maxine."

Holy hell, the woman would have his balls in her distiller for that comment.

He glanced toward the door, praying she hadn't heard him. The bead of sweat broke free and dripped down his temple.

"You okay, boy?" the judge asked. "You don't look too good."

A loud bang made both men jump.

"What was that?" Now the judge looked completely suspicious and stepped back over the threshold.

Puzzle raced through the foyer toward the kitchen and both men chuckled. "Damn cat," Jay joked. "He's always causing mischief. Larkin moved him over here when they started working on renovations."

The judge nodded. "Good idea, keep the poor guy from getting lonely."

Jay looked the man over. He'd never pegged the guy as a cat lover, but it was obvious he was averse to being lonely. Probably why he let Maxine run him around so much.

"Where'd you say Maxine went?"

Jay swallowed the guilt tightening his throat. "I think she said something about going downtown to meet up with Larkin."

The judge nodded as he made his way down the steps toward the circle drive. "If she stops by, let her know I'm looking for her."

"I will." Jay waved then closed the door with a solid thud. Turning, he leaned against it with a sag of relief.

"Nice save, dummy." Maxine stepped through the door to the cellar stairs. "I said don't let him in."

Jay shook his head and gestured toward the photo. "I got distracted. And FYI...you delivered the albums to the Cape if he asks."

She glanced at the photo, then harrumphed. "You lied to a judge, hope it was worth it."

Jay took in the smiling face of Blayne one more time then slid the photo into his back pocket. The idea of seeing that smile every day for the rest of his life fueled a determination in him so strong he wondered if he'd ever really wanted anything before. His struggle to work past his selfish tendencies lost ground every day he spent with her. He wanted, needed Blayne in his life.

And he wasn't going to stop until he made it happen.

"Oh, it is."

CHAPTER 10

*B*layne stood outside of the Cape lighthouse and searched the horizon of the Atlantic as the salty sea spray floated up from the crashing waves. Her sister Emma's voice was clear through the phone. "He hasn't said anything. I'm sorry."

"But you told him about the launch?" She hated the insecurity in her voice, the weakness, but damned if she could stop it.

Emma remained silent for a beat. "I did."

"And what did he say?" Blayne ran her finger over the old stone framing of the red front door. It was cold and uninviting, but she still couldn't wait to go inside. Inside was a whole different story.

Her da was like that. He was a big, gruff bear of a man on the outside, but when you really got to know him, really looked into his heart, all you saw was love and affection and gratitude. Even though they'd lost ma, he'd always taught them to be grateful they had each other. Life would have been horribly different if not for the way their da handled the heart-wrenching tragedy. She dropped her chin to her chest and closed her eyes.

She yearned to be back in a place where he'd shine that light on her once more. Before she'd taken him for granted.

Emma delivered the words she had been afraid to hear. "He said you were a different Blayne than the one he knew."

"What's that mean?"

"I don't know, B," Emma said, the sympathy in her voice making the words a little easier to hear.

"He hates me." Tears welled in her eyes, and she had to swallow hard in order to speak again. "Will he ever forgive me?"

"Aw, come on. He doesn't hate you. He's just—" Emma paused "—hurt. And you know how he is when he's hurt. He builds up walls...retreats."

Blayne blinked away her pain and gave a quick nod for her own benefit. "I do."

"You're just like him you know."

"I'm not," Blayne said.

"Yeah, okay. You're not. Look, I've got to go. Do you have your tickets yet?"

"The launch gala is two weeks from yesterday. I'm on a plane the next morning."

"I'll pick you up at the airport."

"Okay... Thanks, Em."

"Love you." Her sister said softly.

"Me, too, you."

She disconnected the call and rapped her knuckles on the door. Jamie would be a good distraction from the heavy weight of shame in her chest.

The red door swung open, revealing a broad, very naked chest and biceps bulging with every stroke of the towel over his wet head. "Come on in. You were earlier than I thought."

She followed behind Jamie, watching the sinewy muscles of his back flex as he walked, especially the ones that disappeared beneath the band of his loose-fitting sweats.

She wanted to jump on in.

And if there wasn't enough room, she'd make some.

She was done holding back, done waiting, done punishing herself for her stupidity. It was time to embrace it.

They made their way to the main living space, which was light and airy with all the windows open, encircling them with the most incredible views she'd ever seen. The Atlantic sprawled in one direction as far as forever, and the Fountain of Youth in Cape Van Buren square was visible in the other. She'd never tire of this town.

Jamie threw the towel on a stool by the tall counter and swung around. The fresh, just-showered scent of him mixed with the ocean air coming in the open windows and clouded her brain like an aphrodisiac.

"Want some coffee?" he asked.

Blayne nodded, afraid her voice would squeak if she tried to speak. His abs were like the ocean waves, rippling down his body toward the shore of those damn low-hanging sweats.

"Hey, remember this?" He tossed a photo on the counter, his large body taking up space and overwhelming her senses.

Playing it cool, she picked it up and slid onto the stool. She remembered that night. "Oh, I loved that hat."

"What do you mean *loved?*" He looked disappointed, and she held back a grin. Where the hell had she put it? She needed to dig that sucker out. "We hit that one out of the ballpark, didn't we?"

The picture tossed her back ten years and a broken heart ago. They'd worked together, raising money for the kiddos of the community.

"How's your thigh?"

"Sore but getting better." Jamie handed her a coffee in an Archer Conservation Park of Cape Van Buren mug as he unconsciously rubbed his thigh.

"I still say you're crazy, your leg could've been broken." She hoped it was healing fast. She still couldn't believe he risked himself like that.

"What's this?" She looked at the logo—a lighthouse rising out of the ocean with waves splashing around the base.

"It's just a prototype. I was playing around with some designs to show Ryker and Larkin. We need to shorten the full name a bit for merchandise and such."

She looked at the logo, turning the cup from side to side. He stepped close to her as if to see what she was seeing. His clean, masculine scent wafted through the air, tickling her nostrils. More than anything, she wanted to freeze this moment in time and allow herself the simple pleasure of just breathing him in.

"Add birds."

He cocked his head to look at her. His lips were so close it would hardly take any effort to close the distance and take what she wanted so badly.

With a swallow, she blinked and pointed to the logo. "Add the silhouette of birds around the top of the lighthouse in the sky. It'll add some visual interest and use the space a bit better."

He studied the design. "Good idea." Nudging her with his hip, he asked. "You like it?"

She grinned. It was time to give the poor guy a break already. She'd been sharp and short, pretty much a bitch since he'd arrived in town when all she'd seen from him was hard work and a lot of care.

"It's really good. Seriously. I love you."

His grin was quick and wicked.

A wash of horror closed her throat and she choked on her coffee. She grabbed his arm. "*It!* I love it." She coughed through her words, her eyes watering and her throat convulsing to move the fluid to its rightful place.

The skin under her fingers was taut and hot to the touch, and the vibrations of his laugh rippled up her arms, leaving goosebumps in their wake. She shook her head. "Shut up."

He looked down at her hand, which squeezed his arm as if on its own accord. His eyes darkened in a way that promised a storm—one she would love to ride out. "What's happening, Blayne?"

An intense look shone from his gaze, and his jaw flexed rhythmically as he studied her.

She swallowed hard. The desire to feel pleasure, to feel *alive*, slammed into her as she held his gray gaze with hers. Memories of their love, the happiness they'd found with each other flooded her with wanting and hope and fear. "I don't know," she whispered. "But I know I'm tired of fighting with you. I think we've both had enough."

"I don't know what you want here..."

He knew. She could see it in his face, but he was going to make her say it.

If she could take what she wanted on the rink and in life, then she most certainly could do it here, now, with Jamie.

"I want you."

The flash in his eyes sent a warning shot of adrenaline through her body. He grabbed her waist, lifting her to the countertop as if she weighed little more than the box of files she'd schlepped over from the community center.

"Are you sure?" he growled, his lips a whisper from her own. She could already taste him, feel him, and he hadn't even touched her mouth yet.

"Yes. Bleedin' hell, kiss me already, Jamie." It was as close to begging as she'd ever get.

His hesitation was brief, then he overwhelmed her with his taste, his heat, and his own wanting. What she was doing went beyond crazy and well into insanity, but she wanted this man to her core.

His mouth slid across hers in a hungry exploration. Completely new and at the same time familiar. There was a strength in his touch, a challenge and demand that hadn't been there once upon a time. Whether maturity or urgency was the cause, she didn't know and couldn't care less because the result was pure sensory overload.

He slid the ribbon from her head, tossing it to the side, leaving her dark locks to tumble around her face. Gathering her hair in his hands on either side of her face, he brushed it against their cheeks, setting off waves of sensation along her neck and collarbones, until he finally grabbed it all behind her head in a tight hold.

With a gentle tug, he eased her head back until she looked him in the eye, both gasping for air and grasping for footing that never existed between them. Their chemistry had always been explosive and thick, needing to be managed in order to keep from shutting out the rest of the world. God, she'd missed this. Missed them.

She tugged him closer, wrapping her bare legs around his waist until that part of him she craved the most pressed against her, hard and hot and throbbing.

"Jesus Christ, Blayne." He gasped as she ground into him as much as her tenuous balance would allow.

Her navy and white polka dot halter dress suddenly seemed way too constricting.

"Get it off," she begged.

He chuckled, running his hands up her sides until they found the aching fullness of her breasts.

The need to feel his skin against hers, to drown in every sensation created by his touch, drove her mad. Jamie grabbed the billowing bottom of her large skirt while she unbuttoned it from around her neck, then together, they pushed it down over her hips. She stepped out of it, and he froze.

The cool breeze rushed across her bare, heated skin in a delicious caress, and her body gave a shiver of anticipation.

"Holy hell, you didn't have anything on under that thing." He pointed an accusing finger at the dress, and she giggled at the look of shock on his handsome face.

His eyes devoured her from her white-painted toenails to the top of her head, lingering on her tattoo, making her thankful there was a breeze to keep her from combusting. She bit her lip and looked him over, stepping close. Placing one finger on his collarbone, she dragged it over the warm, slick silk of his skin toward his chest. Over one pec to the top of his rippling abs.

"You've filled out in the time we've been apart."

His response was something between a laugh and a strangled choke as he yanked her to him. The heat of his erection set off tiny pulses of excitement between her legs.

She glided her finger lower, down the center trench of his abs to his navel, then lower still until she hit the elastic band of his sweats. His muscles rippled beneath her touch, and as she tugged the waistband out from his body, he gave a warning growl.

A teasing glimpse of what he had to offer rushed her initial intention of teasing him bit by bit. She couldn't take it when her body screamed to feel him now, so she dragged his sweats past his hips, pushing the fabric to the floor.

And there he was.

Straining to make contact, golden skin and an iron promise.

She dropped to her knees.

"Blayne." He could barely get out her name.

Without a word, she closed her mouth around him and sucked him in hard.

He grabbed the counter behind him as if trying to find steady ground. She cupped the base of him and stroked along with her mouth, working his slick skin, reveling in the sweet, heady taste of him.

He fisted her silky hair, assisting a rhythm known long before the two of them had ever met. The sounds of the ocean crashing its waves against the rocky base of the lighthouse surrounded them, demanding they keep up. Setting a pace she was all too happy to match.

"Shit, Blayne." He tugged gently on her to rise.

"I'm not done."

"You have to be, or I will be." He lifted her to face him. Before she got her footing, he stepped into her, yanking her body against his, and up into his arms.

She wrapped her legs around his waist, using his shoulders as leverage to rub against the length of him.

"God damn it, I've wanted to bury myself inside you every God damn second since seeing you in those damn skates with your tattoo peeking out from your skirt."

"I can put them back on." Desperate to feel him, she ground against him harder.

"Fuck me. You need to slow down, woman, I have a plan," he demanded as he tightened his hold, helping her increase the pressure between their bodies.

"I can't. I want you too much. You need to keep up."

His bark of laughter filled the room. "I'd never make the mistake of thinking I could."

With her wrapped around him, he moved to the stairs. "I have something I want you to remember for a lifetime." He stopped briefly by his wallet and grabbed a condom, then took the circular stairs toward the lamp.

"Jamie," she pleaded.

"Almost there." He set her down at the base of the lamp room ladder and spun her around. She grabbed the rungs, shocked by the cold metal against her skin. He stood close behind, that part of him she craved so strongly rubbing along the base of her back.

He slid his mouth along her clavicle to her neck and bit into her skin gently. "Go. One rung at a time." His whispered demand sent a shiver up her spine.

"Jamie."

He gave her ass a sharp tap. "One rung."

She stepped up, never realizing before how amazing the metal could feel against the sensitive arch of her foot. His fingers drifted down her arms in a light caress as he placed a kiss in the middle of her back.

"Another."

She stepped higher, this step lifting her backside to his eye level.

"Now, take your right foot and hook it around the outside rung."

She glanced down at him like he was crazy, but the look she found there made her knees go weak, and she held on with all her strength, moving her leg around the metal as she was told.

His gaze was intense, and his breaths came out in rapid succession. His lips traced the design of the Celtic knot of her tattoo, each rose, the entwined ivy, then he leaned forward and flicked over her clit with his hot tongue.

"Fuck," she cried, her body shaking but wanting more.

He laved at her folds, dipping inside then swirling around her clit. She squeezed her eyes shut, trying to keep a hold on the ladder. Her legs shook. Her breasts rested over the top rung, leaving the other to press cold and hard against her midsection. The sensations were out of control, making her lose hers, and spinning her toward a precipice she wasn't ready to fall over yet.

Then he stopped, resting his forehead against her left leg. "God damn, woman. You taste like heaven." He stepped up behind her. "Climb before I can't."

They stepped up into the lamp room on shaky legs, then Jamie led her to the outside walkway.

It was decadent to be naked with a bird's-eye view of the world.

"We shouldn't be up here. What if someone sees us?"

He flung his arm out toward the Atlantic. "Who? Besides, since when are you shy?" He swung her around, pressing her into the glass windows and giving her a panoramic view of the ocean.

Her body pulsed with his touch, with the ebbing and flowing crash of the waves so far below.

Stepping into her, he lifted her against his chest once again. "Wrap your legs around me, Bean."

She met his gaze and saw the look of love she'd recognized so many years before. Nothing could stop her from taking what she wanted, what this man made her feel.

In one swift motion, she was in his arms, her back pressing against the cold glass, her breasts and stomach one with his heated body. The contrast stole her breath.

He rubbed his hard, hot length against her center, having donned a condom at some point in their journey. "Are you sure?"

Was he mad? "Fuck all could make me stop now." Her body screamed for the release, her heart screamed for the connection, and her soul screamed for the acceptance that this man was and always had been meant for her.

He positioned his head at her entrance then slid slowly in, the girth of him stretching her wide with a pressure that made her cry out in ecstasy.

Inch by inch, her body welcomed him, waves of pleasure spiraling through her. When he was seated fully, deeply inside of her, he took her mouth, stroking his tongue along hers as he began to thrust in and out of her, setting off every nerve in her body in a quaking, joyous celebration.

She held on, meeting him stroke for stroke, as her pleasure built beyond anything she'd ever known.

"Jamie!" she cried.

"I'm here. I'll always be here. Let go, Blayne." He rounded his upper body, pressing his lips to the side of her neck as they reached the promised precipice and flung themselves over.

She opened her eyes to see a world of blue waters with white-capped waves crashing toward the base of the lighthouse as her orgasm slammed wave after wave of pleasure into her.

"Oh my God." She gasped, digging her fingers into his shoulders to meet his demanding strokes and to make some of her own. This was bigger than anything they'd ever shared before.

An ocean of love engulfed her as the world went white in a blinding surge of pure bliss.

He'd wanted her to remember this moment forever.

If she survived it, she'd never be able to think of anything else.

CHAPTER 11

*B*layne's heart spasmed as if trying to understand the emotion bombarding the poor distrustful thing as she grabbed Jamie's offered hand and laughed. "Why are you walking so fast?"

"The sooner I can get you to your apartment the sooner I can see how great that dress of yours looks on the floor."

A rush of heat spread across her chest with the image he'd put in her head. She'd like to see it, too. The past twenty-four hours had been a marathon of re-exploration for the two of them, and every single orgasm had been more exquisite than the one before.

"My apartment? Why not the lighthouse? It worked so well the first time." Her suggestive brow wiggle was answered with two strong arms hauling her close.

"Apartment's closer." His wolfish grin was quick and hit her right in the panties.

He led her down the sidewalk of Cape Van Buren Drive toward the Fountain of Youth. The sun was high in the sky, making the brick sidewalks radiate a luxuriant heat up her flowing white skirt. Seagulls called out as they circled above, and a cool, salty breeze traveled with them as they approached the square. "Let's get this townhall over with, and I'll show you how great the view of Van Buren town square can be."

111

She threw him a coy look. "How about I'll show you?" With a firm slap on his ass, she rummaged through her bag. "Now quit distracting me. This meeting is important. The bigger buy-in we get from the townspeople right off, the more successful the gala launch will be."

He dipped his chin. "I can't believe it's in less than two weeks. Your connections in town are saving our ass with the food and entertainment. It would have taken me weeks alone to figure out who was available for either anymore. Van Buren has changed a lot."

Her gaze drifted up the tall trees of the park, then to the top of the old stone arch at the Fountain of Youth. "And in so many ways, exactly the same."

She allowed the wash of pride and contentment to wrap around her. The townspeople really knew her and would do anything for her. She'd made her mark in Cape Van Buren over the past ten years. She'd made it her home. Being able to stand in front of these beloved folks who had become her family and announce the new board for the Archer Conservation Park of Cape Van Buren would be one of her greatest accomplishments both professionally and personally.

Larkin and Ryker joined them on the stage. Ryker, with his dark bushy brows drawn together, had a possessive arm wrapped around his wife's generous waist.

"Why so grumpy? This meeting is a huge milestone for the launch of the center." Blayne nudged him in the arm but looked to Larkin for the answer.

"Too many people trying to rub my stomach."

"Since when is it alright for anyone to walk up to a person and rub their midsection?" Ryker demanded.

Jamie stepped forward with his hand out but stopped at his buddy's growl.

"I'll break it right off," Ryker promised.

Jamie laughed and slapped him on the arm with a wink to Larkin. "He's so easy to rile up these days."

"Just remember, I have to live with him," she teased, but the warm glow in her eyes acknowledged that she was loving every minute.

"Are you ready for your baby shower?" Blayne asked.

"I can't wait. Having it at Delizioso's is brilliant."

She preened. "It really is, isn't it? Though Claire gets credit for all the fun you're going to have. I was simply responsible for a venue that provided great food and sophistication per her instructions."

Claire had jumped in with both feet, planning for the shower. Blayne had worried a bit about her, but instead of dragging their friend down into the sadness like they'd feared, she really seemed to be thriving in all the details instead. At least, Blayne hoped it was thriving. Now and again she worried it was overcompensating.

"Well, good call." Larkin rubbed her belly. "The time has gone way too fast. I can't believe she'll be here soon." A worried frown wavered on Larkin's dark green gaze.

Blayne kissed her cheek. "She is going to be fine."

Larkin shook her head. "I just feel like she's safer right where she is."

Losing a child then having to face the reality of another child's mortality was way more than Blayne could wrap her own head around, so her heart broke for her friend. Larkin was scared, and she didn't blame her. She'd love to brush her fears away with a dismissive joke or banter, but that wouldn't help anyone.

"Look." She turned Larkin to face her, speaking in a soft but certain tone. "This baby has a huge bear of a man for a father who'll spend every waking moment working to keep the two of you safe. Not to mention her mama. This baby is going to have an amazing life. She already has the most amazing guardian angel. Archer won't let a thing happen to his little sister."

Tears glistened in Larkin's eyes, but she blinked a few times and held them in check. "That is very true." She sniffed. "Enough. I'm just overly emotional these days."

Blayne rolled her eyes. "You're a rock."

Jamie waved at Blayne to join him.

"You two seem to be getting along really well these days," Larkin suggested in a quiet voice.

Bittersweet emotion rolled through Blayne as she agreed. "Ryker was right. We do make each other better. Everything with the launch is moving right along." Including the days she had left in town.

And all the greatest sex in the world didn't right the wrongs of ten years ago. She wished they could.

Larkin looked her own husband up and down. "Oh, I think I have a pretty good reference to go by."

Blayne forced out a light laugh. "That you do. Okay. If I don't see you after the meeting, I'll see you Thursday at your shower."

"Thank you. This really means a lot to me," Larkin whispered.

"Me, too."

Pulling in a breath to ease her excitement, she joined Jamie at the microphone, center stage. It looked as if everyone in Cape Van Buren had shown up. The crescent-shaped rows of seats were full, and a crowd of people was left standing in the back.

She grinned with a wink at Jamie then, placing two fingers between her lips, let a quick, piercing whistle rip.

Silence was immediate and filled the air with the sudden lightness of quiet.

"Good afternoon, ladies and gentlemen. We are delighted that so many of you were able to come out over the lunch hour to meet with us. You all know me by this time, but for those of you who may not recognize this guy..." she dipped her chin in Jamie's direction, "this is the esteemed heir to the Astor Estate, Mr. James Alexander Wilmington Astor the Third."

A growing murmur rose in the crowd, taking her by surprise. She figured they'd be interested in seeing him in town but hadn't counted on quite so much enthusiasm.

"As many of you know, Jamie and I have vetted out the board for the Archer Conservation Park of Cape Van Buren."

She tried to ignore the pointed stares she was getting from the North Cove Mavens as she spoke. If looks were a physical thing, she'd be tied up in ropes by Maxine's gaze alone.

Jamie stepped a little closer, distracting her for a moment with his nearness. His scent drifted around her, creating a haze of memories that was in no way PG-13 or appropriate for a community announcement.

Dropping a heavy arm around her, he leaned in toward the microphone. "Blayne has been an absolute pleasure to work with. Her specific expertise along with my extensive corporate experience allowed us to create a system that will keep the conservation and community center sustainable..."

He continued to break out exactly how over his next few sentences, but she was caught on his description of her talents compared to his own. She had corporate experience as well, just not as long. Working for Deloitte was an opportunity many in the business world would die for.

With a shake of her head, she focused again on the task at hand.

Jamie continued. "This board of directors will be responsible for making sure the future of the center is not only upheld but expanded in a way that supports Larkin Van Buren's vision and the memory of her son, Archer Sinclair."

The crowd nodded in agreement. She loved how much the community rallied around Larkin, how they really understood the magnitude of her loss and the generosity of her heart to create something that would continually give to the town.

It was time to announce the citizens of the town who would become an intimate family of their own. She felt as if she could fly. Soon, she'd be able to share all of this with her father. This was the kind of thing that would certainly make him proud. "Ladies and gentleman, without further ado—"

"Hey, James!" someone from the crowd called out.

She stopped, searching the crowd to see who'd interrupted.

Schmidty Ames, the owner of South Cove Lobster House continued, "Have you run your choices past your father?"

She blinked. What the hell did Astor senior have to do with any of this?

"Mr. Ames, I can assure you—" she began.

"I want to know," he returned. "James, what is your family's take on your choices?"

His choices? His family?

She forced herself to breathe against the pain in her chest.

Cape Van Buren were *her* people. She was the one who'd stayed. She'd served this community, befriended this community, and loved this community every day over the last ten years. Why the hell did they care about the opinion of the Astors?

But if an Astor opinion was what they wanted, then her pride aside, that was what they would give.

She firmly pushed the microphone toward Jamie with a smile on her face. It was so fake she was afraid it might crack, but by damn, not a single soul in the audience would know how they hurt her.

Jamie looked at her in question. "What are you doing?" he whispered with a hand over the mic.

Mr. Ames pushed. "We've heard the rumblings that you'll be stepping in to continue the Astor family business in your father's place. Considering the families long history in good investments, did that have anything to do with your choices and how you'll serve the community going forward?"

At first, it seemed like Jamie wanted her to continue making the announcement, but when the words "family" and "serve" hit his ears, the questioning look in his gaze focused on the crowd and off her.

Stepping away, she gave just enough room for Jamie to have center stage but not enough that anyone would think she wasn't just as engaged as when they started.

Her face remained serene and happy, though the rejection cut through her in a painful swipe. The community she loved so much wasn't interested in her opinion. Apparently, her thoughts didn't hold quite the same weight as the Astor name.

Or as that of the Astor prodigal son, come home to take over the family monopoly. He took his time and offered a little insight into his father's opinions and the Astor family stance on the center.

It was silly to feel abandoned all over again, but as she watched Jamie's beautiful smile win over the crowd at their feet, she was thrown back to ten years before.

And her heart broke once more.

$\sim$

*H*e was a selfish sonofabitch.

Jay twisted the top off the blue jar that Maxine presented her moonshine in and took in the sharp, sweet aroma of blueberry and hibiscus. He'd scored big working for Maxine as the lookout at the Cape house, even if the last time had been a bit of a close call with old Judge Carter getting nosy.

He took a fortifying swallow and steadied his breath against the satisfying heat that rose in his throat. Dropping his forearms to the kitchen counter of the lighthouse, he stared out the window and across the choppy waves of the endless ocean. It was rough, the white-capped waves crashing against the rocks at the base of the house emitting a steady roar not unlike the one he imagined he'd get from Blayne when he finally found her.

The board announcement had clicked along like a freight train and he'd grappled—badly—with trying to get it under control. His gut twisted with the image of her as the crowd had asked about the Astor business.

The intoxicating rush of being center stage had kicked in, a high only rivaled by being with Blayne. He'd waged a war with his need to serve his family name and erase the ashen hue that had come over her face. She'd been so excited, and she still should be, but since she'd disappeared immediately following the close of the meeting, he had a pretty good idea that she wasn't in a celebratory mood.

He pinched the bridge of his nose and racked his brain for all the places she could have gone. Desperate to find her and make her understand he'd never meant to hurt her, he'd already checked her apartment downtown—so much for seeing how great her dress looked on the floor—but she hadn't answered.

The rink had been packed with every other badass in Cape Van Buren, but not the badass he'd been searching for. That was decidedly not a safe place for him to patron alone. Not because he was just so damn irresistible, as he'd like to think, but because the ladies on Blayne's team were so competitive, his value skyrocketed due to her interest alone.

With his shine in hand, he took the stairs up the perimeter of the lighthouse toward the lamp room, hesitating at the bottom of the ladder and the memories they'd recently made there. His body tightened with the phantom sensation of her warm smooth skin, the heady scent of her wanting, the sharp dig of her nails into his skin as he

"You do know when dogs start staring off into corners it's a sign of some sort of brain damage, right?"

Blayne's voice should have startled him, but instead a deep sense of relief settled in his chest. Her brogue seemed a bit thicker than normal and slid across his skin like warmed dark chocolate—deep and rich and with just a hint of sweet.

He drank in the sight of her standing at the top of the ladder, shadows bouncing about her as her skirt fluttered with the current of air that always flowed through the lighthouse. "How'd you get in?"

She shrugged. "I'm in good with the owner."

Questioning his sanity for the thousandth time since meeting her, he hauled himself up the ladder, careful not to spill his moonshine.

She moved through the lamp room to the overlook deck outside without bothering with whether or not he'd follow.

Studying the tilt of her chin, the square set in her shoulders, a rush of possessiveness swamped him. She was determined to hide her feelings, which was new and required a strategic approach.

Back in the day, before he'd fucked it all up, she was passionately loud with every emotion that ran through her. Though some might have found it scary, he'd found comfort in always knowing exactly where he stood with her, how she felt, how she felt about him. She'd met him toe to toe, nose to nose.

There was nothing sexier than a confident, strong woman.

But this new Blayne, this calm, thinking Blayne...this seemingly rational, serene Blayne...remained as sexy as ever but terrified him.

"Look." He reached out to her, but she stepped to the railing. Dropping his arm to his side, he joined her. "I didn't mean to take over the announcement."

She tilted her head, looking at him from the corner of her eye. "Which means you know it was wrong."

"I didn't—"

Turning, she said. "This project is my chance to show my father that ripping my family apart and leaving for the States was worth it."

"Blayne, come on."

She grabbed his moonshine, then moved through the doors toward the ladder.

"What the hell?" All he could do was follow...

Down the ladder, down the stairs. "Where are you going? I just got that from Maxine."

"Yeah, and color me suspicious. She doesn't move off her stock for nothing, so whatever you've been doing for her is probably illegal."

He couldn't help the chuckle that rumbled through his chest. Maxine had gotten more than one of them in hot water with her shenanigans when they were growing up.

Once outside, she climbed the rocks out to the water's edge, then lowered to her bottom, tucking her skirt under her legs and wrapping her hands around his moonshine. After a few deep swallows, she blew out a breath and let her head drop back. "God, this stuff is bleedin' amazing."

Dropping down next to her, Jay agreed. "It is. Now give it back." He tugged at the jar, but she resisted.

"You owe me." She stared at him. Challenging him.

He pinched the bridge of his nose for three counts, praying for patience.

"First of all, of course coming to the States was worth it. Just look at what you've achieved."

She narrowed her gaze.

"I only wanted to answer a few questions then get them back on track, but they had a mind of their own. And my family—"

"It doesn't matter."

"I swear, I—"

She pushed the jar toward him, and as ridiculous as it was, he sighed in relief as he took a sip.

"It doesn't matter," she said. "Nothin' I do'll ever really make my da forgive me, and I was foolish for ever thinkin' this community was mine in the first place. In the end, I felt like an idiot and had to work past blamin' ya for it. The shine helped." Her accent thickened the more she drank.

She hiccupped and lifted her chin at the same time.

And his heart turned over in his chest. Leaving her would forever be his greatest mistake. Years of meaningless hookups and ambitious grabs at impossible deals all to fill a void that never could be relieved. He'd never been the same since, and if he had to go forward without her, he never would again.

Leaning closer, he tucked a few stray hairs behind her ear. Her light eyes were crystal clear and reflected the late afternoon sun, bouncing off the waves. He'd seen her mad, furious even, but never dejected.

And he never wanted to see it again.

He placed the jar of moonshine in her hand.

She looked down at the jar then to him in surprise. "Really?"

He rolled his eyes. "Just drink it."

With serious eyes, she scanned his face. Too many emotions flashed through hers, and he felt each one deep in his chest. It was as if he kept falling and hitting the ground again and again, but damn if he didn't get back up just to do it once more.

"Your dad loves you. He misses you, that's all. And this town loves you, too."

Her scent drifted along the breeze, teasing him, then the soft, plush feel of her lips brushed along his.

"You're sweet for saying so, but I know the truth."

"I feel awful about the trouble you're having with your dad. But whether you and I were together or not, he would have had a hard time. Coming here will always be worth it."

Anger sparked in her eyes. "You don't get to say that. You left me!" She slapped the stone, then grabbed her hand to nurse it in her other one.

With a curse, he reached to check the damage, but she yanked away. Watching the woman he loved struggle with such pain, knowing he was the cause, tore at his soul.

"Don't. You didn't care then, you don't get to care now."

"That's not fair."

Her laugh cracked in an echo off the rocks and base of the lighthouse. "Fair? You want to talk to me about fair? You broke my heart."

And his joined hers in two.

"I was eighteen! Selfish, arrogant...I know. I regretted it every day. Still regret it, and I'm sorry. That's why I'm here. That's why I returned. Do you know how hard—" He grabbed her, resisting when she tried to move it away.

"Let me go."

Determination set upon him, and he met her gaze straight on. "No. Don't you get it? I'm never letting you go again."

Something shifted in her gaze, like a tide returning to the sea, and she retreated. He experienced real fear for the first time in his life.

"But that's it, Jamie." She gestured between them. "This thing is nothing more than the closing scene of an unfinished story. Not the beginning of a new one. You don't have me to let go of."

CHAPTER 12

*P*ulling from the reserves of her strong Irish blood, Blayne pushed Jamie from her mind for the billionth time as she and Claire held onto each other in a tight, excited squeeze.

They peered over Maxine's terrace to watch Larkin follow the old woman into the entrance of the Town Square apartments. Larkin thought the baby shower was later in the week, but everyone agreed the Sunday before the gala was the perfect time to celebrate.

One week before the gala, a celebration of the opening of her little boy's impact on the world, and two weeks before her daughter would bless them again.

Claire sighed then led Blayne to the side of the sliding doors that led out to the festivities from Maxine's living room. "It's beautiful." She glanced around the space.

Blayne took in the sweet smile of yearning on her friend's face. "Are you okay?"

"Me?" Claire scoffed. "Of course! I'm celebrating one of my best friends' biggest moments with my other." She slid her arm through Blayne's.

She wasn't fooling anyone. At least not Blayne. Claire smiled and planned and gushed and prepared, but through it all, there was a glimmer of sadness in her blue eyes, a hint of yearning.

Having lost her unborn child after the death of her fiancé, Larkin's pregnancy and baby shower had to be harder than she let on. The Claire from last year would have given Larkin the finger, but the Claire today gave her a baby shower.

And Blayne worried.

Better she worry about Claire and celebrate with Larkin than obsess about Jamie and his smooth lips and strong hands...

...and the fact she was leaving in a week.

She felt his sincere regret deep in her heart. The truth of his feelings didn't ghost between them like apparitions; they were solid, tangible actions, but they didn't change the past.

The town meeting showed her that. It was one thing to want to change but something altogether different to really make the change stick. And she was terrified that if Jamie ever had the right opportunity present itself, she'd lose again.

She ached with exhaustion at constantly striving for first place in the lives of those she loved but always coming in second.

No more.

She resisted the self-deprecating chuckle. It was good to have goals.

"It turned out really pretty, didn't it?" Claire asked.

Blayne followed the strings of globe lights that hung from one end of the terrace to the other, then the fairy lights wrapped around the bases of the potted palms. Black, white, and aqua pillows and throws made the couches and lounges inviting, and a large champagne fountain on the round marble table glittered. Light reflected off the collection of strawberry-filled flute glasses.

Two long tables were set with aqua dinnerware and silver utensils that sparkled, framed by centerpieces of baby's breath and silver streamers. Yogurt-dipped, dark chocolate desserts shaped like baby feet were tied with an aqua ribbon on each plate.

Nora Jones sang in the background, accompanied by the comforting trickling of Maxine's outdoor waterfall.

"It's beyond pretty, Claire, it's stunning. She's going to be blown away," Blayne assured her.

Claire grinned then yanked her down.

Blayne almost fell on her ass but was able to right herself before turning her ankle on her new stiletto Mary Janes. "Hey!"

"She's coming," Claire whispered, seemingly not caring at all if Blayne fell.

She shook her head with a smile.

"Girls!" Evette yell-whispered from her very awkward position behind Janice's red curls. "Shut up. She's coming."

Blayne could only roll her eyes at these women she loved so much and, rubbing the warmth spreading through the center of her chest, peeked through the windows along with everyone else as Larkin followed Maxine through the kitchen toward the terrace.

"You have to see the little garden I managed out here. Of course, I don't grow anything quite as well as Janice, but don't tell her that. Her head's already way too big for those narrow shoulders," Maxine rattled on.

Evette, eyes sparkling with humor, grabbed Janice to keep her from reacting to the made-up slight. "Shhhh."

Larkin's mom hid behind one of the plants. Mae, Janice's daughter, squeezed as far as she could past her mother, and Shelly Anne tried to tuck down as far as she could behind Blayne.

The large sliding door whisked open and as Larkin stepped through they all jumped up, tossing handfuls of white bird seed into the air. "Surprise!"

Larkin slapped her chest and looked around with a startled expression. Her eyes immediately filled, and her lowered lip trembled. "You guys." She took in every detail of the terrace and her friends then turned to Claire and Blayne. "This is more than I ever imagined. I thought we were planning on celebrating at Delizioso!"

"We wanted you to have something private and special," Claire said.

"No worries, Delizioso will come later for after-party drinks and tiramisu," Blayne promised.

Their friend shook her head and held her now very large and very round tummy. "Wow. It even matches the nursery."

Claire nodded. "Of course. It had to be perfect. Come here. I have sparkling grape juice for you." She poured Larkin a glass.

Blayne joined them and topped two strawberry-filled flutes with champagne. She shoved one at Claire. She may not admit anything was wrong, but the over-bright look in her eyes told Blayne something else altogether. "Here. Drink this."

Claire resisted. "What? I'm fine."

"I know. Drink."

Maxine joined them. "I'll have one too, sweets."

"Sure thing, Maxine." She eyed the cool, straight edge of her friend's silver hair and it reminded her of Jamie's strong jawline. "By the way, how'd Jamie get his hands on a whole jar of your moonshine?"

Maxine raised one arched salt-and-pepper brow. "Well, a certain young man shouldn't have shared the possession of said jar in the first place. Even with the woman he's sleeping with."

Blayne choked on her champagne as all the ladies turned toward Maxine.

"I'm not...he's not...I mean." Her stomach dropped. All she needed was Larkin's hope getting raised that she'd be staying Stateside now that she'd played naked hide-in-the-sheets with the bloke.

"What's this?" Larkin grabbed her arm. "How could you not tell me?!"

Janice, curls bobbing, slid her arm through Evette's and leaned forward. "It was only a matter of time. I always said you were never over him."

"You never said any such thing." Maxine snorted, grabbing a baby foot from a plate, then chomping off a few toes. "I did."

Blayne blanched at the idea that her sex life with Jamie was part of anyone's conversation, period. Though, truth be told, sex with him was goddamn Pulitzer-worthy. The way he used his hands and tongue at the same time was complete genius, not to mention...

"Blayne!" *Snap. Snap.* Larkin's fingers came into view.

Shit. She hadn't seen him in almost four days but hadn't stopped yearning even for one.

This was going to be a problem.

After the talk they had, she wouldn't be surprised if he avoided her until the gala. Pain had left her tongue sharp, but she'd been desperate to protect herself from his apology and regret. He had to understand that what was between them didn't change anything. Not in the way he seemed to hope.

"Anyway," she gritted out. "We have a party to get back to. Claire didn't work so hard on all of this for it to go to waste." She turned to her friend. "What can I help with next?" She sent her a help-me-or-die look.

Unfortunately, Claire didn't care.

"Oh, no rush. I'd love to hear about this new development."

Blayne clenched her teeth.

"Was he as good as you remember?" Mae asked with hope in her eyes.

"I want to know if his you-know-what seems bigger," Janice inquired.

"You can say penis, for goodness sake," Shelly Anne added.

"Penis? Hell, say dick. That's what we're all thinking." Maxine tossed a champagne-soaked strawberry into her mouth. "We all like a good, hearty...dick." She finished the sentence with a loud lip smack.

Oh my God, kill me now.

Larkin laughed so hard Blayne was afraid she'd go into labor early, and Claire was no better. Uh huh. She saw how they were. Paybacks were a bitch. "You are all children." She shook her head.

Maxine's doorbell rang, grabbing her attention. "Ahhh...the entertainment!"

Blayne looked at Claire, but the look she got in return was a blank stare and a blink.

Claire took advantage of the interruption to bring out a tray of butternut squash ravioli appetizers, and Blayne controlled a very quiet sigh of relief.

Maxine burst through the doors, tugging a surprised and unwilling Mitch behind her. "Here he is, ladies!"

"What the hell?" The look on Mitch's face was a mix of get-me-the-fuck-outta-here and how'd-I-fall-for-this-again. Blayne would have felt bad but she was too relieved the attention was off her to care. She'd consider how that might affect her karma later.

Claire spun around with a ravioli between her fingers, then shoved it in her mouth in a nervous reflex. Blayne stared at her, trying to figure out what was going on.

Maxine grabbed Mitch and tugged him to the middle of the terrace. "Time for the fun and games. The first up is Mr. Blue-Balls."

"Aw, hell no." Mitch swore.

Blayne shoved Claire forward. "Claire volunteers."

She resisted with a screeched, "The hell I do."

Janice's eyes lit up. "It's like you were made for each other."

Blayne couldn't help the guffaw that flew from her mouth. She shouldn't take so much pleasure from the predicament Claire now found herself in. Janice has been trying to marry her playboy son off for years.

Larkin slid in beside Blayne and hip-bumped her. "Made for each other." She tilted her head. "Huh, kind of like you and your Jamie."

Blayne's chest squeezed tight, and she tried to speak past it. "He's not my Jamie." And he couldn't be. She'd always feel less than, passed over, unnecessary. Like when he left, like when she had to share the opportunity at the community center, like she did on stage when the town preferred to hear from him instead of her.

She'd willingly surrender her body to him, that was something she wanted, something for herself. Giving him her trust was another thing altogether.

Larkin squeezed her arm. "But you want him to be."

She formed the word "no" with her lips but before she could get it out, her friend shoved a strawberry in it.

"Eat this. It's not nice to lie in front of the baby."

~

*R*yker threw a rope toward Jay. "Here, make yourself useful and tie that down. Max and Martha will be here any minute."

Jay wound the rope in a figure-eight around a dock cleat. "I tried to get the conversation back on track, but people had questions, and you know how important my family is. There are expectations that must be met as an Astor. I mean, what the fuck was I supposed to do? But you should have seen the look on her face. I've been kicking myself in the ass ever since."

A sharp pain flared along the side of his head, and he spun around to see a deck brush skid across the teak. "What the fuck, man?"

"My thoughts exactly," Ryker growled. "At the rate you're moving, we won't have enough daylight to get the boat out in the water." Leaning against the helm, he twisted the cap off a beer.

"I want to marry her, Ryker."

His buddy grunted. "Good. Can you do it after we sail?"

He had a point. Since arriving, Jay had rehashed every moment—well, almost every moment—with Blayne since he'd returned to town. Ryker wasn't really interested beyond a "good luck, buddy" kind of way, but Jay needed to work it all out in his head in order to figure out what to do.

It killed him to see the defeat in her eyes. She'd always been a fighter, and the idea that he'd had anything to do with stripping that away killed him. He just had to help her see that she was loved by the town and together they could accomplish what she wanted to do.

She didn't have to do it alone.

He'd be with her every step of the way. He was her future because God knew she was his.

He wanted to make her his in every possible way.

Then someday, he'd get her to Ireland and make her dad see in her all the amazing qualities that had been there all along.

A future without her left his gut twisted more than a day out in rough seas ever could. He released a pent-up breath in a grunt of agreement to Ryker.

But for now, he'd shut up and focus on getting the mayor to expedite a few last licensing issues they had for the community house.

Max Stanton and Mayor Sebastian Marth stepped aboard with Judge Carter right behind them. "Look who we found." Sebastian jerked his thumb over his shoulder at the judge.

The judge stepped aboard. "I saw the boys out on the boardwalk and thought I'd stop by and say hello."

"You a little lost without Maxine, Judge?" Jay teased.

Ryker snorted. "You're one to talk."

"What the hell ever, you've been nothing but rainbows and sunshine since meeting Larkin."

Tipping his beer back for a swallow, Ryker grinned. "Sounds like me."

Max raised an accusing brow. "I thought we were heading out?"

Van Buren jerked his beer toward Jay. "This one's been sharing his goddamn feelings, so she isn't ready."

On the word "feelings," Sebastian swung away to step off the boat.

"Get the fuck back here, Martha," Ryker demanded.

Dropping his square chin to his chest, Sebastian hesitated at the nickname, then glared at him. The name started in high school before his growth spurt then stuck—at least with his closest friends. The rest of the town didn't dare. "I came here for beer and poker. I've had enough feelings to last me a lifetime today at the office."

Max shoved him in the chest and teased in a high-pitched voice. "Oh, Mayor Marth, I need your help."

Sebastian shoved him back, sending Max over the stanchions and onto the wood deck

"Fuck, man," Max yelled.

Sebastian laughed and accepted a beer from Ryker.

"I'm not talking about my feelings, jackass." Jay grabbed a bottle and tried to force the tightness in his neck to relax. "You know how Blayne is—"

"I'm out." Sebastian stepped toward the dock again.

"Fuck you." Jay grabbed the deck brush and threw it at the mayor. It bounced off his meaty body without effect then smacked the judge in the arm.

"Shit." Jay scrambled to catch the brush. He'd never get another sip of moonshine again if Teddy went to Maxine telling her he'd been abused.

"You should have aimed for Martha's head," Ryker deadpanned.

Jay shot his buddy a look. "Not helping."

Max grabbed his own beer. "Clearly, we aren't going out in the water. Are we at least playing a game of poker?"

"Waiting on Mitch." Jay sunk down on one of the deck chairs.

"Just the five of us. Sorry-ass got tricked into helping Maxine out with Larkin's baby shower." Ryker's eyes glinted with humor, and Judge Carter shuddered.

Max sunk into a chair with a shake of his head and judgment in his tone. "You're a bad wingman."

"Better him than me. I've dealt with much worse with my grandmother."

Jay nodded. "We all did, but damn if she doesn't make the best moonshine in Maine. One sip from her most recent batch and I promised to be her slave for life."

Sebastian shot him a look, and Max coughed in his hand.

What the hell? It was bad enough Blayne had her eyes all over the mayor and his *big sacks* the other day—the idea he even thought of censoring Jay, irritated him on every possible level. He shifted forward in his chair.

"What?" He challenged.

"I thought Maxine wasn't making her concoctions?" Judge Carter questioned.

Oh. Fuck. Jay could feel all the blood drain from his arrogant brain. What the hell did he just do?

Blayne didn't know it yet, but the town would surely welcome her over him after what he just did.

And if the look on Mayor Marth's face was any indication, he didn't have a chance in hell getting anything expedited besides his own ass out of town.

He was on the losing end of two for two in the past week.

As much as he loved Ryker and Larkin, he could handle screwing up the launch.

What he couldn't handle, wouldn't allow, was failing on winning back Blayne. The past ten years had shown him what a future without her was like.

He'd follow her all the way to Ireland if he had to, because there was no way he was letting her go—no matter if she felt there was nothing to let go of.

She was everything.

CHAPTER 13

*L*ate Wednesday evening, Blayne dug her heels in. "Why are we here?"

To her surprise, Jamie hadn't avoided her at all, on the contrary. He'd been at her beck and call, handling any detail. Competent. Capable.

Dependable.

Her heart wanted to believe it, but her brain warned her that history repeated itself, it never learned.

They'd been working non-stop at the center, and any free moments she did have had been preparing Eclectic Finds so it would keep thriving while she supervised from abroad—only made possible with good help.

The thought brought her round again to Jamie.

The Astor estate loomed above her like the Disney Castle. At least, what she imagined the Disney Castle would look like from a two-year-old's point of view because that's exactly how she felt at that moment as Jamie propelled her along the river-rock walkway toward the large, double front door.

She wanted her mother's skirts to hide behind but, instead, self-consciously smoothed the red polka dots of the one she wore. Losing her ma hurt the most when she needed her. In a way though, it had gotten easier over the years to not constantly think about the fact she was gone.

Now at least, a soft reminder in the background, like windchimes on the breeze, rather than an unceasing, clamoring loss. And every time she missed her da. But with him, the pain ran deep. He was alive. He was there.

He told her to never come home.

Inspecting the shine of her patent leather, high-heeled Mary Jane's, she gained strength from the powerful red that matched her silk, off-the-shoulder blouse, and instead of cowering like she wanted to, or hitting Jamie like she yearned to, she tilted her head to take in the property straight on.

She'd hit Jamie later.

The home was reminiscent of a French chateau in a towering, crescent shape that mimicked the coastline of the North Cove, about a mile up the coast from where Larkin lived. From the first time she'd ever laid eyes on his home, she'd never seen anything so grand in her life and never expected to again.

"It's called dinner. We've been so busy confirming all the last-minute details for the gala that I thought a home-cooked meal would give us a chance to catch a breath. Besides, my mother missed you and asked me to bring you by."

She scoffed. "Your ma does not miss me, and you know it."

Jamie looked at her as if she were crazy, and opened his mouth to speak, but the front door was yanked open and a small squeal came from inside.

"Blayne!" Margaret Astor gripped her hands together, taking in the vision of Blayne as if Christmas had come early.

A rush of nostalgia filled her at the sight of Jamie's mother, when happily ever after had seemed like a reality instead of the hard, cold joke she knew it to be. Mrs. Astor hadn't changed a bit over the last decade. Still as elegant as ever, though at the moment, not quite as poised as she usually presented herself.

Warm, small hands grabbed Blayne and drew her in for a fierce hug. She didn't remember his mother being quite so strong, but the wind nearly got knocked out of her in the embrace.

She almost made the mistake of melting into those motherly arms but stopped herself just in time. "Hello, Mrs. Astor. It's been awhile." Awkward didn't begin to describe her feelings as she disengaged from the warm welcome.

Her da had been like that.

Every friend she and her siblings had dragged home like stray puppies off the street were given a place at the table and more attention than they ever expected...or probably wanted.

He'd tell great stories of deep sea fishing with his father back in the old days and jokes that left the kids laughing, but what was more, he'd ask questions, and when the kids answered, he'd listened.

Leaning in, those deep blue eyes focused as if nothing else in the world mattered. "What happened next?" he'd say.

That was always his question. He wanted to hear more. And in that moment, each kid felt as if nothing else in the world mattered but them and their story.

What happened next.

Well, that was the question, wasn't it?

Visiting the Astor home with its photographic history of belonging displayed along the hallways only reminded her of how painfully apparent it was that she didn't—at his house, in Cape Van Buren, or in the States at all. This evening would simply prove it and allow her to move on. Maybe the visit was exactly what she needed.

Margaret led her through the large foyer toward the back of the house. "Far too long." She tossed an accusing glare at her son. "You know I wanted to kill Jay for leaving you like he did."

Blayne tripped on her own two feet.

"Mother." Jamie grimaced.

Margaret steadied her. "Are you okay, my dear?" She continued to lead them toward Blayne's favorite room in the beautiful house.

His mother hadn't agreed?

It was as if she'd been knocked in the head during a roller derby match and had woken up in an alternate reality.

They entered a round sitting room with pillars along the walls that flanked floor-to-ceiling windows overlooking the Atlantic Ocean. It had gold drapes and marble floors, and the view of the moonlit, white-capped waves rolling in from the ocean was the most breathtaking ever.

Well almost.

The lighthouse view gave this one a run for its money, especially with Jamie wrapped around her.

She blinked, trying to make sense of everything that didn't. But she wasn't sure how to handle the swirling in her chest that invited her stomach in to join the dance. What did Mrs. Astor mean she wanted to kill Jamie? Surely, she'd had a huge sigh of relief that their only son hadn't married at eighteen, and to a poor Irish girl who abandoned her family at that.

Abandoned.

Damn it.

Peeking at Jamie, she followed the line of his profile while he poured them wine from a beautiful teardrop decanter that had been the center display on a silver terrace bar cart. His jaw clenched rhythmically, and his shoulders seemed tenser than usual. She didn't even bother to suppress the grin that strained her cheeks.

He deserved any discomfort that came from this little impromptu visit.

"Thank you, darling. Don't forget Father." Jamie's mother took the offered glass of wine then dipped her chin toward the arched opening into the library as Astor Senior joined them.

"Blayne." He embraced her smelling of old money and worldly experience before she could decide how to greet him.

He'd dropped a few pounds over the years, probably from his surgery. From what Jamie had told her, the doctors had been on him to start slowing down and thinking of his heart.

"You are looking quite fit, Mr. Astor."

He patted his chest, smiling at his wife. "It was either do what the doctors say or get on the wrong side of Margaret." Leaning in, he gave her a wink. "No one wants to do that."

Margaret laughed, swatting her husband on the arm. "James, please. I'm the easiest-going woman you know. Which is the only reason you're still married. Who else would put up with you?"

They teased in that good-natured way that was full of love and admiration and wrapped her in a blanket of warm emotion. Her parents had been the same way once upon a time.

Mr. Astor kissed her cheek. "That is the truth."

Blayne didn't know everything that may have transpired over the years, but the two of them continued to thrive in their relationship. She went a tad green. A connection like that was rarely seen off the movie screen or pages of a book.

Jamie handed her a glass of wine, whispering under his breath, "She had to be easygoing. He was always gone." It sounded like an accusation but Blayne couldn't quite pin down his meaning.

"Obviously, they are still madly in love. It's nice to see."

He dipped his chin. "My dad's lucky she didn't walk out years ago."

She shook her head, peering closely at his face. "What are you talking about? They've always seemed to have a wonderful relationship. Your home life was pretty idyllic, if I remember all your stories correctly."

"And it was. But everything comes at a price." He stepped close behind her, holding her hips as his parents continued their verbal play. The sensation of his fingers pressing into her flesh sent tingles spreading over her that had no business in his parents' company.

She discreetly shoved his hands away. "Don't you dare," she hissed.

"What was that, my dear?" Mrs. Astor asked.

"Oh, I said, I'd love a little air." She hiccupped, which was quickly joined by a quiet rolling laugh from Jamie.

Margaret opened one of three sets of large French doors. "What a great idea. Jay, open the others, please."

A light, breeze floated in with the rumble of waves and a call or two from the seagulls.

Blayne stepped to the door's threshold. "I've always loved this room. This view."

Margaret joined her. "You could have visited any time," she said softly.

The offer was sweet but unrealistic. Eighteen-year-olds did not keep in touch with their ex's families. That had crazy ex-girlfriend written all over it, but the thought was kind all the same.

And unexpected.

Nothing about this visit, their warm welcome, or the feelings stirred up by being in the Astor home was what she'd been ready for, walking through the front door.

Her brain tried to sort out her feelings from the facts—or at least what she'd thought they were. But instead of dropping into place and clearing up, it all got fuzzier.

"Tell me more about the gala," his mother murmured. "I'd love to help in any way I can. I know a lot of people."

Just the mention of it pushed Blayne's mind to start racing with possibility. She couldn't remember the last time she'd been so excited about something outside of when she'd opened Eclectic Finds. "I have a lot of it planned already, but there might be something you can assist me with."

Jamie cocked his head. "I didn't realize we were that far along?"

She shrugged. "I've had a vision of what Larkin wanted from the beginning, so I've been working on it as we went. Seemed smarter than trying to plan it all at once."

His eyes narrowed at the jab.

Mrs. Astor smiled. "I wish I could see your plans. I know your mother is smiling down, proud as any parent ever could be."

The words settled like the gentle sweep of a mother's fingertips along her brow, and she blinked rapidly to hold it together. She'd always hoped her mother would be proud of her but gave up after following Jamie to the States. No mother would be proud of that.

She smiled tremulously. "I hope so."

"Hope? I don't understand that at all. It's a fact," Mrs. Astor declared. "I know, I'm a mother, and I'm proud of you."

With a small shake of her head, Blayne argued. "I don't think my mother would be very happy with all of the decisions I've made. But you are sweet."

Margaret clasped Blayne's hand between her own. "No, you are. And a mother doesn't have to like every decision her children make, it isn't her life to live, but theirs. When they find themselves and embark on the path that was meant for them, there is no way but to be proud. Hear me when I tell you...she's proud of her beautiful daughter."

An image of her mother clapping for her from the audience of the myriad school events of her youth overwhelmed her in a wave of homesickness.

"Mom." Jamie's voice broke through, saving her from an embarrassing display of pent-up tears. She blinked rapidly to clear her vision and sniffed.

Margaret gave a determined nod. "Now about that gala..."

Blayne sipped her wine to settle her emotions, allowing for the possibility that Jamie's mother might be right. Getting caught up in the excitement of it all, she lifted her phone. "I can show you."

"I didn't know about any plans," Jamie accused with a look that promised he had ideas of how she could make up for it later. Or maybe it was a trick of the light and her own twisted wanting playing with her libido.

She spared him a brief glance as his mother clapped in anticipation.

Mr. Astor poured more wine and settled into one of the tufted, high-back chairs. "Sit with me, son. They might be awhile."

Margaret sat on a cushioned wrought iron chair at the table and gestured to another. "I'd love to see."

Blayne opened her files. Globe-lit canopies, ocean rock fire pits, and torches for lighting, red and white wine and champagne wishing-well fountains in honor of Archer. Silent auction items from the most exclusive establishments in the community with the proceeds going directly into the Archer Sinclair Scholarship Fund.

Food catered by Delizioso, coffee from the Flat Iron Coffeehouse, and Cupcakes from the North Cove Confectionery. The only thing she still hadn't nailed down yet was the entertainment.

"I have a few bands pre-booked, but they don't seem quite right. This isn't just a celebration, this is a birth of something bigger than any one of us and will serve all of us."

Margaret squeezed her hand. "Yes. It is so lovely that you see that."

She smiled at Jamie's mom and some of the fuzziness cleared. This woman not only seemed genuinely happy to have her in her home, but she seemed excited to share in the details for the gala, and a timid flare of happiness warmed Blayne from the inside out.

Jamie had always made caveats and explanations for the way his family lived, for his mother's role in it all, his father's expectations. So often, Blayne had assumed he was trying to manage *her* expectations on ever being accepted in the family.

She glanced at the man who held her heart, the man she used to dream about calling her own so many years ago, and possibility fluttered. A feeling she'd never believed she'd feel again.

In less than a week, she'd be on a plane to Ireland. All her yearning for home, for her da, came crashing down to remind her why she had to leave Cape Van Buren.

But the encouraging motherly hand covering hers and the gray-eyed gaze of her one true love studying her from across the room reminded her of why she so desperately wanted to stay.

~

*J*ay sipped his wine as he half-listened to his father retell the ins and outs of his most recent doctor's appointment for the hundredth time. It wasn't that Jay didn't want to know, but at this point, he could recap each and every detail right down to the socks the old man had worn that day.

Blayne and his mother were elbows deep in gala details. From what he could tell, the event was practically ready to go, and after seeing what she'd put together, it would, without a doubt, be the most glamorous event Cape Van Buren had ever seen.

"She's quite something," his father said.

Competent, professional, savvy, and fierce. There was nothing to do but agree. "I don't deserve her."

"No, you don't."

Jay jerked his head toward his father.

"But I hope you get her anyway." His father's tone was sincere, which was both an insult and encouraging. "You should never have left her like you did."

Jay agreed, but try telling that to his eighteen-year-old self. "I was an ass and an idiot. My ambition called. Duty called. My family, our business, has always come first. Always trying so hard to prove that I deserved to be a part of it. All I ended up proving was that I didn't deserve the greatest thing I ever had."

His father studied him over the rim of his wine glass, then took a sip. "You had to make your mistakes to really see what you wanted. We always encouraged you to return to her."

Jay shot his dad an incredulous look. "Look at her. I couldn't until I proved I was worthy."

His father's sigh came from the deep recesses of his chest. "Jay, someday you're going to have to let go of the guilt of privilege you've wrapped yourself in." He raised his glass toward the women.

"Keep giving, like you are with the center. Like you did in Haiti after the earthquake, or New Orleans after Katrina. From a young age, you've always jumped in. But someday, you're going to have to stop punishing yourself for being an Astor...for leaving her."

"Family comes first," Jay said.

"You're right, your mother and I have always preached family-first, but that's always included those we were bringing into the fold."

"But that was part of the problem. I realized I couldn't do that to Blayne."

His father's brows furrowed. "Do what?"

Jay shook his head. There was no way to explain his feelings to his father without hurting the man, and that was not his intention. He just didn't think his father ever really considered how hard his being gone all the time had been on his wife.

James Alexander Wilmington Astor II was a great father and a loving— though absent—husband who had worked his whole life to give his family every opportunity to thrive in this community and around the world. Jay saw that. He just hadn't always agreed.

"It's nothing. We travel a lot for our business—"

"You are full of excuses, son. She's from Ireland. Europeans travel all the time. What are you really afraid of?"

Jay scrubbed his fingers through his scruff. Stepping into his father's shoes after proving his abilities was what he'd been working for in order to return to Blayne. But he still feared he wasn't enough, of not being worthy of a woman like her, of his selfish streak hurting her again.

Of never being worthy of her, no matter what he did. He finished his drink, welcoming the burn.

"Look, never mind. I was eighteen. There's no explaining the rationale of a kid."

His father slapped him on the back with a chuckle. "Now that I get. Do you remember when you were determined to graduate at the top of your class, you got it in your head to paint your room black, including your ceiling?"

Jay nodded.

"You thought that blocking out the world would allow you to be more successful, let you focus. You had your mother put up black-out drapes. We were worried you'd suffer from vitamin D deficiency, but a week with no sun, and you were taking down the drapes and repainting the room yourself since we refused to fix it for you."

Jay remembered all too well. "If you remember, I left the walls black."

"Fair enough, but my point is...you sought the light. You've always had this funny idea that you had to suffer to deserve your success. But you still graduated in the top what, three percent of your class? Even with the distractions of life and the responsibilities of our family? I've always thought you were doing the same thing when you left Blayne."

Jay stared at his dad. He'd never thought of it that way before. There was truth in his words that Jay couldn't quite explain. He'd always felt as if he had too much compared to his friends, to the world. And he still wanted more. That's what bothered him the most.

But it wouldn't have changed the fact that Blayne would have had to spend a lot of time alone while the Astor men ran the business. It was just way too archaic of a lifestyle to expect a woman like her to thrive in. At least, that's what he told himself when he was too much of a coward to run to her right away and beg her forgiveness.

He'd told himself he couldn't do that to her.

Watching her with his mother, seeing her plans for the gala, working alongside her for the launch, had shown him a whole other side of the woman he loved that he'd never seen before.

She was a powerhouse all on her own.

And as archaic as it might seem, he wanted her by his side.

Being with her again, making love with her, holding her in his arms, filled the emptiness inside him, that void that had been gnawing at him all these years.

From head to toe, he looked his fill. She was magnificent.

He had to find a way to show her that side-by-side was exactly where they belonged.

He'd never deserve her, but he wanted her anyway.

It was time to quit punishing himself for having it all, because the fact was that without Blayne he had nothing.

She was his all and everything. And it was time to tell her.

CHAPTER 14

*B*layne slid her hand into Jamie's as they walked along the grass-topped cliff overlooking the Atlantic behind the Astor estate. Their chef had outdone herself with dinner, and so Jamie's parents had retired to bed, leaving Jamie and Blayne to enjoy the rest of the evening alone.

They were a distance from the house, the golden wash of the exterior lights casting them in a warm glow and throwing shadows along the grounds as if part of a large soirée.

She imagined there'd been many as Jamie grew up.

A low rock wall bordered the drop-off to the sea below, and three iron benches that had born witness to thousands of stunning sunrises sat a few feet from the protective barrier marking the beginning, the middle, and the end of the safety net along the length of the cliff.

She couldn't help but appreciate how it mirrored her time with Jamie. Their tumultuous wild ride, the beauty, the raw energy, and the often inflexible truths of reality. No matter how hard she tried to stop herself, she felt as if she stood at the edge and was about to fall to the crashing waves below. But with her heart facing his, there she stood.

"Thank you for bringing me to see your parents."

She loved the feel of their palms together. The grip of his calluses, the warmth of his skin. She never noticed how sensitive her hands were until Jamie held them.

That was how it was with him. His nearness brought her to life, made her world buzz with energy. She bit her lip. How was she going to ever leave him?

He slid his fingers up her arm then under her hair and gently gripped her neck. "Then why do you seem so sad?"

She shrugged. She needed to tell him she was leaving. It was no secret, but they'd also never talked about a future together, and the chance of being rejected by the man she loved—again? No, she couldn't take that.

She also wanted to enjoy the last week they had and revel in the excitement and plans for the gala.

But there was more. Talking to Mrs. Astor about her ma had made her think of how short life could be. They were all on borrowed time with no knowledge of when that time was up.

She trailed a finger along his cheek, across the chiseled edge of his jaw, the rough scruff tickling her fingertips and sending goosebumps along her skin. "Talking about my ma. It feels like forever since she passed. Makes me miss my da even more."

His eyes took on that heavy-lidded darkness of wanting from her touch, and her heart answered by speeding in her chest and stealing a bit of her breath. She continued, "I'm sad about the time we wasted being apart. The time I wasted being angry and hurt."

Jamie drew her close, but she pressed her palm against his chest, trying to steady her emotions as she got lost in the steely gaze of the man she was head over heels for, forever lost to, and—God help her—still hopelessly in love with.

They'd lost so many years together. And she still didn't clearly understand why beyond the naivety and immaturity of youth. His...and hers.

Because, let's face it. If he had returned and he said he'd wanted to, would she really have taken him back? Or, in her pain and fear, would she have rejected his apology, too hurt to save herself from herself?

She, too, had already lost so many years with her father, her siblings. Ireland.

All this time, she'd worked her ass off to do something that would be special enough to show her face again to her father, but now she felt worse than ever.

There was no achievement in wasting so much time. In being a coward. In putting her pride above family.

Enough was enough.

It was time to go home. Her heart broke a little with each beat of Jamie's against her palm.

It was time she made amends, no matter how difficult it would be.

But first, it was time to take advantage of every opportunity that was left to experience life with Jamie until she had to step on that plane.

It was time to fall over the edge.

"Jamie?" Her whisper barely carried above the din of the crashing waves along the rocks below.

He slid his fingers along her cheeks and into her hair, lifting her lips toward him. "Blayne, I—"

Suddenly afraid of what was to come, of what had come before, she pressed her finger against his mouth.

"The gala is ready, our plans for the launch will sustain Larkin's amazing vision for this community. Let's just sit in this moment, okay? Celebrate it. Just you and me." She searched his face, desperate for him to agree. "I need you—"

A deep growl rumbled up from his chest. "I've been waiting for you to say it."

He slammed his lips to hers with an element of possession that set off a rush of adrenaline and sparked her desire like never before.

His heat and taste enveloped her in a heady cocoon of want. He wrapped his arms around her, lifting her to her toes.

She gripped his shoulders, kneading the mass of muscles, and bringing him closer still. Her skirts fluttered about her legs as his delicious fingers dug into the flesh of her ass, tightening his hold on her. An intense, swirling pressure built between her legs with every kiss, every caress, every groan of pleasure from his lips.

Yes, this was what she needed.

The night was warmer than usual, especially for May, the ocean barely cooling the air from the afternoon sun. The humid breeze weaved between their bodies as they moved, melting into their heat, and leaving their skin to glide effortlessly with each caress.

Jamie walked her backward toward a bench until he dropped down to the seat, encouraging her to follow, to straddle his lap with her thighs.

The hard iron dug into her knees but only heightened the pleasure of his heat between her legs, his muscled flesh in her hands.

She dove her fingers through his hair, gripping with a tug to better angle his face for her kiss. Her tongue teased and tasted. She'd never tire of his unique flavor, would dream of it for the rest of her life.

He slipped the edge of her blouse over her breasts, baring them to the moon and the stars. Her nipples tightened under his gaze, and his hands filled with the fullness of her as if he couldn't wait if his life had depended on it.

With each gentle massage of his strong fingers, her nipples stiffened into impossibly hard peaks, and the tightness coiling inside of her intensified. She ground down against his hard length, trying to ease her body's demand for more.

She didn't want it to be over too soon. This was a night she wanted to take with her, to warm her when she was alone, to comfort her when she ached for him.

"God damn it, woman." His gravelly curse pushed her, promising more.

"I need to feel you." She worked the buttons of his shirt, but in her fevered state, fumbled with more than she released. On a groan, she bunched the hem and dragged the material over his head.

His soft chuckle washed over her as he helped to get the shirt off. "Easy."

She gripped his hair again. "It's never easy with us." She slammed her lips against his, just as he had before, reveling in the power of it all. With him, she was invincible to everything but his touch, and the contrary fact made her even more desperate to take and to give until they were both helpless.

Lifting her breast to his mouth, his lips found her nipple, sucking, then swirling his hot tongue in an eternal circle of pleasure. From one breast to the other, he worked the weight of them in his hands and drew a moan from her lips.

Her head dropped to the side as a barrage of sensations roared through her. The night sky was an audience of flickering lights, celebrating the concert of their lovemaking. She bit her lip and groaned. With her blouse now bunched around her waist, her upper body completely bare and exposed to the universe, she let her arms drop to her sides to simply feel every caress, tug, and kiss from Jamie's talented mouth and hands.

"You taste so good." His voice was thick with wanting and skittered along her skin in a velvety shiver.

Abandoning her breasts, Jamie dropped warm, wet kisses along her chest to her collarbone as his fingers dug into her hips. Fisting her skirt, he tugged and pulled until the fabric floated about them like a cloud. His fingertips found the edge of her panties, dipping beneath the lace at the juncture of her thighs.

Her breath caught, and she lifted a bit to give him more access. The feel of his feather-light touch along her soft flesh ignited her senses, then he touched that part of her that craved him the most. "Jamie!"

"I'm here." He lightened his touch even more. Just barely skimming her peak with the pad of his thumb. His chest rumbled. "I want to bury myself so deep inside you that you can't imagine how you ever lived without me. But first, I want to feel you, to have you feel me. To remember. And never forget."

His words were already too close to the truth for comfort. She pressed her lips against his neck, taking in his scent, memorizing his texture and taste. With shaking hands, she worked at his belt then, with his help, shoved his pants down to his thighs.

She took him in with hungry eyes, her body clamoring to take him inside and let him do just as he wanted. The thick length of him rose between them, setting her core off in a series of tiny contractions in reflex to the sight. "I want you."

"Good God, woman. I've never stopped wanting you."

He grabbed the back of her head with one hand, drawing her in to take her mouth, while his other slid her panties to the side.

She gripped him, squeezing against the solid heat, and rubbing his tip against her.

Her body buckled at his touch, and his hips jerked up toward her. His low growl elicited an elated, breathless giggle from her lips as she did it again.

"Blayne," he warned.

Her body was slick and ready for him. Primed to more than finish this ride, but rather take control of it and make it one he'd never forget.

Holding him to her, she lowered over the head of him, just enough to feel the ridge of his length, then she lifted.

His dick throbbed. Teasing him was fun, but it tortured her as well.

Holding his gaze with her own, the moon and stars blanketing them from above, the ocean waves buffeting their ears, his heat, his taste, his scent—her senses were in overload, and a heightened urgency for release exploded from her center.

She slid over him, taking his body into her as far as she could before she lifted and did it all over again.

As she moved over him, he growled against her lips. "Fuck me, you are too much."

Their lips met, desperate to take in every flavor the other offered, and she slid along his length again and again, harder and harder. His fingers dug into the mounds of her ass, and she gripped his shoulders, trying to gain momentum and seeking control that was neither hers nor his, but only belonged to both of them together.

Together.

The beauty and perfection, the dark and the pain, all rolled into one reality of life, and with one last thrust from his hips and drop of her body, they soared over that cliff together in a never-ending white light of pulsing sensation.

Jamie swallowed her cry of release as his own groan rumbled from his chest. She ground against him, riding the waves of pleasure that washed through her in an ongoing ripple of clarity.

"You're mine, Bean," he said in a fierce whisper against her lips.

In the U.S. or Ireland, it didn't matter. She *was* his.

With or without honor, there was no one else.

~

*J*ay stared at the warm glow of the sun as it slowly peeked from over the horizon and grinned with contentment.

Contentment.

A feeling so foreign to him over the past ten years, he was surprised he remembered the sensation.

Blayne's warm curves melted into his own hard angles on the hammock in the yard just south of the cliff. Only now her polka dot skirt covered them like a blanket instead of settling about her waist. Exhausted, they'd found their way like drunken sailors to the softly woven bed and had fallen asleep in each other's arms. They had a few days left before the gala, and for the first time, he felt as though he could breathe.

They'd achieved more than he'd originally envisioned when he'd taken on the project. She was a sharp and savvy businesswoman with an intense work ethic and tireless effort.

And she was finally his.

If he'd ever doubted their future before, he didn't now.

A surging need to protect her swamped him. From him or herself he didn't know, but what he did know was she was his, and he'd forever be hers. There was no one else.

He would never hurt her again and do everything in his power to earn her trust. And if it took every day for the rest of his life, well, that worked for him just fine.

Settling in deeper, he reveled in the fresh citrus and ocean scent of her hair. That combination had haunted him all the years they'd been apart. Her smell had been as much a part of him as the berry red of her lips and the crystal-clear green of her eyes.

Her no-nonsense demands and the compassionate, over-protective nature of her friendship had made every other woman he'd ever met seem lacking.

How had he ever left?

She stretched alongside him, and her eyes fluttered open.

"Good morning," he whispered.

Her lips spread into a wide grin. That self-satisfied grin often attributed to the Cheshire cat.

"Good morning."

She didn't jump up and worry that they'd fallen asleep or that his parents might find out. Her sense of self had always been a part of her he'd loved and admired. Instead, she eased into him, gliding her lips along his. "I haven't slept that hard in ages."

"That's because you missed me." As soon as he said the words he regretted it, but to his surprise, the warmth in her gaze remained.

"I did," she returned softly.

"Blayne." The need for her to fully understand him became urgent. "When I left, at first, I only thought of myself, then I only thought of saving you. From me."

Her gaze wandered across the yard to the ocean and the sunrise beyond. "You've told me this before."

"I know, but there's more. You know I was selfish and ambitious. Filled with an almost desperate need to prove myself."

"Almost?"

He squeezed her. "I always had a problem with how often my mother was left alone. Marrying into the Astor family comes with drawbacks, and I couldn't ask you to be with me only to be left all alone."

She propped up on his chest, her dark, silky hair falling about her face. "But leaving didn't save me from that. I was still all alone."

Pressure in his chest made it hard to breathe.

"Honestly, you don't give your mother or me enough credit." She slid a finger along his lower lip. "But it doesn't matter now. I wasn't in a place to understand anything but my own pain back then."

She sighed, then looked him in the eye. "It's okay."

Weightlessness washed over him. The idea of her forgiving him had never been on his radar, only a life of proving he'd never leave her again. "It's not okay. I—"

She pressed a kiss to his lips. "What I mean is...I forgive you for leaving. We were eighteen. Too young to make the decision to cross the ocean and too young to commit to forever. I was as much to blame for my circumstance as you. More so, if I'm honest and really take responsibility." Her warm gaze held his. "It's just that with how much I love you, it was too devastating to handle with any kind of poise."

He was so caught off guard by the words "I love you" that he missed her when he tried to keep her from moving away.

She stood beside the hammock, righting her clothes. "Let's face it, I am not known for my reasonable temper."

He watched her run long, slender fingers through her hair, then tuck her silk blouse into her skirt. Right before his eyes, she transformed from disheveled lover to his sassy, face-the-day, vintage Blayne. Though he loved the look, he couldn't help the feeling of immediate loss.

With a tilt of her head, she asked. "Why the look? I'm saying I forgive you."

Dropping his legs over the side, he sat up, visions of everything he ever wanted flirting with his mind's eye. "I know I don't deserve it, but I swear I'll spend every day earning it."

She stilled, a shadow crossing over her face.

"What's wrong?" He hated not knowing what was going on in her mind.

Shifting from one foot to the other, she shrugged with a whisper. "I wish we could freeze time and just keep last night, this moment, forever."

His relief was swift. "We can, but your clothes are on." The sullen tone in his voice slipped out before he could disguise it.

Her burst of laughter lit her face, and it was as if a tether had been cut and he was floating. Grabbing for him, she tugged him to his feet, then wrapped her arms around his waist.

It was a feeling he'd take to the grave. This woman in his arms, against his heart.

She tugged the top of her blouse over her breasts until they stood in their full naked glory under the glow of the rising sun. "Well, then, we'll just have to remedy that fact once we get to town."

He grabbed for her, but she was quicker and snapped her blouse into place. Sticking her ass high in the air, she bent to slip on her shoes. She was teasing him, and he loved every minute.

"First, I need coffee, and we need to go meet with the musicians your mom referred me to, then you can show me how good this skirt will look on my bedroom floor."

She sashayed toward him. "And you need to make sure you keep the judge away from the Cape house or lose all access to the moonshine." She winked then brushed past him toward the front drive.

His grin was quick, and he followed right behind her, taking in the sexy sight of her ass in that damn skirt. Oh, he'd show her alright.

She forgave him.

He still couldn't quite take in the enormity of that fact.

The sun never seemed brighter, their future never seemed more sure.

Coming home to Cape Van Buren was the best decision he'd ever made.

CHAPTER 15

"*P*inch me," Blayne demanded as she went over her inventory list of party rentals one more time the day before the gala. She anticipated the coming sting like a masochist, yearning for the pleasure-pain validation that this moment was actually real.

She'd done it.

Well, she and Jamie. A thank you to Ryker was on tap, but she didn't want to make his head any bigger than it already was with Larkin by his side and a house full of people as witnesses.

"Larkin." Snapping her fingers in quick succession, Blayne refused to stop until she had her attention.

The bright green gaze of her well-beyond pregnant friend drifted to hers in a lazy haze of love and possibility. "What? I'm sorry. I was—

"Daydreaming?" Blayne said. "Yeah, I can see that." She grabbed Larkin's arm and gave a small shake. "I said, pinch me."

Larkin blinked. "I certainly didn't think you were serious."

"Well, I am." Blayne shoved her forearm under Larkin's perky little nose.

"I am not going to pinch you."

"Oh, for fuck's sake. Don't be ridiculous and pinch me."

Heat flared in Larkin's eyes and she grabbed a chunk of skin and squeezed.

"Ouch!" She yanked her arm away, rubbing the spot with a grin on her face. "Thank you."

Larkin returned the smile but shook her head. "I may never completely understand you."

"Ha, yes you do. Which is why you're worried." Adjusting her clipboard in her arm, she balanced a few boxes in the other and walked them to the front room of the Cape house, Puzzle weaving his furry little body around her legs as she went. The cat really seemed to thrive with all the different people coming in and out of the house.

She couldn't believe the transformation of the bold, almost gothic color scheme from Maxine's home into the fresh and modern seaside escape surrounding her now. It was just as warm, just as inviting as the home had always been, but a bit more approachable. A crisp and clean amalgamation of nature and industry. The perfect place to create art, hold meetings, give a workshop, or enjoy a holiday get together. A fresh start and a new beginning in a place that already resided in every Cape Van Buren heart.

And she was responsible for the launch. Possibility rushed through her in a wave that left her feeling a bit buzzed and out of breath, better than winning a roller derby jam on the rink.

Setting the boxes down, she spun to Larkin. "Can you believe this is really happening?"

"I never doubted it. Why do you think I wanted you to head this up? I wouldn't trust anyone else to understand my vision and make it real more than you." Larkin's answer was softly spoken, but her eyes held Blayne's in an iron grip.

Ryker joined them, sliding his arm around Larkin's very round waist and placing a kiss on her temple. "I completely agree." His deep voice rumbled, and a smile broke out under dark bushy eyebrows that always seemed furrowed in a scowl. It almost made him look friendly.

Her heart did a little flip-flop of envy as it celebrated in their joy. She, too, had found the love of her life, but not every love was destined for forever. The idea of leaving Jamie behind stole the air from her lungs.

Trying to breathe through the pain, she focused on Larkin. Seeing her loved and cared for gave her such peace. She could go home to her family in Ireland without any worries about her friend. In a moment that seemed impossibly dark, Larkin had found love on the Cape.

With a wink, Blayne couldn't resist one last chance to tease. "I've even picked out the perfect pair of skates for tomorrow night."

The grin left Ryker's face so fast that both women giggled. On a sigh, he grabbed a stack of dish towels off the sofa. "Don't you dare. All we need is you to break something...or someone." He gave her a pointed look.

"Oh, please. Tell me you're worried about Jamie, and I'll know you're lying. By the way. Are those towels going in the kitchen?"

He glanced at the load in his arms. "Yes. Why? We agreed on white. I have all the cupboards loaded with dishes, utensils, platters, and an assortment of other serving ware. We've also stocked paper products and snacks. The community kitchen will be in full working order."

She just wanted to hear him say it. "Don't forget, as you get the programs up and running, you'll need to approach Janice about the community gardens and farm-to-table initiative we're thinking about."

He dipped his chin. "We will. What about Claire? Have you spoken to her about any of the art classes?"

Larkin and Blayne exchanged glances. "We're easing into it," Larkin said.

Ryker tilted his head. "Why? What's the problem?"

Blayne peeked past him to make sure they wouldn't be overheard. "She's been a bit too eager and bright with, well, everything. The baby, the community center. She planned the baby shower down to every last baby's breath in the centerpieces."

"So...again, what's the problem?"

Larkin slid her arm through her husband's. "We're worried that she isn't really dealing with everything that's happened. That she's hiding behind all the work and the excitement to avoid how hard it really must be to see us married...and pregnant after...well, you know. She swears she's fine, but..." Her voice trailed off.

"Maybe the work is just what she needs." Lifting the stack higher against his chest, he added, "Tell me if I can do anything else to help. And, Blayne?"

Opening the boxes she'd brought in from the other room, she turned. "Yeah?"

Ryker looked through the large front windows toward the lawn and circular drive. The fountain was in perfect working order and white globe lights were strung like a canopy across the lawn toward the sea of wild blueberries.

As he turned to her, she smiled, awaiting the words of praise for the incredible transformation the cape was going through for the gala.

"I told you so," he quipped.

She watched his retreating back, then stepped forward. "Why that..."

Larkin grabbed her arm. "He's right, and you know it. You and Jamie are better together."

Blayne's reflexive posturing of self-righteous indignation melted as soon as it started and was replaced with a swirling, bittersweet warmth radiating from deep within her soul. Jamie did make her better, and she liked to think she made him better, too.

Nope, scratch that. She absolutely made him better.

With a wink, she grabbed Larkin's hand. "Come on. I want to show you something."

The low din coming from the kitchen suddenly went quiet.

"Maxine!"

Judge Carter's booming voice carried in as if from a loudspeaker.

Larkin's eyes grew wide with concern. "Oh no."

Blayne followed Larkin into the kitchen that was already packed with what seemed like half of Cape Van Buren. With all the renovations, they'd left the kitchen virtually unchanged with its white tin ceiling that mirrored the huge white granite island. Black cupboards rose from the counter, flanking each side of a large commercial stove, and the black-and-white checkered tile floor wrapped it all together. She'd always loved this room.

Maxine stood frozen, taking money from Shelly Anne's outstretched hand. And in the Flat Iron Coffeehouse owner's other arm were two cobalt blue jars of moonshine.

"Shit," Larkin whispered, grabbing Blayne.

"It'll be okay. Don't worry," She assured her. And it would be as long as Judge Carter backed off immediately. But he had another think coming if he thought to showdown with his lady love in front of a crowd.

"Don't you dare use that tone with me, Theodore Carter." Maxine wouldn't accept that from anyone, not Ryker, not Stuart, her deceased husband, and certainly not the judge. No matter how much she loved him, Maxine had fallen into her own woman a long time ago. It was something Blayne had learned from her since moving to the Cape and strived to achieve every day. She was both in awe of and terrified of the woman.

As the judge should be.

Jamie came whistling in through the front door then strolled on into the kitchen while texting on his phone.

"Jamie!" Blayne's whisper was more desperate than quiet and could be heard throughout the kitchen, but not a soul looked their way. All eyes were on Maxine.

She was splendid in a white shirt with a popped collar that met the sharp edge of her shiny silver hair. Her cut was blunt, longer in the front and shorter in the back, and today was set off by a pair of gorgeous silver hoops. With groomed, arched brows and a bright red lip, Maxine looked like she'd just finished lunching with Raquel Welch rather than boot-legging her moonshine.

Judge Carter drew his bushy brows together and slapped his hat upon the island top. "I knew you were still up to your tricks. It has to stop now. I cannot be married to a woman who breaks the law as casually as Mitch Brennan picks up women."

Mitch's head snapped up from the string of lights he was testing. "Hey!"

His mother slapped him on the arm.

Claire joined Blayne and Larkin, mumbling, "He's not lying."

Jamie stepped close to Blayne, his heat enveloping her like a safety net. "What's going on?"

"Moonshine."

Jamie's grin dropped. "Aw, hell."

"Exactly."

Maxine winced. Nothing very apparent, but Blayne saw it. With her painted lips in a thin line, she rolled up the bills. Then, while defiantly holding the judge's gaze, opened her clutch and dropped them in. "Then it seems your social calendar has just opened up, Judge Carter. The wedding is off."

Larkin gasped in unison with a low expletive from Ryker. He stepped between the judge and Maxine. "Grandmother, now wait just a second."

"No, Ryker. I don't think I will." She tucked her clutch under her arm. "No one tells me what to do." She walked toward the front door but stopped in front of Blayne. "I'll be here tomorrow, but you can cancel my plus one."

Blayne grimaced. There were no reservations to begin with. But when Maxine wanted to make a point, she'd make a point.

The front door slammed, leaving the house in an awkward silence.

Jamie stepped up to Shelly Anne and tapped one of the jars in her arms. "Now it's a party."

"Jay, now's not the time," Judge Carter snapped.

Jamie chuckled. "Sorry, Judge, but Maxine's moonshine is the finest kind. It's always the time."

The love of her life was sorely forgetting he wouldn't be getting any in the near future. He'd had one job as far as Maxine was concerned. Blayne sighed. Now he'd be expecting her to share.

Not bleedin' likely.

Shelly Anne raised her brows, then moved toward the sliding doors. "Anyway, I'll be going now. Needed at the shop." She found Blayne's gaze in the crowd. "I have everything ready for the coffee tomorrow so don't fret."

Snapping to attention, Blayne stepped into action. The judge looked like he was in a state of shock, and the best thing she could do for the poor guy was to get him out of the spotlight.

"Great. Thanks, Shelly Anne." She clapped. "Alright, there's nothing to see here. Mitch, finish hanging the lights. Miss Janice, the rest of the flowers for the arrangements are in the honey room, and, Jamie, you need to tell me what's going on with that eyesore of a tarp in the side lawn."

With a worried look at Larkin, Jamie nudged Ryker. The tarp was over Archer's wishing well. That thing had been the center of Larkin's life back when Ryker was thinking of parceling off the land. The boys had promised they'd have the sod replaced and everything completely taken care of by the gala.

"Yeah. We've got it covered," Jamie said.

"I can see that. I'm hoping you won't by tomorrow." What was wrong with him? They could not leave it like that for the party.

Ryker swung his arm around Blayne and guided her away from Larkin. In a low voice, he said, "We're taking care of it."

"By tomorrow, it'll be pristine."

She gave him a solid side-eye. "It better be." She tried not to let it bother her, but she'd asked him to take care of it weeks ago. Shaking the disappointment away, she nodded. "I mean...okay." It was time to fight against her knee-jerk reactions of irritation with him. So much of that stuck around from when he'd left and was no longer fair.

She couldn't look away from his intense gaze, and he took it as an invitation. Stepping close, he placed his hands on her hips.

Ryker saluted. "I'm out. Going to check the beehives."

With a chuckle, Jamie placed a warm kiss on her mouth, lingering against her bottom lip. Her heart fluttered opened a bit more, and she had to fight the sigh of contentment that wanted to escape.

"What are we going to do about the judge and Maxine?" she asked him.

He shrugged. "We can't fix it. Only they can. I'm more worried about me in this instance."

She worried her lip, giving him a nudge. "I can't believe Judge called her out like that. I mean…"

"Can you blame him?" He tucked a loose strand of hair behind her ear. "He's a judge. There's no integrity in breaking the law. It's like she's laughing at his life's work."

She tensed, feeling a bit of an itch hearing a woman she admired being spoken of in anything but admiration.

"Don't pull away." Jamie tightened his grip. "Look, it was a fair assessment of me when I'd left you, and I've been trying to make it right. And it's fair for the judge to feel the disappointment…even with Maxine."

He was right. And she decidedly did not like how it felt. Maxine was treading a bit on the judge's life's work, whether she saw it that way or not.

Relaxing into Jamie's arms, she looked up at him with a bit of a frown. "I'm not sure if I like this new, thought-provoking side of you."

His grin was swift, and she felt it clear to her toes. He stole a kiss. "Yes, you do. I've been working hard to change so I don't make the same mistakes again. So I don't hurt you. Honor is my new middle name."

Blayne's laugh was strained. He'd worked too hard to change, to be a man she could love. And he'd accomplished it. Deep down, she knew she'd never stopped.

But her return home was imminent. Too important to change over the chance at love. Not when that love had hurt her once already.

They just needed a chance to sit down and work it all out. After the gala, they'd make a plan.

"Seriously, though." He held her tighter. "I think we have a real chance to make our future really special." He glanced around the kitchen. "Look at what we've done together."

She shook her head with a feeling of awe, replaying the scene of when she ran into him and fell ass-over-end his first day in town. They'd come a long way in a short time. She'd never imagined anything like it. "You're right...again. I want to resist, I want to fall into my old patterns and argue, but the truth is all around us, isn't it?"

And it was. From everything she'd heard from Emma, her father seemed detached from the relationship she thought they'd had. It killed her, and as Jamie had worked so hard for her, she needed to do the same for her da. Her regret caused an ache unlike anything else. She'd always been her daddy's little girl.

Resting her cheek against Jamie's chest, she concentrated on the steady beat of his heart, wanting to remember the sound, allowing it to ease the sorrow of her own. Yesterday was lost to change, but the possibility of tomorrow opened with endless options.

If only the timing was different.

Everything she wanted was right here. Working for the center, her friendship with Larkin, and just maybe, a future with the only man she'd ever loved.

She hated to admit to being afraid of anything, but she also hated being fake. The truth was, she wanted a future with Jamie so much she was terrified stepping toward it for fear of losing him again.

Picking herself up once had been a hard-fought battle of wills and survival in a country of strangers. Having to do it again...

She couldn't even finish the thought.

She loved Jamie. The words were wrapped tight in her bruised and tender heart, but they were there if she let herself really listen.

But it was time to quit putting herself first. That's what had hurt the people she loved from the beginning. Her da deserved so much more than she'd given him.

Turning her face into Jamie's neck, aching from the impossibility of the situation, she whispered, "You and I make each other better."

And with the acceptance of those words, her heart fluttered in eager and ecstatic anticipation for the man she was afraid she could never have.

CHAPTER 16

*D*etermined to enjoy the celebration regardless of her own conflicted emotions, Blayne stood on the front porch of the Archer Conservation Park of Cape Van Buren's community center and forced herself to take in every inch of the unforgettable sight sprawling out before her.

It was like a dream.

The sun was slowly exiting the day beyond the trees west of Cape Van Buren, leaving a warm, hazy, golden glow upon the lawn. Globe lights were strung back and forth across the west lawn of the cape from gas-lit torch to gas-lit torch.

Large potted plants flanked the corners of the space, and tall bistro-style tables created islands of opportunity to eat delicious foods, partake in exotic drinks, and enjoy the best company that Cape Van Buren had to offer.

Jamie's big, strong arm encircled the waist of her lustrous metal satin Zac Posen gown. The off-the-shoulder sweetheart neckline was supported by sculptural pleating at the bodice with a mermaid silhouette, and flanked on each side by banded short sleeves, leaving the pale skin of her shoulders open to receive the warm kiss of his lips.

His touch made her love leap to life in her chest, and she couldn't help but turn to him.

"You look stunning." His voice was deep and thick with emotion. "I don't know how to explain it, but everything with you is different from with anyone else. Life..." He trailed a finger along her collarbone. "Each breath, each moment..."

She captured his wandering fingers and pressed them to her lips for a kiss. "I feel it, too." Letting herself get lost in his intense gray eyes, she sighed. "Believe me. I tried to find someone to replace you, but with every encounter, I faced a lonelier future. There was never meant to be anyone else but you, Jamie."

His jaws flexed as he listened to her words and his free hand drew her toward him.

She grabbed the silver train of her dress and swung it around to accommodate the need to be closer.

"I love you, Blayne."

She closed her eyes. Could there be a more perfect moment than this? Breathing in the sweet scent of the cape and the salty ocean breeze, her lips trembled. Though she'd always considered her heart her weakest muscle, she finally had the strength to ask for what she wanted. On a swallow, she quietly admitted, "I love you, too, Jamie."

Jamie's eyes flared wide. "Bean—"

A quick slap and shake of Jamie's arm had him stepping from the warm cocoon he and Blayne had made.

Ryker stood grinning from ear-to-ear, and it was as startling to see now as ever. "You two did it. I mean, damn. I knew you would, working together, but this..." He arced his hand out toward the yard. "This is more than I'd ever imagined, and I think exactly what my gorgeous wife was hoping for."

Larkin joined them on the porch, taking the steps one at a time while holding the full skirt of her lime green halter dress. The color brought out the bright green of her eyes, making them sparkle so bright the setting sun had competition.

Her breath came out in little pants by the time she reached the top step, and she rested her hand on the swell of her belly. "It's more than anything..." Emotion left her eyes bright and her words stuttering.

Blayne abandoned Jamie's side to embrace her friend in a hug. "It's all for you and Archer. He'll live through this center forever, Larkin, making each and every life in Cape Van Buren better."

"Shit." Ryker scowled with concern.

There was the man they all recognized and loved. Blayne grinned as Ryker grabbed a handkerchief from his pocket.

"I knew with the two of you, I'd need this." Carefully, he blotted the cloth to the corner of his wife's eye.

Larkin laughed and grabbed his hands in her own. "Just look at it, Ryker."

The four of them watched as the town of Cape Van Buren joined them in all their decadent, sparkling glory for the gala.

Along the edge of the property, by the entrance, a lone figure stood almost invisible in the shadows.

Jamie swore under his breath. "Is that—"

"Don't give him a second thought. Sheriff Davenport is watching from the lighthouse. There won't be any problems. My father isn't stupid enough to try anything with the whole town as a witness. He prefers small groups, so he has some semblance of deniability," Ryker said.

Larkin patted his arm. "Not a second thought." Then she leaned up and placed a kiss on her husband's cheek.

Blayne's admiration for Ryker increased at how easily he dismissed his abusive father. That had been a long struggle for hard-fought success.

They still had a few minutes from the official start time when the first chords of a silky jazz song filled the air.

She leaned close to Jamie. "The band your mom hooked us up with is amazing. I was able to listen to them live at an event at Delizioso a few days ago."

"I'm glad." He smiled. "Speaking of my mother." He nodded toward the lawn. Mr. and Mrs. Astor emerged from a limo in their finest, and their look of pride wouldn't go unmissed by anyone in attendance. Their son played a large part in the splendor and it was written all over their faces.

Blayne shook off a twinge of loneliness. Her da had never witnessed what she was capable of, and her ma's ethereal view was sweet but out of reach.

"Come on." He grabbed her fingers and led her down the stairs with Larkin and Ryker close behind.

Larkin slowed as they closed in on the well. "What's going on?" She pointed to the tarp over Archer's wishing well. "Take that tarp off, Ryker. No one is going to damage the new well, it's a sophisticated party, not a college brawl...or construction site." She made her words at the end very gentle and added a wink.

Ryker winced all the same.

159

"This is what we wanted to show the both of you." Jamie's eyes danced, and Blayne could barely handle how adorable her big, muscly man seemed in that moment.

"What did you do?" she asked, smoothing her hair, a line of dark vintage waves, along one side of her face.

He patted Ryker on the back. "Do you remember that idea I'd mentioned to you?"

She racked her brain. "Jamie, over the past few weeks, you and I have discussed a lot of things."

Larkin laughed. "Look, the gala is beginning and I'm due any second. We don't have time for guessing games."

"You heard the woman." Ryker grabbed a corner of the tarp.

Curiosity tugged Blayne closer as the men pulled the tarp off the well.

Larkin gasped.

Blayne's hands came together over her chest as if trying to hold in the swelling of love that she felt for Jamie in that moment. Now she remembered.

Archer's Angels.

"What's this?" Larkin whispered as she stepped up to the well.

Blayne had so many memories of visiting the Cape with Archer and Larkin. He'd loved the well and dropped pennies over. But he had a rule. No wish could be made until it reached the bottom. She'd never seen a five-year-old boy as patient as he'd been, his blond hair ruffled by the wind and that huge grin with the dimple in his chin, just like his mom's.

Ryker stepped behind Larkin then wrapped his arms around her waist as well as he could.

"Well, as Blayne and I were navigating our way through the policies and procedures and board responsibilities, it occurred to me that time and again you've mentioned wanting to make sure that kids had a voice on the Cape," Jamie said.

Larkin's nod was slow but steady.

Blayne couldn't help the feeling of pride she had for Jamie and joined him at the well so she could better see Larkin's expression.

"I thought that it only made sense to have a secondary set of board members made up Cape Van Buren kids called Archer's Angels."

A sob broke from Larkin's lips and her fingers flew up to press against them.

Ryker retrieved his handkerchief again, which she snatched quickly and without moving her eyes off the new stone sign that stood next to the well.

"Archer's Angels will keep us honest when it comes to the vision and priority of the center. Kids first, the residents first, not bottom lines or profit margins. Though we want this to thrive and need money to make that happen, that is my responsibility." His warm fingers wrapped around Blayne's wrist, drawing her closer.

"*Our* responsibility."

Tears of love and regret welled in her eyes as well, in empathy with Larkin but also from a deep-rooted sense of well-being she hadn't felt since stepping onto U.S. soil ten years ago with Jamie. Well-being she had to walk away from.

"The kids will have an advisor, but there are rules put in place to make sure the children's voices and needs are not only heard, but listened to when it comes to our programs, events, and opportunities."

Jamie sucked in air as if he'd forgotten to breathe, then let it all out in a long huff.

Music drifted around them, accompanied by the din of happy conversation and the breaking waves of the ocean against the rocks surrounding the cape.

Blayne swore a delighted echo of laughter floated above the trees as they stood, waiting for Larkin to speak.

Her friend's eyes widened, and she lifted her face toward the sound. Whether it was their imagination, their joy, or possibly their hope, Blayne would never know, but she'd never deny the moment as long as she lived.

"Are you okay?" Ryker asked.

Larkin gripped the hands around her and smiled at Jamie. "Never better. There are no words, Jay…"

She stepped away from Ryker and wrapped her arms around Jamie. Holding him, she dabbed at her tears before they ran down her cheeks. Jamie patted her, looking toward Blayne for help.

She smiled at him and mouthed the words. "Hold her."

Jamie wrapped his arms around her pregnant form and let her take the time she needed.

Larkin went on to express her heartfelt thanks, then the night rolled on in a waterfall of well-wishes, volunteer and financial commitments, and promises to help make the vision of the center a reality.

Blayne and Jamie presented both the official board and Archer's Angels to the town. They presented the donor program and announced the first official gift by none other than the Astor family.

The food was spectacular, the music perfection, and Maxine's moonshine found its way into more than one glass.

Blayne and Larkin watched as Judge Carter stared after Maxine with the forlorn look of lost love. Blayne understood the feeling, and her heart went out to the man. "Just look at him."

Larkin sighed. "I know. I feel awful. I tried talking to Maxine but she's being as stubborn as ever and even threatened to leave me out of her moonshine will."

"Her what?" Blayne laughed.

"You heard me. I dropped it. Going without over the last nine months was hard enough. I wasn't risking it."

"She'd never."

Larkin raised a brow. "Are you going to test it?"

Blayne pretended to study her manicure. "Hell, no."

"Exactly, but I know she's hurting."

"Yep." Blayne waved to where Maxine, Evette, and Janice were doing the Charleston. Maxine was laughing as she tapped forward, then tapped back, her hands swinging side to side with the move, but there was tension in her eyes, and her voice was a bit too bright.

"She's miserable. And unfortunately, he wasn't wrong."

Larkin shrugged. "Try telling her that and risk your future of any moonshine enjoyment."

"What are we going to do?"

Suddenly, Blayne was swept onto the dance floor by Jamie.

"Not so fast, I can only move my legs so much in the narrow skirt of this dress!" But she laughed, unable to stop or catch her breath.

Jamie broke out into one of the best versions of the Charleston she'd ever seen. She'd never known such a big man could move so fast.

And, man, did she like what she saw. The lazy *lub-dub* of her heart sped up as she took in the breadth of his shoulders encased in a tuxedo jacket that looked as if it had been made for him.

On second thought, it probably had been.

Her mouth watered at the sight of his chest muscles flexing under his crisp white shirt and his thighs bulging in the most delicious fashion every time he stepped forward. If she didn't get a few minutes alone with the man, she was going to spontaneously combust.

Grabbing his hand, she tugged him from the floor. Besides, she had to talk to him and figure out what they were going to do before she went mad.

"Wait, where are we going?"

She tossed him a wink. "You've hung out with Ryker long enough to pick up a few tricks. I want you to show me how to extract a little honey."

The look in his eyes went from heavy with desire to delight with such speed she would have dropped his tux pants right then and there if it weren't actually against the law. She didn't need anything else getting in the way of her future.

They burst through the front doors of the house as quickly as her skirt and train would allow her to go, past the kitchen, and down the hall until they found the honey room.

Once inside, she slammed the door shut then locked it.

The click sounded loud in the quiet of the room.

They could hear the crowd outside. The music, the joy.

This was her town, after all.

"What are we doing in here?"

"I told you. I want you to extract some honey."

He stared at the large stainless pots in bewilderment. "Seriously, I have no idea—"

"Jamie, we need to talk." Her voice was low, but the tone caught his attention.

She ran the tip of her finger along the upper swell of her breast at the neckline of her dress. "And I *want you* to extract *my* honey."

"Well, fucking hell," he growled, reaching for her. "I might have to be told twice, but I only have to hear it once."

"Wait, I—"

His lips found hers in a kiss that was as sweet as it was hot. All thoughts of conversation flew from her head as she promised herself that one day she'd get him in one of the bee suits just so she could take it off him again.

The subtle scent of honey in the air and the soft jazz filling the room from outside was the most delicious backdrop to her guaranteed *happy ending* that she could have ever imagined.

~

*J*amie turned Blayne around and unzipped her gown to discover she was completely naked underneath. With an urgency that was foreign to him, he didn't waste any time helping her step out of it and into his arms. The thing was an amazing contraption that somehow stood on its own as if it had an audience.

He didn't give a fuck if they had a stadium. He was about to give the best performance of his life, and if anyone even thought of interrupting, he'd kill 'em, then spend the rest of his life in jail warm with the memory of Blayne's heat, the scent of her sweet, ocean breeze skin, and the unique flavor of her mouth that he craved like an addiction.

She spun on him in a frenzy, launching into his arms and making him land hard against the countertop. His arm flung out, sending a pot crashing to the ground, but the commotion only seemed to excite her more.

A desperation seemed to push her along as if they didn't have the rest of their lives to love one another. There was nothing he'd rather do than answer every kiss, every bite, every tug with equal fervor. Cradling her face, he took command of her mouth, tasting, sipping, drinking her in as if he'd never have the chance again.

She shoved his jacket from his shoulders then yanked his shirt from his pants. She had his fly open and the hard length of him in her hands before he could fully register the direction of her efforts.

"Blayne. Fuck."

She squeezed him, stroking from the tip to the base, and his sight went white. There was no slowing the woman down when she got her mind set on something, and he'd learned a long time ago not to try. Besides, any ride with Blayne was a ride he wanted to be on. No matter how fast or slow.

He slid his fingertips along her body, taking in every familiar curve and dip, knowing every sigh and every breath hitch before she gave it. He knew this woman.

Knew her body, her heart, her mind, and her soul.

He was beyond proud of what she'd accomplished and that he was able to be a part of it.

His chest swelled with the love that had never died, had never wavered, and he yanked her up against him.

She had to let him go and catch herself at his shoulders, wrapping her arms around him.

"Stay," he said.

As her heated gaze held his in question, a few wisps of black hair fluttered around her face. She whispered, "If only I could."

She was the most beautiful woman in every way, and he didn't think he could ever feel more passionately for her than in that moment.

"I'll always be here for you, Bean. Never leave you again." His breathing labored. "You're amazing." His statement was half-growl, half-moan, as she rubbed her breasts against his chest. Trying to focus, he gave a small shake to his head. "I'm serious. Your mom, your dad would be so proud of you."

She stilled, her eyes glistening with the threat of tears.

Setting her to her feet, he cupped her face again. "I didn't mean to upset you, I—"

"I love you," she whispered. "I always have. Remember that. Okay?"

His mind, heart, and soul tripped once more. Wondering if he'd misheard her, he just stared like he had on the front steps, afraid she was simply caught up in the excitement of the gala.

He'd hoped, but he'd never let himself truly imagine that she'd ever forgive him for his royal fuck up. And even now, having heard her words again, the fear that he was wrong, that he'd mistaken her meaning, kept him silent.

Finally, he found his tongue. His voice, hoarse with emotion, dragged past his lips and he demanded, "Say it again."

Her berry-painted lips spread into a grin but trembled with something else.

"I love you." She kissed his forehead. "I love you." She kissed each brow. "But—"

"I love you, too," he cut her off.

Wrapping her legs around his waist, she used his shoulders to lift her body until she was poised to take him inside her. "Don't ever forget," she whispered, worry clouding her eyes with something he couldn't understand.

His body on fire and his love burning brighter than ever before, he gave a fierce shake of his head, then rested his forehead against hers. "Never."

"Promise?" The uncertainty in her voice killed him as much as the waiting to feel her around him did.

"I'm yours, Bean. And you're mine."

"Yes." Her answer was solid and sure, allowing his pulse to settle into the rhythm she'd set with her body.

Two steps had her pressed up against the wall where he could find his bearings and move with her toward the pleasure they both wanted.

His body tightened with every stroke, every touch. Her hands and lips were everywhere. She overwhelmed him, humbled him...she loved him.

Reaching her peak, she moved faster, harder, grinding on him with a strength he'd always admired. Her heels dug into the backs of his thighs, her legs clamped around his hips like a vice, and on a groan, she sailed over the precipice.

And he was right behind her. Side-by-side.

Like he said.

With passion he didn't even try to subdue, he shouted her name as the wave of his orgasm slammed into him, measuring hers beat by beat.

He didn't understand how it was possible, but the only woman he'd ever loved, loved him once again. She was in his arms and in his life.

And this time he wouldn't fuck it up.

CHAPTER 17

*B*layne would have laughed in the face of anyone who told her they could see hearts floating about her head, but with each step across the gala dance floor in Jamie's arms, she swore, she could see the little pink shapes out of the corner of her eyes.

As it turned out, honey was quite the aphrodisiac, and they hadn't yet had a chance to talk, but they had time. She wasn't leaving until the morning.

Another heart came into view. Or maybe she was high on life, or Jamie's kiss, his touch, his love...

"You look happy," he whispered against her ear, sending a shiver up her spine.

She raised a brow. "Don't get cocky."

"Me? Never." Feigning a look of innocence, he slapped his chest.

"Truthfully? I can't remember the last time I felt this good," she confessed, though it was only partially true.

Jamie winked, sending a thrill that raced along her nerve endings, reminding her she was quite naked under her dress. "I can. About fifteen minutes ago, as a matter of fact." His tone was decidedly suggestive.

"Fifteen minutes ago?" She tapped her chin. "I'm confused."

On a low grumble, he gathered her close to show her, beyond a shadow of a doubt, exactly what he was talking about.

The hard length of him burned through his tuxedo pants and her dress as if nothing separated them at all. There was no getting enough of him.

Never was.

Which was why she'd tried with such determination and persistence. Larkin once joked about her never having a relationship longer than the length of a man's dick, and she was right. But that was only because Blayne had never found anything interesting beyond that point.

Except with Jamie.

Always Jamie.

Claire glided up, gorgeous in an ice blue, floor-length, strapless dress that set off a tiny waist that defied physics and would entice even the most steadfast man.

Stepping between Jamie and her friend, she teased, "Don't you be coming up here, seducing my man with those big blue eyes and rockin' bod, my friend."

A decidedly unladylike guffaw escaped Claire's lips, and she slapped her gloved fingers over them. Rolling her eyes, she said, "Knock it off." She jabbed a thumb at Jamie. "This one's never had eyes for anyone but you, even when he was propositioned with every possible temptation in every possible manner down at the rink a couple weeks ago."

Town gossip spread fast and the Van Buren Roller Beauties were a gorgeous bunch. So much so that Blayne joked about switching teams more than once. But they were a crazy lot, too. When it came to those ladies—men were safer.

But knowing he went looking for her warmed her in an unexpected way. She refused to look at him for fear that he'd see just how hopelessly, head-over-ass in love she really was. For fuck's sake. She literally crossed an ocean for the man.

"Anyway, I was in the house and your phone kept ringing. I answered. Your sister's been trying to get a hold of you. Something with your dad?" Claire's gaze wavered in concern.

Fear twisted in her stomach. If Emma was calling, and it had to be Emma because their older sister, Ruby, had barely spoken ten sentences to her since she'd left, she must have news.

Which also meant it was time she and Jamie had that talk. No more interruptions, no more distractions.

"Thanks, Claire. I'll go call her right away, just give me a minute with Jamie."

"He'll have to wait, she's waiting on the line."

Jamie moved to go with her. "I can come with you."

"No." She patted his chest. "Go find Ryker, have a drink. I'll find out what's going on, then come find you."

"Are you sure? I'm here if you need me." His gaze showered love on her in a way she'd never tire of.

With a smile, she nodded. "I'm fine. Go. We'll have another honey tasting when I'm through." She winked.

His eyes dilated immediately, and he stepped toward her.

Throwing both hands up, she laughed. "Go!"

"Fine. But that wasn't fair."

She gave him a saucy grin. "And you love it." Sliding her arm through Claire's, she headed toward the house.

"There's a honey tasting?"

Blayne laughed. "I'll explain later. Thanks for letting me know about the call."

Claire nodded. "Of course. I was worried since the same number kept calling, otherwise I wouldn't have bothered you on such a special night."

"It really has turned out to be magical, hasn't it?" She looked across the lawn. Now that the sun had dropped below the trees west of the town, the cape was blanketed in the velvet of night but bedazzled with strings and strings of white globe lights. Music was in the air, the waves crashed off the shore, the scent of the ocean mingled with the sweet and savory foods along the perimeter of the dance floor.

And to top it off, Jamie had shared the donor report to start, and it was beyond anything she'd ever imagined.

All the dreams she never dared to dream just might come true.

Turning to Claire, she nodded toward the dance floor. "Go dance. I know there's no shortage of Van Buren men out there just itching to get a little attention from the sex-pot Claire Adams."

Claire's eyes grew wide then narrowed. "You're as awful as you've ever been. I like it." On a laugh, she made her way to the party.

Blayne hesitated, worried about how she was going to tell Jamie, worried about what news her sister could possibly have for her.

Slipping her heels off at the door, she walked barefoot into the large kitchen to settle in at the island, comforted by Puzzle's purring, furry presence as the cat jumped to the table top and rubbed his whiskered face against her arm.

Arranging her silver mermaid skirt to accommodate the stool, she picked up the phone. It was 2 a.m. in Ireland, so either it was important, or her sister was bored. She'd been calling Blayne all hours of the day and night since she'd learned how to use a phone.

"Blayne?" Emma's whisper floated across the line.

"Em, I'm here. What's up? Why are you awake?"

"I was waiting to call you until Ruby fell asleep. She didn't want me to bother you."

"Typical." She rolled her eyes. Her older sister would probably rather not claim the relation at all if she could help it. "What's so important that you couldn't tell me once I got in? I'm leaving tomorrow."

"Da fell and broke his hip."

Blayne straightened in her stool. "What? When, how…I mean."

"He was pruning the ivy along the front of the house and fell from the ladder. It's pretty bad. He's having surgery tomorrow. A hip replacement."

Hip replacement? That's what happened to old people, grandparents, not her father. Noah MacCaffrey was a bull of a man. Big, strong, and more capable than anyone she'd ever known.

Hell, he raised three daughters and a son all on his own after their ma had passed.

He was a saint.

He was all they had.

And she'd left him.

Tears stung behind her lids and she ached with shame. "Is he going to be okay? Can he walk?" Her voice rose with each word.

"Calm down. He's okay. It's just…I knew you'd want to know. There's no way to get you here earlier at this point, so you'll miss being here to see him when he gets out of recovery. But I wanted you to be prepared." Emma's voice wavered.

She swallowed hard. She walked toward the front of the house, to the large window that overlooked the party. Searching through all the townspeople, she spotted the broad, steadfast shoulders of the man she adored. He was laughing, enjoying a toast with Ryker if the tap of their glasses was any indication. Her heart swelled with love and squeezed with agony at the same time.

The intensity of it all was an impossibility, and she grabbed a chair for support. Everything was here, but everything was also in Ireland.

She'd finally found a love that was ready for forever, but her father deserved more from her than a get-well card, and there was no telling how long he'd need her to be there.

Sometimes the universe spoke—it was about time she listened to the needs of her family instead of her own desires.

This was the true bitch of karma.

"Of course. I'm coming home, Em."

~

*J*ay accepted the glowing praise from Ryker as they toasted once more to a successful launch. The gala was still in full swing. He'd had some of the hottest sex in his life amongst the greatest edible gift of nature—apart from Blayne, that was.

He grinned.

Ryker tossed back his drink. "What's that look for? I'm getting a little uncomfortable if it's directed at me. I mean, I know we're close, but I'm a married man."

"I'm gonna ask her, and I want you to be my best man."

Ryker slowly lowered his glass from his lips. "Are you fuckin' with me?"

"No. And I'm not *fuckin'* this up again. I let her go once and lost ten years with an amazing woman. I refuse to lose another second."

"That's the smartest thing you've said since returning to the Cape." Ryker said.

Shaking his head, Jay shook him off. "Please, I outlined a strategy for a donor program that has already accepted enough in gifts to keep the center in the black for the next five years."

His buddy dipped his dark head in agreement, then accepted two more glasses of Scotch from a passing waiter and handed one to Jay.

"Damn right. And yet this proposal is still the smartest damn thing you've ever said."

"You approve?"

Ryker's dark brows furrowed. "She's family."

"You yell at her all the time." Jay laughed.

"Because she's a pain in the ass. And we wouldn't have her any other way. Do you know she never left Larkin's side when Archer died? She stayed, she pushed, she persisted. Hell, when Larkin would have run from me, Blayne encouraged her to stay and fight. She's changed our lives."

They clinked glasses then sipped from the rims. "Besides, she's your pain in the ass, and she suits you."

They turned to see the object of their conversation approaching them from the house, and Jay raised his glass to her. "Yeah, she does."

"Now you need to convince her to stay."

"Wait, what?" He wanted to question Ryker further, but he didn't get the returning grin or wink from her as he'd expected.

"Fuck."

Ryker followed his gaze. "What happened?"

"I don't know, but the look on her face tells me it isn't good news. Something's happened in Ireland."

His buddy clapped him on the back again. "Then you'll help her through it."

Jay threw Ryker a look of bewilderment. "Help Blayne? Are you crazy? When she's vulnerable, she pushes people away as if her life depends on the isolation."

He tried to decipher the resigned set of her expression. "God damn fucking hell," Jay whispered fiercely as he held the engagement ring inside his jacket pocket like a lifeline. Everything he ever wanted was going to come together in this great culmination of fate tonight, but the scared and reserved look in the love of his life's eyes had warning bells clanging in his head.

His gut grew heavy with dread.

"Calm down, man. Let's see what's going on."

Jay stepped toward her, but she stiffened. "Bean? What's wrong?"

She studied his face as if in pain. "I, uh…" She swallowed hard on the waver in her voice.

"Let's go talk in private." Jay slid his hand up her arm.

She eased away with a shake of her head. "No. I need to tell you here." She waved toward Larkin and Claire to join them. "I'm afraid if we talk in private you'll try to change my mind, making this harder than it already is."

The blood drained from Jay's head and the roaring grew louder.

Larkin and Claire stepped into the circle of friends with worried looks in their eyes.

Blayne lifted her chin. The quiver in her lower lip told Jay the news was worse than he expected. "My da's hurt. I'm leaving tomorrow, but I need to go home and pull myself together."

Both Larkin and Claire broke into a barrage of heated denial, but she shook her head until they stopped. "You guys. Come on. Don't make this worse." She looked at Larkin. "You've given me the greatest gift as a friend and opportunity as a business partner. And it kills me that I won't see this sweet baby the day her face is first warmed by the sun." She gently placed a hand on Larkin's round belly.

"You can't be serious. What about the grand opening? I kept hoping we'd have more time or that you'd change your mind." The pain in Larkin's eyes was obvious and Jay could relate.

"Larkin, you knew I was leaving."

What the fuck?

His heart split in two and a pounding started slow and low in his skull building with each passing second of this new revelation. "What the hell do you mean, she knew you were leaving?"

"I'd decided before you came to town. It was my plan all along. But then—"

"When the hell were you going to tell me? What the fuck has this all been about, Blayne?" He'd never felt so much pain in his life, and he squeezed the engagement ring box so hard in his hand that the corner of it dug painfully into his palm. He welcomed the burn.

"Jamie, I'd been trying to tell you. You know that I love you, but it's my da."

He tried to reach for her again, but she stepped away. "Why the hell are you pulling away from me? If it's something with your dad, let me help. We can do this together."

Tears welled in her eyes, and his heart broke in another way. Her voice was thick with emotion and regret and something that sounded too much like good-bye. "I can't let you touch me. If you do, I might not go. Can't you see? This is killing me, but I have to go. He broke his hip and is having surgery in a few hours."

She swallowed hard. "And you can't come with me. We hurt my da...no." She swallowed and clarified. "That's not fair. I. *I* hurt my da when I left home. I abandoned him and our family and broke the trust between us. I can't go home to his side with you by mine. I don't know when I'll be back. And I can't ask you to wait. I want to, but it wouldn't be fair." Her voice caught. She was hurting, but he was in agony.

Shoving his fingers through his hair, he tried to subdue his panic. "This is crazy. This doesn't have to be the end."

"But it does. If I go home, knowing you are waiting for me to return, I won't be able to focus on helping him recover, helping him heal. I'll always have one foot in the Atlantic ready to swim back to you."

She grabbed his arm, her eyes begging him to understand. "These past few days have been everything I've ever wanted. I wanted more time to explain but... My da, he deserves more than a half-assed attempt to help him and try to mend what I broke ten years ago." She sniffed, her tears falling freely now.

Her touch was more than he could bear, and he shook her from his arm.

Larkin wrapped her arms around Blayne. Claire stood with her own wrapped around her middle as if she didn't know what to do or how to help.

Jay could relate. What the hell was happening?

"I'll wait. There is no rush. No pressure. Don't you understand? I can't lose you again."

She winced as if in pain. "I should never have moved here in the first place."

"That's it? Your family calls and regardless of what we have together, you're done. You're leaving. Just like that?"

"Jay, calm down." Ryker grabbed his arm, but he yanked away.

"It's not just like that." She shook her head. "I've been planning to return after the launch. Everything between us was unexpected and new. I'd hoped to have a chance to talk about it, figure it out, but it's too late. Don't you see? Every time we try, the world tells us we shouldn't."

He ignored the tears running down her cheeks, they meant nothing in the face of reality.

She was leaving him.

It was everything he'd already done to her being thrown back at him, and irrational anger burned through his chest. "Was this your plan all along? Is this your payback?"

Her eyes grew wide with shock. "What? Planned? I'd never—"

Jay scoffed. "You'd never what? Lash out? Fight back? Make someone pay? That's been your whole M.O. since we've met."

"I've grown up. Clearly, I can't say that for all of us. This has nothing to do with you."

He yanked his hand from his coat pocket. That was the final straw and the truth of it all. Her life, her terms. None of it had anything to do with him. He'd fucked that up ten years ago when he left. Apparently, there was no going back. "Of course, the fuck not. It never does, does it? The truth of the matter is you don't trust me...you don't trust us. And you're running away."

She lifted her chin. "No, I'm going to help my da. Running away is your job."

His mother stepped up to the group. "What is going on? You're causing a commotion."

Jay ignored her and threw the engagement box at Blayne's feet along with his fucking hopes and dreams and sorry-ass fool of a heart. "Sincerely, I hope your dad's going to be okay. But if you can't see that we could get through this together, that you can trust me to be there, there truly isn't anything between us worth fighting for."

CHAPTER 18

*B*layne stood outside the home that was a part of her heart and soul. As she stared up at the sharply-peaked, thatched roof then down the more moderate slopes along each side to the stone that gave the true life to her home, she was hit by a wave of nostalgia for the night she'd had dinner with Jamie at his parent's home.

The thought of him made her ache, and she closed her eyes against the pain.

Her father's house was way more modest but had more character than any other she'd ever seen. It had been the home of his parents and his parent's parents, passed down through the generations and unfailingly maintained with integrity and grace and honor.

Honor.

That word had haunted her for a decade. It was funny how so many words went in one ear and out the other, and then one came along that was more powerful than time, distance, or even love.

The ivy he was so proud of was perfectly groomed and pristine.

No one would ever guess that it had laid up her big, burly father inside.

She'd arrived later than she'd planned due to weather and delays and general airport fun. And her father, being her father, had refused to stay in the hospital opting to recover at home with a visiting nurse.

Typical Noah MacCaffrey. Stubborn, mule-headed, and he refused to listen to anyone.

The awareness of the apple not falling far from the tree left her restless and on shaky legs. Not a good combination.

"Are you going to just stand there staring or are we going to actually go in?" Emma tapped her bright pink high-top sneaker. Her skinny jeans were covered by a flowy white spaghetti strap tank top, and her brown curly hair was piled on top of her head.

Blayne had always loved the sprinkling of freckles across the bridge of her little sister's nose, but at the ripe old age of twenty-five, they were beginning to fade. Her pink baby cheeks were now sculpted with a bit of bronzer, her once upon a time out of control brows now groomed to model perfection. Emma was quirky and artistic and as beautiful as ever.

"I'm scared, Em."

Emma slid her arm through her sister's. "I know. No one knows you're here, but I'll tell ya this. When da was comin' outta surgery, he asked for ya. Pissed Ruby off, it did."

Shit. Blayne could only imagine. And she didn't blame Ruby. Their older sister had taken up to helping their da ever since losing their ma when Dylan was born. Having their da ask for Blayne after all Ruby had done for him probably hurt like hell.

But she couldn't lie. It gave her hope.

"Okay, let's go." Emma led her through the front door.

As soon as she stepped over the threshold, she was hit hard with memories, with a feeling. The taste and smell and sound of home.

It was as if she were thrown back in time, losing all the lessons she'd learned, forgetting all the experiences she'd had, leaving her a vulnerable and stubborn eighteen-year-old. She raised her chin. She could do this.

She wanted to run.

With a self-conscious pat, she checked her cream necktie blouse, then made sure it was securely tucked into her navy blue high waisted trousers. It was now or never. Facing down mistakes didn't have a good time.

"Ya can do this." Em gave her a smile.

"Where's Ruby and Dylan?"

"Dylan has class. He'll be home after. Ruby ran to the pub to grab some dinner. Let's get you in to see Da before she gets home and starts yellin'."

Blayne's heart pounded in her chest as if it were trying to jump free, leaving her light-headed and a little woozy. "I think I'm jet-lagged."

"Na, just terrified."

They quietly entered their father's room. His large, four-poster bed still rested adjacent to the big, arched window with the crosshatch design of the diamond window muntin, facing the back garden.

He looked so peaceful that she hated to disturb him. His beard had grown white as had his brows, but they were both as thick and luxurious as ever. The Donegal tweed cabbie cap that always adorned his head was hanging from one of the posts on his bed.

She smiled. He was never without his flat cap. When she was little, she always imagined him sleeping in it, but when she'd climb in with him to snuggle on an early morning weekend, his head would be bare of it. She was always so surprised to see he had so much hair.

And there he was, almost just as she left him. Love burst through her chest at the sight of him. She'd missed him, but she'd never fully understood how much until he lay in front of her. All the years now behind her, wasted years without her da, burned her with shame and sadness. It hurt so much she had to swallow the sob that threatened.

His expression was so soft and peaceful, she hated to disturb him. With hesitation, she turned to leave, but Em stopped her with a firm shake of her freckled face.

Damn little sisters.

Noah MacCaffrey had taught her to be strong and now was the time to show him she'd learned a thing or two when she'd been home.

"Da. I'm home. It's me, Blayne." Her whisper carried across the quiet room as she moved next to him then lowered gently to the edge of his bed.

His eyes blinked before he focused in on her. They were still the deep blue she remembered as a child but missing a bit of the spark her memory teased her with.

His voice was rough with sleep and pain meds and trembled with disbelief. "Blayney?" Tears immediately filled his eyes.

"Ya. It's me, Da." She was afraid to move, wanting to hug him but not sure if she had the right, not wanting to hurt him more or ever again. Her throat tightened, and her eyes stung. How had she ever left him?

"I'd prayed and prayed, my girl. You've finally come home," the gruffness in his voice deepened with emotion.

"I didn't think you wanted me here." Her whisper barely slipped past her lips in her sorrow.

He opened his arms, and she sunk into his big, burly chest just as she did when she was a little girl. The spice of his cologne wrapped her in a warm embrace along with his arms. He kissed the top of her head. With a hitch in his voice, he said, "Blayney, I never wanted ya to leave me in the first place. I hoped every day to see ya walk through the front door."

She couldn't help the sob that escaped her chest, and her da's arms wrapped around her tighter still. "I'm so sorry I hurt you."

"Shhh. None of that now." He dragged a hand over her hair. "The blame isn't yers to carry alone, Lass."

"But I said such awful things that I didn't mean. I've missed you so much," she whispered.

"As did I. A pain I've carried in my heart since the day ya left." He nudged her to look him in the eye. Cradling both cheeks, he said, "I'm sorry, too, Blarney. So, so sorry."

Regret tore through her with such force she broke down in her da's arms. The kind of cry that said so much but made no sound. All the memories, time that was lost, Jamie, Larkin, losing her ma, and leaving her da crashed into her with the ferocity of the Atlantic Ocean against the lighthouse rocks in January.

Either coast left her missing the ones she loved.

Going home was everything and nothing. It was here and there, both far and near.

But at least wherever she rested her head, she would know she was finding her honor once again.

*B*layne checked her text messages, but save for a few from Larkin, making sure she was safely on Irish soil, there was nothing there.

And the fact that Jamie wasn't pressuring her should leave her relieved and thankful that he respected her situation, but instead loneliness left a heavy weight in her chest. It was her decision, and the right one, but walking away from him had been excruciating.

As obstacles go, the ocean now between them was nothing compared to the look in his eyes when he'd thrown the engagement ring box at her feet.

Her heart had torn in two along with his, and it was all her own doing. If she'd have made better decisions years ago...

But then she'd never known such love existed.

She yanked her pruning gloves on a bit tighter then, with garden shears in hand, climbed the ladder to the thatched roof. The beautiful vine that mapped out a little life around their storybook home still needed to be groomed along the back of the house.

While her dad slept, the least she could do was something productive, meaningful. And there wasn't much as important to Noah MacCaffrey as his plants... except for his children. He'd always been a tending type of man. He tended his gardens, he'd tended to his wife, and he'd always tended to his children.

When they were little, he'd play board games, or dolls, or have a tea party. Whatever their little hearts desired. He was there.

And she'd repaid him by running away.

She snipped a few wandering vines, careful not to take out her self-reflecting anger on the innocent plant, then wrapped others in a new direction to help manipulate the shape she wanted. She shoved the sleeves of her light jacket to her elbows. The sun was shining, and the sky was clear of any clouds. It was humid but cooler compared to Cape Van Buren.

She glanced around her childhood garden in Glengarriff. Tucked in the woods, but not far from the Atlantic, they were surrounded by a lush fairyland where leprechauns and wood nymphs played. Their home was the quintessential, thatched-roof, stone cottage that brought people to Ireland in the first place.

The breeze off the Atlantic left her feeling a bit nostalgic, but instead of images of her running with her sisters over the little footbridge next to the house, she saw the brick roads of Cape Van Buren and the rocky shore of the coast. Her heart couldn't separate the scent of the ocean breeze or the call of the seagulls just because she was now experiencing them from an opposite shore.

Leaning just enough to inspect her work, she slipped her shears in the pocket of the overalls she'd changed into and made it down to the ground. Everyone was inside, and though the reunion with her sister and brother had been awkward, she'd survived.

She stepped through the large, wooden double doors from the back garden to find her da set up on the couch with pillows and blankets and his favorite beer.

"Are ya allowed to drink on pain medication?" She threw him a side-eyed look.

He waved in dismissal, taking a sip. "It's a pint, that's like mother's milk."

Dylan brushed past her. "Great. She's home less than a day and already trying to tell da what to do."

Her brother's thick brogue washed over her with its beauty even though the words were anything but. He wasn't too keen on her return, if his anger and distance toward her were any indications. But he didn't really know her either. Not really. She left when he was ten. Just a boy. And now he'd turned into a beautiful man-stranger who didn't seem too interested in seeing her again.

Tension strung tight along the muscles in her neck. She'd hurt more than just her da.

Ruby shot their brother a look. "Leave it."

No more, no less.

Dylan muttered under his breath as he disappeared to his room.

Blayne studied the serious tilt of her sister's mouth, the severe, slicked-back ponytail of her cherry red hair that was just like their da's own mother, and the determined fire in her eyes as if she had a mission and no time for anything else.

There was something missing.

Joy.

The light that used to twinkle in her eyes as she chased them around the garden when they were little was gone. Instead, all that remained was resignation.

"Come sit." Her da patted the space next to him, and she settled in, careful not to disturb his hip.

"How's your pain? Are ya hurting? When does the nurse come?"

His lips spread wide, making the whiskers of his beard ripple across his cheeks. "Why did you come home?"

She swallowed hard and played with the tasseled edge of the throw along the back of the couch. "I missed ya. I wanted to come sooner, but I was scared. I needed to do something worthy of coming home first." Her voice was low, almost unrecognizable to her own ears.

Her da's big, warm hand stilled hers. He moved it from the couch and held it between his own.

"I said things I regret the day that you left," he said.

"No, Da. I'm the one who's sorry. I hurt ya..." She glanced at Ruby and Emma. "And the family. I was selfish and—"

"You were so young, and I was scared. But you've always been independent. Strong, feisty. So much like your mother in looks and temperament, but still yer own person. Everything I already knew ya ta be, Blayney, yet I tried ta keep ya. For me."

She leaned into his side. "I wasted so much time not seeing ya." Her throat thickened with emotion.

He beckoned Emma with a wave.

Blayne's sister trailed her fingers along the spines of a few books on the floor-to-ceiling shelves in the alcove in the corner of the room. Removing a leather-bound album from the collection, she turned it over then handed it to their father.

"But I've seen ya." He opened the front cover to reveal photos of Blayne.

She leaned in for a closer look. Page after page of photographs memorializing her accomplishments. Her graduation, first job, Eclectic Finds, and the beautiful photo of the Van Buren house on the cape that she'd sent to Emma.

Running her finger over the photo, she glanced at her little sister. "Ya did this?"

Noah cleared his throat. "You've accomplished so much. I'm as proud as any da could be. But, Blayney..." He rubbed his hand down her hair. "Ya never had ta do any of this to come home."

"But ya said not to come back."

His chuckle was filled with regret. "An old man with a broken heart. I hoped the threat'd keep ya home, but instead it kept ya away."

Emma lowered to the arm of the chair to see the pictures, too.

"By the time I figured it out, I was afraid to call ya home. Ya had to find yer way back on yer own in order for it ta be real."

Closing the album, he handed it to his youngest. "I never meant to make ya feel like ya had to choose. There's no reason it shouldn't all fit. The last thing ya want ta do is ta leave yer bloke the same way he left ya. Family is important, both the one ya have and the one ya want ta make."

Blayne shook her head. "It doesn't matter. If I'm honest, I think I'd always be waitin' for him to take off again. That's no way to live."

"So ya left him first?" He rested his weathered palm against her cheek. "Ya can't live in fear. Listenin' to yer heart's always been the best way."

She hadn't left Jay the same way. Her da needed her. Her family needed her. And it was time she thought of more than just herself. Her da kept staring at her as if waiting for her to see something. He held her gaze with the deep blue intensity of his own.

A wave of realization washed over her, leaving her a bit dizzy.

Her da was right. She'd left Jamie due to her sense of duty, her need to prove herself, and didn't make room for him. But she also couldn't think of how to have done it differently. "Well, it's no matter now," she said softly.

There was nothing left to fit together. She was alone. But at least she was with her family.

"What happened next?" her da said in a gruff whisper.

Tears burned her eyes at his question.

"Jamie asked her ta marry him," Emma said.

"No, he didn't. He threw an engagement ring at my feet." Her chest squeezed at the memory. She'd picked the box up with shaky fingers, but she couldn't look at what was inside. It represented all her dreams that would never be born. There was no way to bear it, so she'd slipped it into his mother's hands, kissed the woman's cheek, then hurried home.

Leaving everyone she'd always loved behind as she ran toward everyone who'd always loved her. She'd never been more conflicted.

"Because ya were leavin' him. Seems the men in yer life have a lot in common." Her da raised his pint in the air. "Ya always were consistent."

She sniffed with a watery grin as her father's forgiveness washed over her, taking a lot of guilt with it. She was lighter than she'd felt in years. There was no getting back the years they'd lost, but she could make sure to take advantage of all the time they had left. "Well, I'm home to stay. There's no tellin' how long it'll be before yer back on yer feet, and I couldn't ask him to wait. I won't leave ya again, Da. I promise."

Placing a warm kiss on her forehead, he smiled. It was the look she'd carried with her over the years whenever she missed him the most.

With a sip from his pint, he sighed. One full of contentment and comfort. "That's a promise I can't letcha keep. Yer flight for Maine leaves in a week."

CHAPTER 19

*I*t had been almost a full week since the gala, since his future crumbled to the cape's fertile lawn, yet the pain in Jay's chest still took his breath away. He wanted to rage at the world, but in the end, it was his own fucking fault.

He should have never left Blayne in the first place.

Lifting a box of supplies, he made his way past the crowd on the front porch and into the Van Buren house. "Get outta my way." He pushed past Ryker, into the kitchen.

"What the fuck, man?" Ryker followed him inside.

"Ryker!" Maxine admonished.

He threw an are-you-kidding-me look at his grandmother. "Are we really going to go through this again?"

"Exactly. One second we're blamed for calling her old, the next for swearing." Mitch rolled his eyes and ducked just in time as a wooden spoon hurtled toward his face. "Hey!"

"Speak for yourself. I've never been stupid enough to imply my grandmother's old. That's all you, buddy." Ryker grinned as Maxine retrieved the spoon she threw, then slapped Mitch on the ass with it.

"What the hell?!" Mitch jumped away and slammed right into Claire. The box she carried fell to the ground, sending small jars of paint and brushes across the tile.

Claire spun on Mitch. "Do you ever watch what the hell you're doing?"

The two took up a verbal sparring match that Jay had no interest whatsoever in, so he set his load by the sliding glass door then ripped the top open.

"See what you started?" Ryker nudged him with the heel of his shoe.

Jay stood. "Don't fuck with me, I'm not in the mood. I didn't start shit."

"Get your head out of your ass, man. The grand opening is tomorrow. This is your show. You can't run it by barking orders and cussing up a storm. Are you trying to sabotage all the work you and Blayne have already accomplished?"

The sound of her name was like a punch to the gut. He steadied himself against the wave of pain, gripping his fingers in fists at his sides.

"Look, man. Obviously, you miss her. We all do. This doesn't have to be the end."

"She made it clear that she wasn't coming back. Not to mention apparently you all knew she was heading home to Ireland, but no one thought to fucking tell me about it."

"Yeah, Jay? I don't think about what the hell is going on in your life every goddamn minute. Get over it. Figure your shit out and start treating all the volunteers helping us set up for tomorrow like it means something to you."

"Boys, the two of you are making a scene." Maxine joined them with Jay's mother at her side.

Ryker looked up at the ceiling as if praying for patience. "You're one to talk, Grandmother. Has the judge showed up yet?"

The question did its job and Maxine's lips clamped closed, but Ryker didn't get off easy, because she grabbed his arm and hauled him toward the front door. Jay did not wish to be in his shoes.

His mother touched his arm. "What're you doing? Maxine said you've been charging through here like a bull all week."

Jay smiled. "Don't worry about it. I'm fine."

"Obviously, you're not. Come." She reached out.

"Mom, I have too much to get done."

"You do, but you're not going to do it right in the mood you're in. Come," she demanded.

"Where?"

"Seriously?" She gave him the look she always gave him when he was dumb enough to argue as a kid.

But he stubbornly resisted.

"Walk with me in the woods. It won't take long."

"Fine, but I'm getting something done while we're out there." He let her lead him out the front door and down the front porch but stopped to grab a wheelbarrow filled with plaques and carved stakes. She headed toward the path into the woods.

As soon as they stepped through the opening in the foliage, the world took on a hushed buzz, softened from the clanging of reality. The light dimmed to a glow, filtered by the canopy of trees. His mother followed a small path to a little bench that had hummingbird feeders around it.

One of Ryker's beehives buzzed in the distance, and Jay remembered watching Stuart Van Buren, Maxine's late husband, working his magic when they were children. Every one of Ryker's friends thought he was a superhero. He could take a bee sting like it was the caress of a feather.

Jay dropped to the bench.

"When you and Blayne came for dinner, you said a few things, implied them anyway, that gave your father and me pause."

The last thing Jay wanted to be doing was having this conversation. "Mom, I say a lot of things." He pushed up from the bench, grabbed a post hole digger, and got to work setting up the informative nature signs that Claire had designed for the grounds.

The work felt good to his muscles, the burn a relief from the heavy feeling in his chest.

"I won't argue with that." She chuckled and sat on the bench closest to where he worked. "But this seemed a bit like an accusation against your father."

He set the carved pole that would support the sign. "Mom, I love you and Dad, but I didn't like how you were always left behind."

"Left behind?"

He gave a decisive nod. "Every time he had a deal, was setting up a new account. He'd be traveling Europe while you were stuck at home, stuck with me. Until I joined the business, then I was guilty of it, too. Though I realized leaving her was a mistake right away, I knew I couldn't do that to Blayne. Couldn't ask her to give everything up because of my sense of duty. Especially not before I had enough to offer her that might somehow make up for it all."

She shook her head. "Give what up? You're not making any sense." Pushing up from the bench, she steadied the plaque he was attaching to the pole as he finished the job.

"I was never left behind, Jay. First of all, and I mean this in the nicest way, I hate to break it to you, but I've never needed to be with your father, or you for that matter, every second of the day in order to be happy. I never sat anywhere, waiting. I worked, and I thrived, and I lived a great life raising my son and nurturing my community. I'm a woman full of passions that reach far beyond the walls of our home. The fact that you don't or didn't see that means I failed you somewhere."

He stared at his mother trying to work his brain around her words. "You've never failed me. I..." A weird pinch intensified between his shoulder blades. No more words formed coherently, though he tried to wrap his tongue around a few. All this time, he thought she'd been lonely. And he wouldn't lie, it was a bit of a kick in the ass to hear she didn't need him to be happy.

What the hell?

He truly was a selfish bastard.

Forcing himself to find an answer, he focused on the task at hand and tested the stability of the sign.

"Mom, I..."

She dropped her hands to her sides. "Look, I love you, but sometimes you're a bit dense."

"Hey!" He rubbed his neck as if she'd tugged his hair.

Handing him another pole, she continued. "Blayne isn't the sit-at-home-and-wait kind of woman. And she certainly isn't the type to stare out a window pining for her love. How could you not know that?"

As he lowered the pole into the hole he'd created, he considered taking its place since he felt like he might as well have dug it for himself.

His mother put her hands on her hips. "Thinking I had no life shows how little you thought of me and, more importantly, how little you actually think of Blayne. Grow up."

She turned and stomped back the way they'd come.

"Mom! Wait!" What the fuck? Was she actually mad at him for caring?

Nothing about this day or week, hell, his whole return to Cape Van Buren, made any sense at all.

He dropped his tools and ran to catch up to her. "Wait." Gently grabbing her by the shoulders he turned her around. "I'm sorry. I just always thought..."

"You mean you didn't actually think."

He dropped his chin to his chest.

"Is that why you left her so long ago? Am I the cause of you losing out on the love of your life? And if I'm honest, me losing out on the daughter I always wanted?" Her eyes had a glassy look as if she might cry. If she did, screw the damn hole he dug, he'd simply throw himself off the rocks by the lighthouse.

"You aren't the cause of anything. I let my own perceptions and ambitions and insecurities cloud my judgment."

"Do you love her?"

"You know I do." And saying it eased some of the pain in his chest.

She shook her head with a shrug. "Then what're you going to do about it?"

"Nothing. She made her choice." And the pain of it all threatened to swallow him whole.

"The only choice she made was to be there for her father. After ten years, don't you think she deserves the time?"

"She said she wasn't coming back!" The shock of his voice echoing against the trees caught him off-guard.

"Because she doesn't want you waiting for her. She needs to be there for her father. Sound familiar?" She raised her brows. "But the question is since when does my son back away from a challenge...especially the hard ones?"

She rubbed his arm. "Someday, you're going to realize the only person expecting you to prove anything is yourself."

He studied the determination in her eyes. How had he never seen it before? He'd been a fool. She was right. He never saw her sitting anywhere—the woman had been a whirlwind of activity his whole life. Not only that, she'd traveled all over the world, sometimes with his father, sometimes with her girlfriends.

He could see Blayne doing that. Hell, with her he'd probably be the one left behind. Not on purpose but because she was such a force in her own right.

His mother was right. A surge of adrenaline rushed through him like it did when he was about to close on a big deal. What the hell was the matter with him? Coming home to the Cape was the whole point of everything.

He may be a selfish bastard, and he never backed down from a challenge, but Blayne MacCaffrey belonged to him. She made him the man he always worked so hard to prove he was to everyone else.

She thought an ocean would keep him at bay? Fuck that. She wasn't getting away from him that easily. Or ever again. He said he'd always be there for her.

Now was the time to prove it.

"I'm going to put a proposal together to share with dad about expanding into Ireland," he said.

"Now it sounds like you're thinking." She removed the engagement box from her pocket. "I think this belongs to you."

"No, but I know who it does belong to." He took the box and flipped up the top. A beautiful green Paraiba tourmaline-and-diamond engagement ring with an antique square cushion wrapped in white gold. The main stone was the exact color of her eyes, a crystal seafoam green unlike any other he'd ever seen before.

"When do you leave?"

"Right after the grand opening," he said.

"I'll help you pack. I'm sorry she'll miss it." His mother kissed his cheek.

"That's okay. If I can make things right, she'll never miss out on anything again, and neither will I."

For the first time in a long time, the tension in his neck eased and anticipation filled his chest.

They belonged together. On the Cape and in Ireland. Home was where their families were, and no one said they couldn't have more than one.

~

The Archer Conservation Park of Cape Van Buren officially opened its doors to the town and hearts and needs of all the people who long before had become family. Jay stepped aside to let one of Cape Van Buren police department's finest walk on through.

Cindy Majors gave him a saucy wink. "Thanks, Jay."

"You're very welcome," he returned with a tip of his head.

"Is Maxine inside?" The hopeful look in Cindy's dark eyes was one he recognized.

"She is, but lay off asking any questions about the moonshine. She and Judge

Carter still aren't talking, which is stressing out Larkin. He's here, too, but lurking along the perimeter."

She snapped her fingers. "Damn it. Okay. Thanks for the heads up. Larkin's due to pop any second, isn't she?"

For some reason, the visual made him wince, and Cindy laughed. "Any day now."

"Moving on so soon, Jay?" Mitch joined them in the foyer.

Cindy stuck her tongue out at him in a playful manner. "Don't be an ass, Mitch…or a sore loser." Turning to Jay, she patted him. "And thank you. I hope you get things figured out with Blayne. You know we all love her."

"Yeah." He gave a nod. "Me, too." Slapping Mitch on the shoulder, he asked, "What the hell is wrong with you? One of these times, you're gonna get knocked on your ass or find yourself at the altar."

Mitch smirked. "Hasn't happened yet."

"It's only a matter of time, my friend."

"Yeah, yeah. I'll leave that to you and Ryker. Watching what the two of you have gone through has cured me of ever wanting a serious relationship."

"The hell it did. You made that decision when your dad had left."

Mitch narrowed his eyes at him. "Watch it."

"Come on. I have an announcement to make."

Mitch stepped behind Jay as if hiding from someone. Jay spun around. "What the hell are you doing?"

"Fucking Claire Adams."

"You're fucking Claire Adams?!" Jay was beyond shocked.

"Hell no, jackass. And don't talk about her like that. I'm hiding from her." The look on Mitch's face as he watched Claire round the fountain in the front drive was a whole different conversation than the words coming out of his mouth. "Every time she sees me it's like she has Tourette's or something and the only words out of her mouth are asshole and motherfucker."

"She does not say motherfucker."

Mitch released a sigh of relief as Claire continued on around the back of the center. "Maybe not, but when I'm around, she sure as hell thinks it."

The laugh that erupted from Jay's chest left him feeling lighter than he had in weeks. "What did you do to make her so mad at you?"

"Not a God damn thing."

"Huh huh. Clearly." Jay shoved him. "Come on, I need to find Ryker to make his toast, then I have something to share as well."

The two men made their way through the front doors of the house to search for Ryker in the kitchen.

The Gothic-inspired Victorian was filled to the brim with people there to celebrate the grand opening. The front room had tables lined with information about the currently offered programs, those that were coming, and request forms for new suggestions.

Delizioso Italian Restaurant had an array of antipasti offered for everyone to enjoy, and Dine on the Vine had provided the season's most popular red and white wines for everyone to sip on. Well, everyone but Larkin, who was currently staring at a bottle with the same look Jay imagined she gave Ryker anytime he had to travel to New York for work.

"You better be careful, someone may mistakenly think that look on your face has something to do with Marco instead of the wine."

Larkin giggled. "Please, even if I did, they'd only feel sorry for me." She nodded toward Mitch and his sister chatting by the sliding glass doors. "Marco Bonamici has never had eyes for anyone but Mae. Not that he has time for anything outside of wine tastings and not that she even seems to notice. Besides, the only thing I'm interested in is getting this baby out of me and a good red in me. Even Ryker doesn't measure up."

Jay shook his head. "Poor guy."

"Which one, Marco or Ryker?"

He laughed. "Both." Pulling in a breath, he directed her to a seat along the wall so she could get off her feet. His whole plan counted on Larkin's cooperation. "Speaking of the poor guy..."

She ignored the crowd in the kitchen and focused on him with a curious intensity. He could see why Ryker loved her so much. Larkin had a way of making you feel like you were the only one in the room. "What's up?"

A small commotion behind him caught Larkin's attention but this was too important for distractions. "I have a plan. I'm going to Ireland to get our girl back."

"Blayne." Larkin whispered. Her eyes immediately filled with tears, and Jay dropped to his knees. "Yes, exactly. This is about Blayne. But knock off the crying. This should make you happy, not sad. Ryker'll kill me if he thinks I made you cry." He ran his fingers through his hair. Truth be told, he couldn't stand the sight either.

She glanced past him, a smile stretching her lips wide. "I'm beyond happy. This is what happens when I'm happy these days." She grabbed his hands between hers. "I knew you couldn't just let her stay away. We need her here."

"Well, that will remain to be seen."

She stilled with a look of confusion. "What do you mean?"

"Her family's in Ireland. I love her, Larkin, and if that's where she needs to be, well then, that's where I need to be."

"Ohhhhh!" Larkin crooned.

A husky voice spoke from behind him, the familiar Irish brogue a bit thicker than usual, and rocketed through him like a sonic boom.

"Is that your M.O. now? Take me all the way across the ocean, away from my family, and then abandon me there?"

He shoved to his feet and swung around. "Blayne."

CHAPTER 20

*L*ove slammed through Blayne as her eyes devoured Jay. He looked a bit pale with the shock of her arrival, but he was as gorgeous as ever, and the vision of him before her confirmed everything she ever thought she knew.

He was her one and only true love.

Her everything.

And please, God, let him love her like he promised to.

"What are you doing here?" His voice was raspy, his hands shoving in his pockets then reaching for her only to drop at his sides.

She swallowed hard, trying to clear her mind of any jet lag so she could say the right things to make up for her epic failure the night of the gala. "I couldn't miss the grand opening."

Over the past week, she and her da had made amends and made a plan. He was determined to see her and Jamie together. If he'd been important enough to leave Ireland at eighteen and she still loved him, then he was important enough to leave for now. Besides, Noah MacCaffrey did not like the idea of his daughter repeating Jamie's offense in the name of family.

She could still hear his thick brogue whispering in her ear as he gave her a hug goodbye. "There is no honor in runnin' away, but there is in chasin' after yer dream, Blayney."

Drawing in a shaky breath, she reached for him. "I'm so sorry, Jamie. I was scared about my da, and I had already hurt him before. I thought since there was no guarantee you and I would work a second time, that you wouldn't leave again, that I had to go."

"But now you're back? For what? How long?" Jamie looked caught in a tug-of-war.

"For you and forever."

His gray eyes flared, and he took her hand. "We can't keep separating our families from our family."

At his touch, a swift relief washed over her, and she went lightheaded. Grabbing him to steady herself, she nodded. "I agree. I—"

Before she could finish, he placed a finger over her lips. Her initial instinct was to bite it, but that was the old Blayne rising up. Pushing that self down, she waited.

"I proposed an expansion of Astor Enterprises into Ireland. We're already a global business and it only makes sense when we have family there."

Surprise rocketed through her. "Expanding? So, you really were coming to get me?"

He held her close. "That was never a question. I can't lose you again, Bean. You're it for me. You'll forever and always be my everything."

Tears of disbelief, of fear, of complete elation filled her eyes. Every dream she ever had ended with this one man. "But your mom and dad are here. It's not fair to make you leave. I…" She was prepared to stay and continue to build a life in the States. She'd already built a home here, she just hadn't let herself believe it.

He pressed a kiss to her lips. "You're my family, Blayne. My most important family, the one I'll grow with and raise children with."

Her heart stuttered at the thought. There was no helping the grin pushing at her cheeks.

"I was an ass ten years ago. I was selfish and underestimated you based on something I had completely wrong all this time. I'm so sorry for hurting you, for wasting so much time. But I have to be selfish again. Because I'm never leaving your side. You are mine as much as I've always been yours."

Wasting time was something she understood all too well. "I'm sorry for turning around and doing the same thing to you. I knew it was wrong, but I couldn't see any other way." An awareness of understanding emerged, ticking up the corners of her lips. "And ten years ago, neither could you. Well, aren't we a pair?"

"Guys?" Larkin interrupted.

But her friend would have to wait. Blayne was finally home where she belonged. In her town with the only man who truly understood who she really was. Happy ever afters were for believers.

And she believed.

"There's no more sacrificing between us or our families," she said.

The kitchen buzzed with the excitement of the grand opening and seeing Blayne, but Jamie seemed to only have eyes for her. "If you think you're up to it, we'll work here for six months out of the year and then in Ireland. You have your store here and this place, but I'm sure you'll find something to add to the colorful town of Glengarriff. We'll figure out the exact logistics as we go along, but, Blayne..."

He got down on one knee...

Every hope and dream that she had ever dared to have flashed through her mind. Was this really happening? She'd have her family and the Astor family and Jamie? After everything was said and done, she knew her place was with him and the amazing, loving people of Cape Van Buren. Her family promised to love her no matter where she called home—and to visit often. Emma couldn't wait.

But now, they'd all get the best of everything.

"I've loved you since the day I watched you throw back a whiskey at the Blue Loo..."

Her giggle was thick with emotion as she blinked away tears.

"Guys!" This time Larkin let loose a shriek.

Ryker came barreling through the crowd, almost shoving Jamie on his ass.

She grabbed Jamie, pulling him to his feet as she tried to figure out what was wrong. "What's happening?"

With Ryker wrapped around her, Larkin panted through her words. "I'm really sorry...whoo, whoo, whoo...and beyond thrilled that you two are working things out...Whoo, whoo—"

"Larkin!" This time it was Ryker's deep bellow that echoed through the room.

"The baby is commmmmminggggg!" The last word ended on an awful scream that made Blayne swear for the second time in her life that she was never getting pregnant.

EPILOGUE

THREE MONTHS LATER

"$\mathcal{R}$emember when Archer was born, and you swore you'd never get pregnant?"

A grinning Larkin settled into a gray tweed chair next to Blayne. The North Cove home she shared with Ryker had been renovated, resulting in a floor-to-ceiling window that opened up the back wall to the rear deck and provided a clear view of the lighthouse across the choppy waters. The glow of the lamp was like a beacon through the large picture window.

Steadfast and consistent, the perfect symbol of love and strength and commitment that the center had for the town of Cape Van Buren.

The Archer Conservation Park of Cape Van Buren was thriving and growing by the minute. They were also in the process of tweaking programs and adding more. Which explained why it seemed like the whole town was visiting at the same time.

Larkin's mother and father were in the kitchen with Jamie's parents, as well as Maxine and Evette. The judge was still on the outs with his lady love, but they all secretly hoped they'd find their way back to one another soon. A grumpy Maxine was scary.

Claire joined them, a big glass of wine for herself and Larkin, and made the new mother scoot over and share a small corner of the chair.

Blayne scoffed. "Archer was child's play. Now, this little nugget..." She glided a finger down the baby's petal-soft cheek and Audrey Maxine Van Buren-aka Baby Max—turned her head toward the touch. "Well, she was a whole different ballgame. I think I'm cured of any threat of the infamous biological clock after hearing you scream."

Jamie grabbed each side of her chair, leaning toward her for a kiss. "You better get reacquainted because I know it shouldn't turn me on to see you holding the baby, but I don't know if you've ever looked sexier."

A rush of heat washed through her at his touch. She hoped the feeling never went away. Refusing to let his head grow any bigger, she simply narrowed her eyes at him, though there was no helping the upturn of her mouth. Damn the man. "Slow your roll there, Mr. Astor, we're not even married yet."

Jamie rubbed his big palm gently over the dark fuzz on Baby Max's head and promised, "Soon, if I have any say in the matter. We've waited long enough."

It was a wonderful feeling that he was so impatient to be her husband. She'd have to remind him of that in a month or two when he realized she was a pain in the ass to live with. "Let me see how soon my da and siblings can get here. After everything that's happened, I can't get married without them."

With a gentle touch, she smoothed the cotton onesie covered in lighthouses along the baby's tummy.

With a dip of his chin, he sighed, but the look in his eyes was happy and bright. "Of course."

Jamie perched on the arm of her chair, glancing out the window. "Is the Hide Away & Stay Inn still running?"

Ryker strolled in from the kitchen with Mitch close behind and handed Jamie a beer. "For the time being. I've heard some talk about the threat of it closing down, but nothing's confirmed."

"No! I love that place. Do you know how many times Blayne and I used to take Archer over there to hang out for the day? We'd grab a picnic from their little cafe and hike through the woods or play in the water along their little beach."

Larkin's eyes turned bright with unshed tears, but she smiled, letting her gaze fall on the baby. "I remember like it was yesterday. He'd loved it there almost as much as the Cape. I hope Audrey Maxine does, too."

She smiled at Ryker and the room went quiet.

Blayne cleared the lump from her throat. "Little Max is our girl, of course she'll love it."

"I haven't been out there in ages," Claire said.

"Well." Larkin finished her wine. "You've got a bit on your plate now that you're taking on the programming at the center. The art classes you proposed to Ryker and me will be amazing."

"Besides, you haven't been 'out there' period. I've never seen a person hide behind a to-do list as much as you." Mitch snorted, tipping his head back for a long swallow of beer.

Claire grabbed the sandal off her foot and threw it at him, knocking him in the chest and making him choke on his drink.

"Hey, what the hell?"

With an innocent look, she shrugged. "Better than being the walking STD of Cape Van Buren."

"Oh!" Blayne laughed behind her fingers.

Mitch's face turned as red as Larkin's chest was known to do. "What did I ever do to you?"

Claire opened her mouth to answer but was interrupted by a solid knock at the front door.

"Who the hell is that? The whole damn town is already here." Ryker frowned but his tone was good natured. Larkin's love softened the man's rough edges, but he sported a frown like no other.

Jamie nudged Blayne. "About the wedding."

"Jamie!" She laughed. "You technically haven't really asked me yet and you've had three months."

A throat cleared behind her, and her heart stopped. She knew that sound, that tone, that timbre.

Turning her head, she shot up from the chair. "Da!" Her head spun trying to reconcile the vision of him before her.

Ryker took baby Max from her arms as if afraid she'd drop the sweet thing.

Blayne rushed forward and threw herself into her da's arms.

"Whoa now, Lass." He steadied himself with a cane. "Just got my medical release."

She glanced down at his hip, then noticed someone over his shoulder. Ruby, Emma, and Dylan stood shyly just past the threshold in the front foyer.

Her throat convulsed with emotion, and she tried to swallow beyond the questions and tears. "What are you doing here?"

"I think yer bloke here might have some answers for ya."

Jamie shook her father's hand. "Mr. MacCaffrey."

Noah dipped his white-whiskered chin.

With an indrawn breath, Jamie glanced from father to daughter. "Sir, I brought you here to apologize in person."

"Wait, what?" She interrupted, trying to understand what was going on. Her family was here...in Cape Van Buren—her home.

Jamie looked her father in the eye. "I'm sorry. We handled things so badly, so wrong when we were young, then I only made it worse when we got to the States, but I promise you, the only woman I've ever loved is your daughter."

Noah pressed his lips together. She could see the pain of the memories in her da's deep blue eyes.

"Thank ya, son."

Jamie cleared his throat. "Blayne had mentioned once that what we did lacked honor, and I'd like to make that right. I would like to ask for your blessing in marrying your daughter." He shot a look at her. "That is, if she'll have me."

Love rushed through her as appreciation for Jamie's kindness swamped her.

Noah MacCaffrey laughed. Outright laughed.

She watched him. He must have gone daft. She looked to Emma for some help, but her little sister only shrugged.

Her father grabbed Jamie's hand and pumped it vigorously in a shake. "Lad, I appreciate the gesture, but three plane tickets is a very expensive price to pay to ask for my blessin'. Ya could have asked over the line."

Jamie shook his head. "No, I needed you here. Does that mean you're okay with it?"

"Have ya met my daughter? If I say no, she'd knock me over the head."

The whole room laughed, but all she could do was stare between her father and Jamie, her heart splayed open, vulnerable...accepting.

This was love.

"Then you see, I needed you here so I could do this right." Jamie turned to Blayne and took her hand. "I've loved you since I was a boy, and it would be my greatest accomplishment if you would let me love you long past being an old man."

Her fingers fluttered to her lips. "Jamie," she barely got out the whisper.

"Blayne MacCaffrey, will you make an honorable man of me and be my wife? I promise I'll never leave you and that I'll get on your nerves more than once."

She choked on a giggle, swallowing hard as tears formed in her eyes.

"I promise to keep you connected with your family and that you'll get sick of mine."

Margaret Astor, leaning into her husband, gave a husky chuckle behind the handkerchief she used to dab her eyes.

"But even more, I promise to make sure you feel at home wherever we lay our heads at night, and that mine will always be next to yours."

She'd never experienced such joy. There was a certain pain to so much pleasure that left her breathless and hopeful and overwhelmed. She glanced around the room at all the faces that loved her, that always had loved her.

Ryker was right from the very beginning. She and Jamie made each other better.

They renewed hope, forgiveness, and second chances at not only love but life.

She grabbed his shirt and pulled him close. Tears now streaming down her face, she laughed and cried and nodded with a flurry of dark tendrils falling about her face. "Yes! I'll marry you." Then she poured every ounce of herself into that kiss. It was more than an answer. It was her promise to stand by him, side-by-side, wherever their future may lead. She wasn't afraid anymore, she wasn't searching for her place. She'd already known where it was long ago.

But there was more. She'd always dreamed of love—even when she didn't believe it would happen for her—but she'd never known to dream of honor...on the Cape.

Did you love *Honor on the Cape*? Reviews make a huge difference to an author's career. I would be extremely grateful if you are able to take a few seconds and leave a review on your favorite retailer!

If you haven't yet, enjoy your introduction to Larkin and Ryker in *Love on the*

Cape **FREE** on all e-retailers. Once you fall in love with them (they're irresistible, LOL!), you won't want to leave Cape Van Buren!

ALSO AVAILABLE IN THE ON THE CAPE SERIES
Love on the Cape
Honor on the Cape
Cherish on the Cape
Draw You In
One Jingle or Two
Love, Honor & Cherish: The On the Cape Trilogy

ACKNOWLEDGMENTS

To my children and husband, otherwise known as my heart and soul, thank you for believing in me and always knowing I could do this even when I didn't. I love you. To my big brothers, Tommy, Todd, and Billy—as goofy as I am, you've always held me up. To Paula, my sister of the heart, I'm forever in awe of you. And to my mom, who's continued to mother me from the other side, I hope I have a fraction of your grace. Thank you.

Thank you to my editor KR Nadelson. Your insight and ability to really understand my story is truly a gift. Thank you. To my copy editor Jessica Snyder, you go above and beyond and are forever in my heart. Dawn Yacovetta, your eagle eye is priceless. Thank you all for being such an incredible team! Errors are inevitable but with your help my readers will be distracted by a lot less.

Thank you to Amy Ball for opening doors of opportunity for me and helping me be a more organized writer.

Thank you to the Romantics, your love lifts me up, and to my fan group, MK & CO, for your friendship and for believing in me. I love everyone in this family, from the very first to the still-to-come.

One more exuberant thank you to the readers of Cape Van Buren. I truly love this town. Experiencing life with you in this way is magical. I hope that at least one scene, one line, or simply one word resonates with each of you.

And to my sisters and brothers in the fight against breast and all types of cancer. I know both sides, having lost my mom to breast cancer at a young age, and having survived breast cancer myself...twice. My writing is one of the things that carries me through. I have many more books to write.

Thank you. Hugs, loves, and peanut butter,

MK

ABOUT THE AUTHOR

 MK Meredith writes contemporary romance promising an emotional ride on heated sheets. She believes the best route to success is to never stop learning. Her lifelong love affair with peanut butter continues, and only two things come close in the battle for her affections: gorgeous heels and maybe Gerard Butler...or was it David Gandy? Who is she kidding? Her true loves are her husband and two children who have survived her SEAs (spontaneous explosions of affection) and lived to tell the tale. The Merediths live in the DC area with their large fur baby...until the next adventure calls.

www.mkmeredith.com

mk@mkmeredith.com

facebook.com/mkmkmeredith

twitter.com/mkmkmeredith

instagram.com/mkmkmeredith

bookbub.com/authors/mk-meredith

amazon.com/author/mk-meredith

ALSO BY MK MEREDITH

THE ON THE CAPE SERIES

Love on the Cape

Honor on the Cape

Cherish on the Cape

Draw You In

One Jingle or Two

Love, Honor & Cherish: The On the Cape Trilogy

THE SCRIPTED FOR LOVE SERIES

There's no place like paradise and the happy ever afters found in the film industry of Malibu, CA.

Love Under the Hot Lights

Just a Little Camera Shy

A Heated Touch of Action

THE INTERNATIONAL TEMPTATION SERIES

A strong dose of decadence along with a side of tall, dark, and sexy in your favorite travel destinations.

Playing the Spanish Billionaire

Seducing the Italian Tycoon

THE SEATTLE CRUSH SERIES

Seducing Seven

~

STANDALONE TITLES

Not Your Usual Boob: The Good, Bad, and Wonky of Breast Cancer